About the Author

Fran Pickering is a London-based British murder mystery writer who's travelled extensively in Japan. Her experiences there provide the inspiration for the Josie Clark in Japan mystery series.

She writes about London art, architecture, gardens, and Japanese food on her blog, Sequins and Cherry Blossom. When she's not in Japan she's usually out dancing.

COPYRIGHT

THE BULLET TRAIN MURDER

A Josie Clark in Japan mystery

Fran Pickering

Also by Fran Pickering

The Tokyo Karaoke Murder (Josie Clark in Japan #0 novella)

The Cherry Blossom Murder (Josie Clark in Japan #1)

The Haiku Murder (Josie Clark in Japan #2)

ONE

Josie picked up the last cardboard box, gasping as she hefted it up from the floor of the lift, and carried it awkwardly down the corridor to their new flat. The door had swung shut; she kicked it open for what felt like the thousandth time that day and staggered inside to drop the box with a bang onto the ragged stack that half filled the room. Then she slumped down onto the floor with a groan, folding her long legs into what little floor space remained, then pushing her unruly hair back off her face and tightening her slipping ponytail.

Dave followed her in, with a cardboard cat carrier under one arm and Josie's old vacuum cleaner under the other, the coils of the tube threatening to strangle him at any moment. His large frame, so different from the delicate build of the Japanese for whom the flat had been built, seemed to fill the available space. He wiped the sweat from his blunt features and dumped the cleaner on the floor but put the cat carrier down more gently, then slumped down next to

Josie and tried ineffectually to brush the dirt off his Metallica T-shirt. Rin's anxious tabby face peered out through the holes in the carrier and she mewed piteously.

'Tea,' said Dave. 'Now. I will die if someone doesn't pour tea down my throat in the next five seconds.'

'You only get tea if I can remember which box we put the kettle in,' said Josie. 'And if it's somewhere relatively near the top.'

She stared thoughtfully at the pile of boxes for a moment then dived in and pulled one out from low down in the stack. The boxes piled on top of it wobbled but held in place.

'Got it,' she said triumphantly, pulling her battered kettle out from the box, along with an assortment of tea bags squished up together in a plastic bag. 'Green tea, peppermint tea, camomile tea or *hoji-cha*?'

'Are you trying to kill me?' said Dave. 'Don't you have any builder's tea in there?'

Josie scrabbled about some more and came up with a battered packet of Typhoo.

'That'll do,' said Dave. 'Make it hot and strong.'

A strangled cry from the cat carrier made Josie jump.

'Poor Rin,' she said. 'Do you think it's safe to let her out now?'

'Hang on,' said Dave, sliding across the floor and kicking the front door shut.

Josie undid the top of the cat carrier. Rin leapt out

and shot behind the pile of boxes like a furry streak of lightning. It reminded Josie of the day she had first seen her, a pathetic bundle of tabby fur cowering in the corner of a windy balcony after her owner had been murdered. She moved the boxes and gently picked Rin up and cuddled her, to be rewarded with a hesitant purr.

'Can you make the tea?' she said 'I need to spend some time being nice to Rin.'

Dave reached out and took the cat from her.

'I'll do being nice to Rin,' he said. 'You get on with the tea.'

Josie delved into the open box again and brought out a couple of mugs, which she took into the kitchen with the kettle and box of Typhoo. As the kettle boiled she pondered whether to tell Dave her news over tea or wait until they'd got things straightened out a bit more. Wait, she decided. Best not to catch him when he was tired. She needed him in a good mood.

She went back in the living room with the tea, to find Dave had moved a pile of boxes off the sofa and was now sitting on it with Rin in his arms. The cat's eyes were closed and there was a look of ecstasy on her face as he rubbed her under her chin. Josie put the two mugs of tea on the floor and sank down onto the sofa next to him.

'You'll have to have it black,' she said. 'We don't have any milk. I'll pop out to the convenience store later and get some.'

'Fine by me, so long as it's hot, wet and strong,'

said Dave, reaching down for his mug.

Josie looked despondently at the chaos around them.

'Do you think we'll ever get it straight?' she said.

'It won't take long,' said Dave. 'And it's so much better than that cupboard in Ichikawa you used to live in. It's got a bedroom and everything. Plus it's in Meguro, so it'll halve your journey time into work.'

Josie felt a flash of guilt. Maybe she should tell Dave now that she wouldn't be travelling into Otemachi for a bit. But the opportunity passed as Dave went on, 'Plus it's no distance from Keiko and Yoshi's place. Given how much time you spend round there, that's probably years of your life saved.'

Keiko was Josie's best friend. Since she'd moved to Tokyo from Sapporo two years before, Josie had spent many happy hours in the flat Keiko shared with her boyfriend Yoshi in Shibuya.

'Oh,' she said, starting up. 'I said I'd ring Keiko.'

'Sit down and relax and get your breath back first. Keiko won't mind,' said Dave, pulling her back down beside him.

'We were so lucky to get this place,' Josie said, looking out of the window at the evening sky and the brightly-lit buildings beneath, feeling happy that she'd left the suburbs and come to live at the centre of things.

'I was lucky to get the job,' said Dave. 'It's only for a year, but at least we'll be living in the same country for once. And after that—.'

Josie knew why he didn't go on. After that he had

a job in London with a guaranteed promotion attached.

'After that,' Dave went on, more gently. 'You'll come with me, won't you? To London? You'll have had enough of Japan by then?'

Josie hesitated.

'You know I don't want to live here forever,' said Dave.

'Yes,' said Josie, feeling guilty again. 'Actually, there's something I wanted to tell you—'

She broke off as her phone rang.

'It's Keiko,' she said. Dave made a 'this'll take forever' face and got up to take their empty cups to the kitchen.

Keiko was keen to hear all about the flat, but Josie's answers were brief and Keiko soon took the hint. Just before she rang off she said, 'Have you told him yet?'

'Not yet,' said Josie. 'I thought I'd wait until we'd sorted ourselves out and do it then.'

'Don't leave it too long,' said Keiko. 'When do you start?'

'Monday.'

'You're kidding,' said Keiko. 'Tell him now. You can't leave it any longer.'

'I know. But I haven't been able to nerve myself to do it. He's not going to be pleased.'

'All the more reason to tell him right away. The longer you leave it, the worse it will be. Do it now. No more excuses. Get on with it.'

Josie put down her phone and looked across at

Dave, who was slicing the first of the boxes open.

'Come and help,' he said. 'The sooner we get this done the sooner we can christen our new bed.'

'In a minute,' said Josie. 'You know I said I've got something to tell you?'

'Yes, so you did. What is it?'

'Come and sit down. It's sort of good news and bad news.'

Dave stared at her and a look of panic came over his face.

'Josie,' he said. 'It's not... You're not...'

'No,' said Josie hastily. 'No, of course not. It's not that. It's something else.'

'Go on.'

'Well, it's to do with work. You know how I've always wanted to work in IT but they put me in Corporate Support instead...'

'You've got a transfer to IT? That's wonderful.' Dave beamed at her and made as if to hug her.

'Well, yes. But they want me to do a sort of training placement first. In Osaka.'

Dave drew back.

'Osaka?' he said. 'That's hundreds of miles away.'

'It's not for long,' said Josie hastily.

'How long?'

'Well... six months.'

'Six months?'

'Starting Monday.'

Dave looked stunned. Josie gulped but pressed on.

'It's such an opportunity for me. You know it's

what I've always wanted. And six months isn't that long. I'll come home at the weekends and you can come over to Osaka and we'll go out and have a good time. You know you said you wanted to see more of Japan. Well, this is your chance.'

'But...' Conflicting emotions chased each other across Dave's face. Disappointment and sadness, then, with an obvious effort, a smile. Josie's heart did a flip as she saw how hard he was trying to be happy for her.

'Congratulations,' he said, with a valiant attempt at hearty sincerity. 'I know what your career means to you and this is the break you've always wanted. We'll find a way to make it work.'

'Thanks,' Josie said, feeling like she might start to cry. She looked around their new flat, the one that was meant to be their first home together. Rin jumped off the sofa with a little thump and came padding towards her to be cuddled. Josie picked her up and held her close as Rin purred contentedly. Dave looked at her with the cat in her arms and looked quickly away.

'I'll make some more tea, shall I?' he said.

'Okay. I'd better make the bed up.' Josie put Rin down, went into the tiny bedroom, which she had been so looking forward to sleeping in after two years in a one room flat, and laid the futon out on the floor, then put a cotton cover bright with spring flowers on the duvet and spread it over the futon. Dave came in and handed her a cup of tea.

'It'll be alright, honestly,' said Josie, leaning

against his broad chest. 'It's only two and a half hours away on the bullet train, and I can catch the train at Shinagawa, which is only a couple of stops from here. I'll come back on Fridays so I'll be here all weekend. They've given me place in the company hostel during the week, and you'll be busy at work, so you'll hardly notice I'm gone.'

'Yeah, I suppose you're right,' said Dave, putting his arm around her and staring over her head.

'It'll be good really – it'll help you with your Japanese, having to manage without me during the week. You know you said you were keen to learn more.'

'That's right,' Dave said. 'It's a good thing, really.'

She looked up at him. Normally she liked it that Dave was taller than her, especially now she lived in a country where it seemed like the whole nation was shorter than she was, but it had the drawback of making it easy for him to avoid her eyes.

'You really don't mind?'

He said nothing, just kissed her in an abstracted way, then went back into the living room where she could hear him opening more boxes. She straightened up and tried to look on the bright side. At least she'd told him. Of course he wouldn't like it right away, but he'd come round. And anyway, it was her career, and her decision. And she'd decided on Osaka.

*

The pale morning light glimmered onto the shiny tiles of the platform at Shinagawa, so clean you could have eaten your dinner off it. At that hour of the morning there were just a few sleepy-looking salarymen lined up waiting for the bullet train to arrive, and the quiet was broken only by the echoing announcements; *don't rush to board the train, it's dangerous; stand back behind the yellow line, otherwise it's dangerous*. Anyone would think that catching the bullet train was some sort of wild adventure rather than something thousands of people did every day.

Considering Josie had had to get up at painful o'clock, she felt surprisingly alert. It was something about the freshness of the air that early in the morning, the hint of sunshine and warmth to come. It was May and the streets were filled with clipped lines of azalea bushes in full pink and mauve flower. A faint smell of warm cake rose from the bag in Josie's hand, which held a freshly baked *melon pan* sweet roll and a coffee she'd bought at the coffee stall in the station entrance. The morning held a bright promise, the first day of her new life.

The announcement changed. Now it barked out urgently that the six seventeen Nozomi super express bound for Osaka was about to pull into the platform, and warned people to take care, though since the platform edge was protected by steel barriers Josie wasn't sure what they were supposed to take care of. The commuters picked up their bags and stood expectantly.

Josie peered down the track as the gleaming white platypus-billed nose of the new N700 series bullet train slid grandly into view. Set high up, like eyes above the curving beak, were the black windows of the driving compartment. The long train flowed endlessly past her, its smooth bill aiming for the far end of the gently curving platform, and stopped with the door to compartment sixteen, where Josie had a reserved seat, precisely lined up with the gap in the barriers and the platform markings showing where to queue. The door slid aside with a gentle sigh and Josie stepped onto the train, which pulled away so gently that for a moment she didn't realise they were moving; then the platform started to slide out of sight and streets full of hurrying commuters, tall glass skyscrapers glittering in the sun and the colourful shopfronts of innumerable convenience stores flashed past as the train gathered speed. Osaka here I come, Josie thought. First day of my new career. I can't wait.

*

Josie stared. Her phone map assured her she'd reached the AZT office but the grey concrete building flanked by a few mournful pine trees wasn't at all what she'd expected. It looked like a municipal furniture storage facility, and the car park, with a peeling barrier manned by an ancient security guard with a whistle and a flashing light sabre, didn't help. She wondered if she'd come to the wrong place, but the sign over the door said *AZT Insurance, Osaka Branch* in old-fashioned lettering so there could be no mistake.

Pull yourself together, she told herself. Just because the AZT building in Tokyo is a modern skyscraper doesn't mean the Osaka office has to be the same. So it's a bit old and battered, so what? It's probably an intellectual powerhouse once you get inside.

But the inside wasn't exactly humming with activity. There was just a drab reception desk where an impassive receptionist looked straight through her.

'I'm here to see Mr Ozawa.'

'Fill in the form. There are pencils on the desk over there.'

Josie wrote *Mr Ozawa, Deputy Director, Technical Support,* in the space on the form for who she was visiting, handed it in and sat down to wait.

Time passed. People came and went, lift doors opened and closed. There wasn't much to look at in the tired reception area – just a battered wooden floor and tall frosted windows that let in light but no view. Just when Josie was beginning to wonder if she should risk the receptionist's contempt to ask if she had been forgotten, the lift door opened and a girl stepped out.

Josie stared at her, then caught herself and tried to look as though she hadn't been staring. The girl was beautiful, as lovely as a Disney princess. Her body was slim and perfectly proportioned, with curves where most Japanese girls had straight lines. Her face was slightly round, her nose small but not flat, her lips finely curved and her brown eyes gently slanted. Her colouring took your breath away – impossibly white skin, perfectly red lips, jet back hair. Not even the grey suit, plain white blouse and low-heeled pumps she wore could detract from her loveliness. But her ears were... well, there was no getting away from it. They were enormous. They stuck out on either side of her head like paddles. Josie tried not to stare at them, but the effort was too much.

The girl walked over to Josie and bowed.

'Josie Clark?' she said in a high-pitched, childlike voice. 'I'm Mimi, the office lady in IT Support. I'll take you up to the office.'

'Thank you,' said Josie, unable to trust herself to say anything more. Mimi? Really? This girl was called Mimi? Mimi was the Japanese for ears, so it seemed beyond cruel of her parents to have given her such a name.

'Have you worked here long?' said Josie as they stood in the lift. It was the most neutral thing she could think of to say.

'Not really,' said Mimi. 'Less than a year, actually.'

'What's it like?'

Before Mimi could answer the lift stopped at the fourth floor and the doors opened onto a corridor painted a dull shade of brown that failed to match the frayed drugget mat that ran along the centre of the floor.

Mimi saw Josie looking at it.

'We're not on the main floor,' she said. 'You'll get used to it.'

'What do they have on the main floor?' said Josie.

'They have proper carpet. The main floor is where the Director and the insurance advisers work. Important people, not like IT Support.'

Mimi led the way into a large room where bits of kit lay around in piles between the desks, and disconnected keyboards and computer mice balanced precariously on top of each other like badly made sandwiches. The room had the air of a semi-abandoned repair shop. Josie's heart sank. She'd thought that when she finally got to work in IT it would be glamorous and cutting edge, leading the way to bigger and better things. But it was all too obvious that IT Support in Osaka was one step up from the caretaker. She'd have been better off staying in Corporate Support back in Tokyo.

There were around a dozen men in the room but they barely glanced up from their screens as the two women entered, which struck Josie as odd. A tall female foreigner walks into your office and you can't even be bothered to look up? She got more attention than that just walking down the street.

Mimi led the way to a door at the end of the room and knocked on it. When a gruff voice called, 'Come in,' she said, 'It's Miss Clark' and stood back to let Josie enter.

The man seated behind the desk, who Josie guessed must be Mr Ozawa, was short and stout with a heavy forehead, thick eyebrows and a permanently downturned mouth. He glanced up as she entered the room and nodded her to a chair. She waited while he finished reading the top paper from a thick file on his desk, feeling the butterflies starting to flutter in her stomach. This man could make or break her future career at AZT. She hoped he was going to like her.

He closed the file and looked up at her.

'Mr Kimura says you speak good Japanese,' he said.

'Yes,' said Josie.

'That's good, because nobody here speaks English. I suppose you know how to behave respectfully to your superiors?'

'Yes, I think so,' said Josie.

'Right then. You'll be working with Mr Shiga on the software upgrade. We're rolling it out to the whole office, so every computer needs to be checked to make sure it's working properly. You'll be doing that. Make sure you don't upset anyone or interfere with their work. Mr Shiga will tell you what to do.'

He opened his file again. Josie stood up, but the interview wasn't quite over. Mr Ozawa gave her a piecing stare and then said, 'Security. Data security is our top priority. Never forget that.'

'Yes, thank you,' she said. 'I'll do my best.'

She walked out, trying to look intelligent and keen and not as though her heart was sinking.

Back in the main office she paused. She wasn't normally very sensitive to atmosphere, but there was something about this place that seemed all wrong. Beneath the industrious silence it simmered like a nearly boiling kettle, as though there were tensions below the surface that might blow it apart at any moment. It felt like she'd walked into a space where a blazing row had been going on a few minutes before, and the silently bent heads were only waiting for her to leave to burst out into recriminations again.

Josie shook herself and took another look around the room at the quiet, industrious people focusing on their work. There was nothing to suggest there was anything wrong. But the feeling refused to leave her. Something she didn't understand was going on here, hidden below the surface. She shivered with irrational fear as a man sitting by the window got up from his desk and walked towards her.

TWO

He was somewhere in his forties, careworn and shabby. His shoulders were hunched as though he'd spent his whole life bent over a laptop and he moved awkwardly, like a jointed doll Josie had been given as a child. His hair was short and plastered close to his head, which he kept bent as if he hoped nobody would notice him, and his black suit was badly cut. He looked like someone you'd walk past in the street and be unable to describe two minutes later.

'Welcome to Osaka, Miss Clark,' he said in a surprisingly high-pitched voice. 'I am Shiga, your immediate superior.'

No chance of first name terms, then, thought Josie.

'Good morning, Mr Shiga,' she said. 'It's a pleasure to be here in Osaka.'

Mr Shiga blinked and swallowed but didn't meet Josie's eyes.

'You'll be working with me on the software

rollout,' he said, staring intently at the floor as though there was something vitally important on it. 'Here's a set of checklists – you'll need to tick off everything on the list for each computer you work on. This is a schedule of the computers we've checked so far and the ones that remain to do. Based on previous experience it should take you forty five minutes to check each computer, though you'll need to allow extra time if the worker isn't at their machine when you arrive or if they're busy and can't be disturbed. Generally speaking I'll expect you to complete ten machines per day.'

Ten machines a day, at, say, an hour each, allowing for moving around the building, amounts to a ten hour day, Josie thought in alarm.

'Er, suppose I run into problems and it takes me longer than forty five minutes?' she said.

'If you run into any problems you can stop the check and call me. I'll come and sort it out.'

'Will you need me to do any of the rollout work?'

'No, the rollout is fully complete. We just need to have the machines checked. Hand your completed checklists to me at the end of each day. I hope that's clear.'

Josie stared at the papers, each covered with a long list of tasks in very tiny *kanji* characters.

'Perfectly,' she said, hoping her voice didn't show her disappointment.

'Right, well, Mimi will show you around and get you set up.'

Mr Shiga walked away.

'You've got this desk in the corner,' said Mimi, leading the way to a battered desk piled high with old computer wiring. 'I'll try and find a home for this stuff but for the time being just push it to the back. There's a laptop, which you'll have to sign for, and you'll need to get a pass made so you can get into the building. I'll take you down and show you where the pass office is when you've had a chance to settle in. I'll get you a cup of tea, shall I?'

'Thanks,' said Josie, slumping into the battered office chair and attempting to swivel it. It didn't move. She switched on the computer in front of her, which asked her for a password she didn't have. She switched it off again and stared vacantly at a notice pinned above the computer saying *Data Security First!*, trying not to look as awful as she felt.

It'll get better, she said to herself. It has to.

*

Somehow she got through the day. Mimi showed her around and got her kitted out with a security pass and a locker in the room next to the ladies' toilet. There was a canteen in the building, but it was nothing like as large or as efficiently run as the one Josie was used to in Tokyo. It had a tiny counter, from behind which an ancient couple dispensed noodles and curry rice.

'People tend to walk down to Umeda for lunch,' said Mimi, seeing the expression on Josie's face.

'Right,' said Josie, resolving to brave the crowded

cafés of Umeda too. Nothing would make her eat in the canteen if she could help it.

She was glad when five o'clock came, but as the clock ticked past five and on to five fifteen, she realised that no one was making any move to leave. Mimi came round with more cups of tea and it was clear everyone was settling in for the evening. Josie went over to Mr Shiga's desk.

'Er,' she said. 'I need to find the hostel and get checked in. Is it alright if I go now?'

'Yes, that's alright, said Mr Shiga. 'Seeing as it's your first day.'

'What time do people usually finish?' said Josie.

'About ten. Unless we've got an urgent job on. Then it's later.'

Josie suppressed a shudder and thought longingly of her modern, comfortable office back in Tokyo where nobody cared if she left at five o'clock every night. Coming to Osaka was looking less and less like a good idea.

The company hostel where she would be staying during the week was twenty minutes away on the Midosuji underground line, and looked to have been built about the same time as the Osaka office. It was dark with dimly lit corridors open to the elements. The metal door to which she'd been given a key opened onto a small square room with a tired carpet, a single bed and a hopelessly small wardrobe. The notice next to the phone said that you could get an outside line by dialling reception. Inside the wardrobe she found a list of times when she could borrow a vacuum cleaner to vacuum her room.

She sat down on the hard bed, trying not to think about Dave and Rin, warm and snug in their comfortable flat in Meguro, with all the amenities of Tokyo on the doorstep. She could have been there too, just setting out to eat sushi or *shabu shabu* or any one of the myriad treats just waiting outside the door. Instead she was here on her own in a cold room in the suburbs of Osaka with a fifteen-inch television that looked as if it had been made in the last century taking up all the space on the only table in the room, and a set of electrical sockets that looked like they might blow if you plugged in a hairdryer.

Welcome to your brilliant career, she said to herself as she opened her bag and took out the meagre selection of clothes she had brought with her. She'd meant to bring more of her things over once she'd got settled in, but now she felt that the fewer of her possessions she subjected to the depressing environment of her room the better.

Feeling too tired after her early start to venture out in search of food, she unfolded the pile of sheets and blankets on the bottom of the bed and spread them out uncaringly. She was asleep in five minutes.

*

The next day wasn't much better. There weren't any other women in the IT section apart from Mimi, and the impassive men studied their computer screens with exaggerated concentration, as though to protect themselves from any human interaction. And the odd feeling of simmering tension persisted, despite Josie's attempts to convince herself she was imagining it.

She looked wistfully across at a little group of three guys about her age working on the far side of the room who seemed like they might turn out to be fun. She'd heard them laughing together when Mr Shiga was out of the room. Apart from them and the guy at the next desk to her who at least said good morning, everyone was older than her with serious faces that never turned in her direction.

By Thursday she was feeling desperate to get back to Tokyo. She trailed around the gloomy building, going through the same set of steps on each new computer and wondering how long she could stand it. But then something happened to break the monotony. One of the young men she'd seen working on the opposite side of the room passed her in the corridor and stopped.

'Hi,' he said. 'You're the new girl, aren't you. I'm Koji Hamada. Pleased to meet you.'

'Josie Clark. Same here.'

Josie felt ludicrously happy to have at least spoken to another human being about something other than work. And Koji seemed promising. He was shorter than average even for Japan, thin and spry looking and seemed to be constantly on the move, an impression reinforced by his bright eyes which darted everywhere and missed nothing. They gave his face an air of animation unusual among the bland impassive faces of most of her colleagues. Even from a distance Josie had marked him out as the ringleader of his little group. He wore the unvarying black suit and white shirt of the salaryman but Josie had the impression that, left to his own devices, he might have an interesting taste in clothes.

'You work for Mr Shiga, don't you?' said Koji. 'How's that going?'

'Okay. It's my first week so it's hard to say.'

Koji glanced at her, his eyes twinkling.

'He's not going to improve on acquaintance.'

Josie smiled, feeling relieved to have someone to be conspiratorial with at last.

'I think you might be right,' she said. 'How about you? What do you do?'

'I do troubleshooting,' said Koji. 'Which basically means explaining to the idiots in this company how to use a computer. Me and Mack and Taro.'

Josie noticed his two companions hovering behind him, waiting to be introduced. Koji beckoned them forward.

'Meet our little team,' he said. 'Makoto Banda - we call him Mack - and Taro Yoshida.'

His two companions bowed to Josie. The one Koji had introduced as Mack kept his head bent, but Josie noticed his hair was stylishly cut and his suit fitted him in a way that salarymen's suits rarely did. When he looked up his face had a chiselled, aristocratic look. Taro Yoshida was a contrast to the other two – tall enough to look Josie in the eye, solidly built, with an air of bovine calm. He had enormous feet, encased in clumpy black shoes, and large awkward hands.

'Mack's from Osaka,' said Koji. 'Unlike most of the people who work here. And Taro is from Toyohashi.'

'Toyohashi?' said Josie. 'Where's that?'

'Not far from Nagoya,' said Taro. 'It's on the bullet train route, but the Nozomi doesn't stop there. I have to get the Hikari.'

The Nozomi was the fastest of the Tokaido bullet trains and Josie always travelled by it to get to Tokyo. The Hikari made more stops and ran slightly slower, while the Kodama, the slowest, made so many stops that in Josie's view it hardly qualified for the title of bullet train at all.

'What about you?' said Josie to Koji.

"Okayama,' said Koji. 'I was hoping to get sent to Tokyo but I ended up with Osaka. At least it's bigger than Okayama, but it's still a backwater as far as AZT's concerned. They keep saying they're going to rebuild and turn it into a big insurance centre, but nothing seems to happen.'

'There's a problem about the land,' said Mack. 'That's what I heard. They've got to buy out the main leaseholder before they can do anything. That'll take years.'

'And in the meantime they're just letting the old office decay,' said Koji. 'You must have got a shock when you saw it.'

Josie laughed.

'Well,' she said. 'It wasn't quite what I expected from a big multinational like AZT.'

'And the IT section is the worst,' said Koji. 'Most of the people who work in it don't know anything about computers. And that includes Mr Shiga.'

'It's true,' said Taro. 'Koji's way brighter than Mr Shiga. Koji should be in charge here, then we'd get things done. He's a wizard, just like Harry Potter. I call him Harry sometimes, don't I, Koji?'

'That's right,' said Koji. 'I keep a wand in my desk drawer, you know.'

Taro laughed, but Josie could see he half believed it.

'Mack is Ron Weasley,' Taro went on. 'And I'm Hagrid.'

'Why Hagrid?' said Josie.

'Because I'm bigger than the others and I don't think as fast,' said Taro. 'You can be Hermione if you like. We don't have a Hermione yet because there aren't any women in the IT section.'

'There's Mimi,' said Josie.

'She's the office lady. She can't be Hermione. It's got to be someone clever to be Hermione.'

Josie thought she saw Mack frown but he didn't say anything.

'Is Mimi her real name?' Josie said.

'No,' said Koji. 'I called her that. It's short for Fukumimi – lucky ears.'

'That's a bit cruel!'

'No, it's not. A woman with lucky ears will bring good fortune and riches to the man who marries her. Everyone wants to marry a woman with lucky ears.'

'Mr Shiga likes her,' said Taro. 'But I don't think

she likes him.'

Once again Josie had the sensation that Mack was going to say something but checked himself.

'Okay,' said Josie. 'I don't mind being Hermione. What does it involve?'

'Not a lot,' said Mack. 'Though Taro will show you round Universal Studios Harry Potter Experience if you like. He knows it like the back of his hand.'

'I bet the one in London is miles better,' said Taro eagerly. 'What do you think?'

'Sorry, I've no idea,' said Josie. 'I'm from London but I haven't been back there in a while and I've never been to the Harry Potter place. But I've seen platform nine and three quarters at King's Cross.'

Taro's eyes grew large.

'I really want to go to London,' said Taro. 'I'm saving up for it.'

'Now you've met us, you should get to know us better,' said Koji. Why don't you come out to lunch one day? There's a place we go to every Monday that I'm sure you'd like.'

'It serves the best noodles in Osaka,' said Mack.

'I can't resist that,' said Josie. 'Thanks, I'd love to.'

'Right, we'll do it next Monday, then,' said Koji.

Josie headed off to her next task feeling distinctly brighter. Maybe Osaka wouldn't be so bad after all.

She was so preoccupied with her encounter that she took a while to register that there was something familiar about a figure at the far end of the corridor.

A thin, ascetic-looking man with a worn suit and tightly knotted tie. His face was turned away from her, but Josie's heart leapt – she could recognise Mr Tanaka, her friend and mentor anywhere. That characteristic slow walk and thoughtful air – it couldn't be anyone else.

'Mr Tanaka,' she called, hurrying towards him, but to her surprise, instead of turning round and greeting her with a smile, the figure turned away and disappeared into a nearby office. She looked at the sign on the door, which said *Global Reinsurance*. That made sense – it was Mr Tanaka's speciality. She wondered whether to follow him, but something held her back. If he didn't want to speak to her, there must be a reason. She'd be seeing him soon in Tokyo – she'd ask him then.

*

On Friday Josie got to the office early, determined to get her allocated number of checklists finished so she could get back to Tokyo and meet Dave for a late supper and a night on the town. She'd thought about it carefully and decided that the ten past six train, which would get her into Tokyo at eight forty three, was the perfect compromise between looking keen and having enough of the evening left by the time she got to Tokyo to make it worthwhile.

Judging by the lightening in the atmosphere in the office, her new colleagues felt much the same. Josie found out why when Mimi came round with the tea.

'Didn't you know?' Mimi said. 'Mr Shiga and Mr Ozawa are off to a meeting in Nagoya this afternoon. So everyone's planning an early getaway.'

Josie mentally kicked herself for failing to find out this crucial piece of information. She could have booked a seat on an earlier train, but it was too late to change now.

'What time are they going?' she said.

'Two o'clock. And it's going to be a long meeting so they definitely won't be coming back afterwards. Mr Ozawa told me so.'

Mimi moved on with her tray.

The man sitting next to Josie, who had overheard, leaned across and said, '*Hana no kinyobi*, you know.'

Josie did know. Friday, when the flowers bloom, the Japanese equivalent of *Thank God it's Friday*.

She looked at her neighbour. He was about her age, with a long chin and narrow eyes that made him look a bit like a fox.

'I'm heading back to Tokyo for a night out with my boyfriend,' she said. 'What about you?'

'I'm going back to Shizuoka. I haven't been able to get away for weeks so I'm determined to be on that train tonight.'

'Shizuoka, where the tea comes from,' said Josie automatically.

'That's right. I'll bring some in for you if you like.'

'Thanks,' said Josie. 'Though I didn't mean to hint or anything.'

'No problem. We like people to enjoy our tea.'

*

That afternoon Josie rushed through the rest of her checks and managed to finish them all by half past five. When she got back to the office it was to find a very different atmosphere to the normal simmering silence. Mr Shiga's desk was empty, his computer screen blank. Some people had obviously left already, and those that hadn't were leaning back in their chairs chatting and idling. There was no sign of her three fellow wizards and she suspected they'd probably been among the first to leave. Her neighbour's desk, too, was clear and the screen dark. Josie left her completed checklists on Mr Shiga's desk and shut down her computer.

New Osaka station, when she got there, was pandemonium. It was the height of the rush hour as everyone fought to get onto bullet trains to Tokyo or, in the other direction, to Hiroshima and beyond. Crowds of people flowed though the ticket barriers that separated the bullet train platforms from the JR lines and spread out to buy bento boxes of food to eat on the train, papers and books for the journey or boxes of sweets and cakes to take back to their loved ones. Then they jammed themselves onto the escalators that led up from the shopping area to the bullet train platforms. A few people were making a last minute dash for the platform to catch the train that was about to pull out. Josie stood aside to let them rush past – she'd got ten minutes before her train left, enough time to consider buying one of the boxes of Osaka specialities, which mainly consisted of soft balls of sweet paste with sweet aduki beans in the centre. There were great piles of them, each box carefully wrapped in coloured paper with just the top one left open to display its wares. She decided against it and headed for her platform.

Her train slid out of the station bang on time, as the bullet trains always did. Her compartment was crowded and far too warm for Josie's liking, though everyone else seemed to find it perfectly comfortable. She handed over her ticket to be stamped when the smartly dressed young ticket collector came round, bowing as he entered and left the carriage, and then drifted into a doze. Many of the other occupants of the compartment were asleep, or else eating the bento meals they'd bought at the station while staring intently at their mobile phones. A young mother with two children read to them quietly from a picture book and two young women had a whispered conversation, careful not to disturb those around them.

At Kyoto and Nagoya a load of passengers got off and another load replaced them. Then it was non-stop for an hour and a quarter to New Yokohama, the dormitory town for Tokyo, where at least half of the passengers left the train. Then Shinagawa, where Josie would have got off if she hadn't arranged to meet Dave in town. Then Tokyo, where everyone got up, picked up their bags of litter and formed a queue waiting for the doors to open.

Josie followed the line of people off the train and down the escalator where they joined a flow of people from other trains heading for the ticket barriers. She waited, shuffling forward, until it was her turn to feed her ticket into the automatic ticket barrier which swallowed it and flashed up a *thank you* on its display as she passed through. Just another Friday night in one of the busiest stations in the world, thought Josie, but then paused as she realised that something unusual was going on. The tide of people was flowing away from the platforms as normal, but for some reason the ticket barriers into the bullet train area were shut and a crowd was rapidly building up.

'What's going on?' she said to one of the waiting commuters.

'There's trouble on one of the bullet trains that's just come in,' he said. 'They're not letting anyone through.'

'What kind of trouble?'

The man just shook his head, but a woman next to him said, 'Haven't you heard? Someone told me they've found a body on a train. Stabbed to death.'

THREE

Josie hurried away from the station, not wanting to hear any more. She'd had enough of bodies – she'd already been involved with too many of them since she came to Japan. She was done with investigations and finding out that people she knew were murderers. Not every dead body in Japan was her problem. She hadn't found this one, didn't know who it was, knew nothing about it and planned for it to stay that way. She and Dave were having a night out and no dead bodies were going to stop her enjoying herself.

All the same, she couldn't stop herself taking a quick look at the television news the next morning. There wasn't much information. The body had been found in a disabled toilet by one of the cleaners preparing the train for a quick turnaround on one of the busiest days of the week. The victim had been stabbed. The police had been called and had held the train in the station, causing untold damage to the operating schedule. The train had come up from

Hakata in the far west, stopping at Hiroshima, Osaka and Nagoya before it terminated in Tokyo. There was footage of the scene at Tokyo station the night before and an interview with a representative of Japan Railways, who said, 'We are happy to cooperate with the police in any way we can,' as the crowds built up behind him.

'The police must do their job. There's nothing to be done,' said one commuter, standing in what Josie recognised as the access area for bullet trains at Tokyo station. People around him nodded, or hurried past heading for the JR platforms where trains continued to run.

'The affected train was taken out of service,' said the announcer, 'so that police can perform more forensic tests. There is no word yet on the identity of the victim. But this morning the bullet train platforms have been reopened and the schedule has returned to normal.'

The report drifted off into a discussion of knife crime and whether it was or was not on the rise. There was a reference to 'Chinese elements' which made Josie grimace. Any violent crime in Japan was sure to be blamed on Chinese elements. It was as though Japanese people couldn't believe themselves capable of such acts.

So it was a stabbing, Josie thought. There must have been some blood, but no one had noticed anyone with blood on them leaving the train. It seemed unlikely that you could stab someone to death on a crowded train, even in the disabled toilet, without anybody noticing, but this murderer seemed to have achieved it. He must be either incredibly lucky or very methodical.

A sound behind her made her turn. Dave came into the room with two steaming mugs of tea. Josie hurriedly switched the television off.

'I was just looking to see what's happening about the trains,' she said. 'Apparently they're back to normal, so I'll be alright on Monday morning. Not that I'm looking forward to going back.'

Dave sat down on the sofa and handed her one of the mugs.

'I get the impression the Osaka office is not exactly what you were hoping for.'

'I'm not sure what I expected,' said Josie. 'But I suppose I thought it would be more up to date and that I'd learn new stuff. But it's so old-fashioned. And it's hard to get to know anyone.'

'Your Mr Shiga sounds like a pain.'

'He's awful,' said Josie. 'We hardly speak, and he goes around with a long face all the time as though he has some dreadful secret preying on his mind.'

'Maybe he does.'

'Well, I wish he wouldn't worry about it at the office. And then there's Mr Ozawa. He's like some caricature of a boss, all barking orders and lurking in his room.'

'What about the other people in the IT section? I thought you said you liked some of them?'

'Yes, though I'm not sure about this Harry Potter business. I know the films are massively popular here but I can't help feeling having a Potter group at work is taking things a bit far.'

Dave laughed.

'Well, Hermione, you can come and work your magic on me if you like. I have this terrible desire to be bad and only you can fix it.'

He grabbed her and pushed her towards the bedroom, growling. Josie laughed. It was good to be home.

*

The weekend drifted past in a haze. They had a leisurely brunch at the local salad bar and Josie spent the afternoon shopping among the fashionistas of Shibuya with Keiko. It was bliss. On Sunday they went walking in Yoyogi Park and had *tonkatsu* pork cutlet in Josie's favourite restaurant, where they gave you your own little bowl of sesame seeds to grind, releasing a spicy-sweet aroma, and you could order endless refills of rice and shredded cabbage. She went to bed that night feeling that she'd been living the good life and wondering why on earth she'd let herself in for six months in Osaka.

'Thank goodness the trains are back to normal,' she said to Dave as she kissed him a hasty goodbye on Monday morning. 'I don't want to be late.'

Dave grunted and turned over.

'Shut the door quietly,' he called after her. 'I'm going back to sleep. Just because you have to get up in the middle of the night doesn't mean I'm going to miss out on my eight hours.'

Standing on the platform in the early morning sunshine waiting for her train to come in, Josie couldn't help thinking about the body and the poor cleaner who'd found it. She'd often seen the cleaning teams, half a dozen women in bubblegum pink uniforms with bulky white bags of cleaning materials slung over their shoulders, standing in a patient line waiting for the train to arrive. They had just a few minutes to sweep through the train emptying the rubbish bins and cleaning the seats before the next cargo of passengers embarked and the train left, with the cleaners lined up on the platform to bow it on its way. Up until now all the thought she'd given them was to wish they'd hurry up so she could board the train. Now she imagined what it must have been like to open the toilet door and find a blood-covered corpse inside. It was enough to put you off going to the loo for life. Josie wondered if the cleaner had screamed and her colleagues had come running to stare at the awful sight, like they did in the movies.

By the time her train glided into the station, its impossibly long snout gleaming white and its front lights shining like fiery nostrils, Josie had put together a vivid mental picture of the moment of discovery. The slumped body, the blood on the floor, the reflection of the cleaner's terrified face in the mirror. She could see just how it must have been. And then, the wait while the police were called, delayed passengers getting ever more restive until finally the announcement over the tannoy that the train was being held indefinitely due to 'an unforeseen problem'. And the patient commuters had turned and filed away, getting out their mobile phones to tell their waiting families they wouldn't be home for dinner.

As always, the train slowed to a halt with the door of her compartment neatly lined up with the numbered gap in the platform edge barrier. Josie followed the queue onto the train, looking at the familiar sight with fresh eyes. A long sleek tube like the inside of an aircraft with rows of seats all along it, three on one side of the aisle and two on the other, upholstered in restful blue. Oblong windows along each side, many of them with their translucent grey blinds already drawn against the weak morning sun. Some of the seats occupied, a few already tilted back so their occupants could catch up on missed sleep on the journey. A peaceful air, with few conversations. Many passengers were already engrossed in their mobile phones, switched to 'manner mode' so as not to disturb anyone around them. It was, as usual, uncomfortably warm and smelled, as always, like boot polish and disinfectant.

The train imperceptibly gathered speed, reaching nearly two hundred miles an hour as they raced through the morning light. Josie, like the rest of the passengers, hardly glanced out the window. Spectacular speed was what they expected; excitement was for tourists. Instead she studied the map of the train on the back of her fold-out tray with more than usual interest.

It was a sixteen car train with unreserved seats in the front three compartments and the more expensive Green Car compartments in the middle. There were twenty rows of seats in each compartment, except for the first and the last compartments which were shorter because they had engines attached. All the compartments had aisles and connecting doors so you could walk the whole length of the train if that was what took your fancy. Every odd-numbered compartment had two high-tech toilets, a urinal and a washbasin at one end. But it was compartment eleven that Josie was interested in – that was where the disabled toilet was.

On an impulse she got up and walked through to compartment eleven. The disabled toilet, with its sliding semicircular door took up most of one end and there was plenty of room inside. Easily room for more than one person. Plus, as there were no seats nearby, and most people preferred to use the ordinary toilets, it was unlikely that there would be many people around to hear anything suspicious. All in all, it was a perfect place for a murder, with running water literally on tap.

Back in her seat, she opened her newspaper, the tabloid *Mainichi Shinbun*, which had gone to town on the murder story. The victim still hadn't been named and no details about him had emerged, beyond the fact that he was a salaryman, but then most of the people on the train probably were, so that didn't tell you much. He'd been found slumped on the floor of the disabled toilet with the door closed but not locked. The knife he'd been stabbed with was in the sink where it had been cleaned of blood and fingerprints. It was a *hōchō* – the kind of large kitchen knife that everyone used for chopping vegetables, sharp, with a pointed end. A *hōchō* was a basic kitchen essential – you could buy them everywhere. Josie had one and had come close to chopping her finger off one time when she wasn't paying attention, so she was well aware of its potential as a lethal weapon.

It had originally struck her as odd that no one had discovered the body before the train reached Tokyo. In Josie's experience the toilets on the train got a lot of use, especially as the train approached its destination, so someone would have been bound to stumble in through the unlocked door. On the other hand, if it had only happened just before the train pulled into Tokyo there'd have been people queuing at the exit doors ready to get off and they surely would have heard something. But now she'd seen the disabled toilet she could see how isolated from the rest of the train it was. And it had been a Hikari train, and most people travelling as far as Tokyo preferred the faster Nozomi. The majority of passengers had probably got off before the train even reached Tokyo.

The *Mainichi Shinbun* didn't indulge in such speculation. Instead it had interviewed everyone it could lay its hands on, from commuters to ticket collectors to members of the cleaning team. The trouble was, no one had very much of interest to say. They all thought it was terrible, feared for their safety, worried about how long it would take the train schedules to get back to normal and expressed relief at how quickly the police were on the scene, but in terms of actual hard facts they were useless. No one had seen anything. No one had suspected anything. But then, Josie thought, it wasn't that surprising. A toilet compartment on a train is a very private place.

But what were two people doing together in the disabled toilet? Either one had gone in and failed to lock the door properly (unlikely) or they'd gone in because they knew each other and wanted somewhere private – to do what? Josie's mind slid over the possibilities, dismissing the idea of a train equivalent of the mile high club. Not in Japan, where public exposure was a thing to be dreaded above all else.

So, a private discussion, then. An argument that went wrong. No, an argument would mean raised voices. A whispered conversation, a surprise attack, leaving the victim no time to defend themselves. The killer had kept a cool head, taking their time to clean their fingerprints off the murder weapon. Then a check in the mirror that there was no tell-tale blood on their clothes, a casual stroll back to their seat, a short wait for the train to reach Tokyo station and then an easy getaway among the crowds leaving the train. The killer could have been in a taxi and speeding away before the cleaner discovered the body. All they had to do was stay calm.

Josie wondered if there was any record of who was on the train. Probably not. On a Friday night there'd be a lot of people catching whatever train came in first and looking for a seat in the unreserved compartments. They'd have bought their ticket from a machine with cash – Japan was a cash society and everyone, even Josie, routinely carried a stack of 10,000 yen notes. She would never have dreamt of wandering around with several hundred pounds in fifty pound notes on her in London, but somehow in Japan it had come to seem normal – everybody did it. Why not, in a low-crime society where credit cards were only just beginning to catch on?

'It's terrifying isn't it?' said a voice beside her, and Josie realised she'd been staring at the same page of her newspaper for far too long and had attracted the attention of the young woman sitting next to her.

'I was afraid to get on the train this morning. He could still be out there, waiting to do it again. I'm not going anywhere near the toilets,' her companion said.

'I'm sure it's safe,' said Josie. 'The police will catch him soon.' Or her, she thought. We just don't know.

*

Josie arrived at the grey concrete entrance to AZT Osaka with a dull sense of familiarity, even though she'd only been working there a week. It was that kind of place – its utter predictability seeped into your soul. She grimly contemplated another week among the battered desks and ancient computers and thought longingly of her gleaming office in Tokyo.

Only five months and three weeks to go.

But when she reached the IT office, it wasn't the way she expected it to be at all. People weren't sitting at their desks but milling around in a confused sort of way, rearranging chairs and moving some of the taller piles of unused computer kit to clear a space.

Josie stood at the door, not knowing quite what to do. She felt she ought to help, but she didn't really know what they were doing, and the fact that she had hardly spoken to any of her colleagues before made her hesitate, so she just stood and watched as a rough circle of chairs was assembled in the centre of the room and people sat down with an air of nervous anticipation.

Josie wondered if she should sit down too and whether it mattered where she sat, so it was a relief when Koji, who was sitting near the front, turned to survey the rest of the room and caught her eye. He waved at her and pointed to the seat next to him.

'Thanks,' she said. 'What's going on?'

'The Director of IT is going to address us.'

'Oh. Does he do that often?'

'Never, in my experience.'

Koji turned to look around the room again as though he was expecting someone, while his hand tapped out a constant rhythm on his knee, which she found it slightly unnerving.

'So why is he going to talk to us now?' she said, hoping to distract Koji from whatever was on his mind.

'I don't know,' said Koji. 'Nobody knows. We were just told to get ready for an announcement. My guess is—' He stopped abruptly as Mr Ozawa came into the room, accompanied by a tall, grim faced man who, Josie assumed, must be the director. The man took his place at the centre of the circle and looked around. Koji took a pair of heavy-rimmed glasses from his pocket and put them on, then stared intensely at the Director.

'I'm sorry to disrupt your work,' the Director said. 'But some news will be announced later today and I wanted you to hear it from me first.'

Oh, no, Josie thought. AZT's gone bust and I'm out of a job.

'What I have to tell you is not strictly work-related,' said the Director. 'But it concerns a work colleague. Or perhaps I should say, a former colleague.'

There was a stir as everyone looked around, trying to work out who was missing. Mr Shiga, who was sitting in the front row, turned round to shush them. His face was white and he looked as though he might be sick.

Someone's run off with the contents of Mr Ozawa's safe, thought Josie. Or got drunk and said something rude about the Emperor.

'You all know…knew…Mr Horii. He joined us at the end of last year and did valuable work on the helpdesk. He was a steady and reliable worker, who will be sadly missed.'

At the words 'sadly missed' there was a collective

intake of breath from his audience and Josie regretted her frivolous thoughts.

'Mr Horii was taken from us on Friday evening and I'm sorry to say that his death was not a natural one. You may have read in the papers about the terrible incident on a bullet train to Tokyo on Friday evening. It is with great regret that I have to inform you that Mr Horii was the victim of that horrendous attack. His parents have been informed and the police will be releasing his name to the press today. May his soul rest in peace.'

There was a murmur of horror from the assembled company.

'Although we are confident this terrible act has nothing to do with anyone at AZT, the police will naturally explore every avenue. Mr Horii's desk has been taken away for examination and the police have told me they wish to interview all Mr Horii's colleagues. We have set aside a room for them to do that and you will all be called in order this afternoon. I'm sorry for the disruption to your work but I'm sure I can rely on you all to work hard to catch up.'

He made a sign to someone at the door, who opened it to allow a number of office ladies with trays of green tea to come in. The director walked purposefully from the room and Mr Ozawa said, 'I realise you will all want a few moments to come to terms with this awful news. But then, let us return to our duties and work hard to deliver the best results we can achieve, in Mr Horii's memory.'

Josie took a proffered cup of green tea

mechanically. Her mind was in a state of confusion and for a moment she couldn't think straight. The murder on the train, the one she had thought was nothing to do with her, had suddenly come very close to home. But who was Mr Horii? She couldn't think, and she couldn't tell in all the melée who was missing. Not that she'd be able to work it out anyway. The only people she knew, apart from Mr Shiga and Mr Ozawa, were Koji, Mack and Taro. And she'd spoken briefly to the guy at the next desk, but didn't know his name.

She turned to Koji, who suddenly looked surprisingly calm.

'What a dreadful thing,' she said. 'But who was Mr Horii?'

'Saburo,' said Koji. 'Saburo Horii. We were the same age. We joined the company together. And now he's gone.'

'Where did he used to sit?'

'You must know. I saw you talking to him on Friday. He sat next to you. You could have been the last person to speak to him. I bet the police are going to be interested in you.'

FOUR

People started to move the tables and chairs back to their usual positions and get back to work. Mimi appeared with a batch of papers which she handed around.

'Timetable for the police interviews this afternoon,' Mimi said as she gave Josie a copy. Josie stared at it unseeingly.

'What do we do now?' she said. 'Just go back to work as though nothing had happened?'

She looked across to Mr Shiga's desk. He was already at work, staring fixedly at his computer screen as though daring anyone to disturb him.

'Just fake it until lunchtime,' said Koji. 'Then we'll go to that place I told you about, just you and me and Mack and Taro. We can talk about it there without anyone hearing us.'

'Okay,' said Josie.

'We'll all leave the room separately and meet up in the foyer. I don't want Mr Shiga to know we're going out,' said Koji. Josie nodded, still too stunned to think for herself and glad to be told what to do.

She sat down at her computer and pretended to do some work, shuffling her pile of checklists from time to time in the hope that she would look like she was doing something useful. She was uncomfortably aware of the empty space next to her where Saburo Horii's desk used to be. She wondered if the police would bring it back when they'd finished with it or if it was regarded as evidence in some way. They'd taken his computer too, of course, and all his papers. They were probably going through it all now, looking for clues that might tell them who the killer was.

Why had he been murdered? she wondered. Did he have enemies who hated him enough to kill him? Or secrets in his life that the police would unearth? It seemed unlikely for an IT specialist in an insurance company, but there must be something to find, otherwise he would still be alive. Josie wished she'd talked to him in the brief window when she'd had the chance. Then she might have had some idea why it had happened. As it was, all she knew about him was that he came from Shizuoka and had a thin fox-like face.

A tap on her shoulder broke her train of thought. Koji walked behind her on his way out. Josie gave it a minute and then got up and went down to the foyer where she found Koji, Mack and Taro waiting for her. Without a word Koji led the way through the heavy doors and out into the street. The pine trees rustled in the gentle wind as they passed and Josie looked up at the sun glinting through their needles. It was going to be another lovely day, as the world continued on its usual course, oblivious to Saburo's death.

Koji moved surprisingly fast and Josie found herself struggling to keep up with him, even though she was a good six inches taller than he was. He led the way down the street away from Osaka station, into a maze of back streets lined with old-fashioned houses where girls on bicycles, with their shopping in wicker baskets on the front, chatted as they rode and old ladies with string bags of vegetables tottered past. Josie felt as though she'd suddenly plunged into a different world, like Alice following the white rabbit down the rabbit hole.

Koji stopped abruptly outside a haberdasher's shop, its bow window filled with a miscellany of ribbons and patchwork, knitting patterns, felt toys and glittering boxes of buttons.

'This is it,' he said.

'Here?' said Josie dubiously.

'Wait and see,' said Koji, and led the way through a tiny shop crowded with rolls of cloth and balls of wool to a door at the back. He opened it and gestured to Josie to go through.

On the other side was an old-fashioned parlour with a big round table covered in a lace cloth where a couple of young men in dark suits were already seated. Koji motioned to Josie to take a chair and sat next to her with Mack and Taro on his other side. A middle-aged woman, wearing the sort of flowery pinny Josie had only seen before in photos from the 1950's, emerged from a door on the far side of the room with two steaming bowls of noodles which she put down in front of the waiting young men. Then she turned to the new arrivals and eyed Josie appraisingly.

'Who's this you've brought with you?' she said to Koji, in a broad Osaka accent.

'This is Josie Clark, Mrs Miyazaki,' said Koji. 'She's just started working in our office and she's had a bit of a shock this morning. We all have. So we need some of your famous noodles to put us back together.'

Mrs Miyazaki nodded but didn't ask what the shock had been.

'Can she eat noodles?' she said.

'I love noodles,' said Josie, tired of being treated like she wasn't part of the conversation. 'And I speak Japanese too.'

'Even *Osaka-ben*?' said Mrs Miyazaki. *Osaka-ben* was the local dialect, which Josie still struggled to follow, though she wasn't prepared to admit it.

'Yes, of course,' Josie said, hoping she wouldn't get caught out.

Mrs Miyazaki nodded and disappeared back into the kitchen.

'Are you sure it's alright, bringing me here?' said Josie.

'Don't mind Mrs Miyazaki,' said Mack. 'It's just that she's fussy who she serves. But you came with us so she knows you're okay.'

Mrs Miyazaki emerged with more steaming bowls. She put one down in front of Josie. It was full of gleaming yellow broth, shining white noodles and beansprouts, and was topped with three thin slices of pork and half a soft-boiled egg. Enoki mushrooms peeped out from just below the surface. It smelled deliciously, saltily, of pork and miso.

Josie took a pair of chopsticks from the jar in the middle of the table and picked up a good pile of noodles, holding them over the bowl to cool before she put them in her mouth. The rest of the occupants of the back room were already tucking in and the air was filled with the hiss of noodles being slurped. Josie tried to keep up with the others but as usual her noodle-slurping skills left her trailing behind. The customers who had been there when the AZT group arrived had already paid up and left by the time she picked up her bowl and drank the last of her broth.

Mrs Miyazaki took away the empty dishes and gave them all a little handleless cup of brown tea. Then she disappeared into the kitchen again, leaving them with the room to themselves.

'It's good, isn't it?' said Koji. 'But you have to know it's here. And Mrs Miyazaki doesn't let just anyone in. You have to be introduced, and she has to like you. We come here every Monday, and Mrs Miyazaki has our noodles waiting ready for us.'

'They're the best noodles in Umeda,' added Mack. 'Better than the specialist noodle shops, even. Plus it's quiet here and there's no queue.'

Koji nodded. 'Mack here,' he said, 'is a noodle

connoisseur.'

'Well, I don't know about that,' said Mack. 'But my uncle runs a noodle bar, so I know a bit about it. I'll take you there sometime if you like. It's in Namba.'

'That would be great. I know Osaka is famous for its food.'

'The kitchen of Japan,' said Mack, with a touch of justifiable pride.

'People in Osaka arc famous for their obsession with food,' said Koji, whose thinness suggested he didn't share their interest. 'Have you ever heard of *kuidaore*?'

'No – what is it?'

'It means to eat yourself bankrupt. It's a saying. Tokyo people bankrupt themselves on shoes, Kyoto people on clothes and Osaka people on food.'

'Dotonbori is the place to go,' said Mack. 'It's the biggest concentration of restaurants in the whole of Japan. You can get anything you want there.'

'You can see Dotonbori Taro and his drum,' said Taro. 'Taro, like me, see?' A big silly grin spread over his face and he started drumming on the table as though his fingers were drumsticks.

'I feel guilty, somehow, eating noodles and talking about food when we've just heard about Saburo,' said Josie.

'We can't give up eating because of that,' said Mack.

'Did Saburo ever come here with you?'

Mack hesitated and glanced at Koji, as though

54

looking for guidance on what to say. Koji replied for him.

'Saburo came here once or twice,' he said smoothly. 'But he wasn't really part of our group.'

'He never had any time for us,' said Taro. 'I wanted him to come out to the arcades and play games with me but he never would.'

'He was okay,' said Mack. 'He wasn't very sociable, that's all.'

'He was the same age as Koji?'

'Yes, Koji and Saburo joined the company together and then Taro and I joined the year after.'

'Saburo was too serious for us,' said Koji. 'We like to have fun once in a while but all he ever did was work. He was just like the old guys – always stuck at his desk. Never took his eyes off the computer screen.'

'He took them off when Mimi was around,' said Taro with a foolishly sly grin.

'Shut up,' said Mack. 'You shouldn't talk about Saburo and Mimi like that.'

Taro sniggered but didn't reply.

'Well, when the police question you this afternoon you can tell them all about it,' said Koji. 'You can include Mimi's list of conquests if you like.'

The mention of the police seemed to silence them all. Koji got up from the table, leaving a one thousand yen note by his plate. The others did the same and Josie followed their example.

'Thanks for taking me to Mrs Miyazaki's,' she said as they walked back to the office.

'Come again,' said Mack. 'Any Monday.'

The grey bulk of the AZT office swam into view, casting a shadow over Josie's mood. There was something unsettling about it – not just the peeling building, left to decay while people wrangled about leases, but the whole atmosphere inside it. It just didn't feel the way it should. People were closed in and secretive, as though they had something to hide When she went into people's offices to check their computers they didn't smile at her or ask her anything about who she was and what had brought her there. They just moved aside and got on with some paperwork while she worked. Which was odd, when you thought about it. She was the only foreigner working in AZT Osaka as far as she could tell, and usually people wanted to know all about her. Especially in a place like Osaka, Manchester to Tokyo's London, full of independent-minded people with strong opinions and no inhibitions about expressing them. Josie had been to the Kansai area before, when she was a fan of the Takarazuka Revue which was based just outside Osaka, and she'd always found people outgoing and friendly. Why was the Osaka office so different?

Back at her desk Josie picked up the timetable for the police interviews. They were starting with Mr Ozawa and Mr Shiga and working their way down the hierarchy until they reached Josie, almost at the bottom. Only Mimi ranked lower. On an impulse Josie headed towards the little kitchen which was where Mimi was most often to be found, making tea.

'Can I have a cup of tea please, Mimi?' she said, squeezing into the limited space as Mimi pressed the top of the green tea dispenser to fill a cup for her.

'You've been out with the boy wizards, then,' said Mimi.

'Oh you saw? Yes, they took me out to lunch. It was very kind of them,' said Josie.

Mimi nodded.

'Very kind of them,' she echoed.

'It's awful news about Saburo,' said Josie. 'Did you know him well?'

Mimi turned away and busied herself opening a new box of tea so Josie couldn't see her face.

'Not that well,' she said. 'Why, did someone say I did?'

'Someone said something, I think,' said Josie, wishing she hadn't asked the question.

'Who?'

'Oh, I don't know, one of the guys I suppose.'

'Taro, you mean.'

'Well, yes.'

'Taro's nosy but he isn't always right,' said Mimi. 'You'd do well not to trust everything he says.'

'Okay,' said Josie. 'Thanks for the tea.'

She took the cup back to her desk, arriving just in time to see Mr Shiga returning from his police interview. He looked sick and sat down at his desk with a heavy thump. Josie wondered if they'd been grilling him. But what was there to grill him about?

All the rest of the afternoon she tried to concentrate on her emails as one by one the members of the IT section were called to their police interviews. But she couldn't stop herself looking up guiltily every time anyone left the room or returned, which was surprisingly frequently. It didn't seem like the police were investing a lot of time in grilling Saburo's colleagues – on average Josie reckoned the interval between each interviewee leaving the room and returning was about half an hour, which meant that the actual interview must have been shorter than that. She tried to get a look at the faces of the returnees to see whether they looked as though they had been through the mill but they all seemed to look much the same as when they left. The only one who looked upset was Mr Shiga, who'd been kept the longest.

By the time it got to Josie's turn, interview time was down to twenty minutes. She couldn't stop herself giving a little jump when her name was called and her heart started to thump alarmingly, but she managed to calm herself by the time she reached the interview room. After all, it wasn't her first experience of the Japanese police. She'd had to deal with them before when she'd had to give evidence and they'd always been perfectly kind and polite. But this was different – this time she was being interviewed at the start of an investigation, could even be a possible suspect as far as they were concerned. It was a novel feeling, the feeling of being under suspicion, and not one that she enjoyed.

Inside the interview room were two policemen, both on the young side. No grizzled detectives with piercing eyes then, Josie thought as she took the proffered seat and waited for the interview to begin. It did without any preliminaries. The policeman sitting across the table from her looked down at his list of questions and began to ask them with an air of performing a well-worn routine, from which Josie guessed that everyone else had been asked exactly the same thing. His colleague, who sat slightly to one side, poised his pen over a sheet of ruled paper, ready to record her answers.

It amused Josie to think that what she said would go down on his sheet in beautifully formed *kanji* characters that she herself would struggle to write. For a moment she had a flash of respect for the police, then she wondered why they were using such an old-fashioned method when they could have taken their notes so much quicker on a laptop. But she knew the answer – change came slowly in Japan, and a bureaucratic organisation like the police would be the last to join the twenty first century.

She was so distracted by these thoughts that she didn't quite catch the first question and had to ask for it to be repeated. The policeman looked confused. Oh no, Josie thought, he thinks I don't really understand Japanese and he doesn't know what to do.

'I'm sorry,' she said quickly. 'It's just that I didn't quite catch what you said. Just ask me again.'

The policeman looked uncomfortable, but repeated what he had said, speaking very slowly and loudly.

'Please state your name and position in the

company.'

'Oh,' said Josie. 'My name is Josie Clark and I'm an assistant in IT Support.'

The man with the pen put two little ticks at the top of his sheet of paper where Josie's name and rank were written.

Were you present on the AZT premises last Friday afternoon?'

'Yes, I was.'

'Did you leave the IT Support office at any time between one o'clock and five o'clock?'

'Yes, I was out the whole time checking computers.'

'From one o'clock?'

'I went out straight after lunch, so yes, from one o'clock.'

'Which floors did you visit?'

'I was working on the fourth floor that day.'

The policeman checked a plan of the layout of the building and said, 'So you were in the Fire and Domestic Damage section?'

'That's right.'

'The whole time?'

'Yes,' said Josie, remembering the tedium of that afternoon. 'The whole time.'

'Did you leave the building at any time between one o'clock and five o'clock?'

'No, I didn't.'

'Did you return to the IT Support office at any time between one o'clock and five o'clock?'

'No, I didn't.'

'Did you see Mr Horii at any time between one o'clock and five o'clock?'

Josie thought back to that day. She'd spoken to Saburo in the morning, but that was it.

'No, I didn't,' she said.

'What time did you return to the IT Support office?'

'It must have been around five thirty.'

'Was Mr Horii present in the IT Support office when you returned?'

'No, he wasn't.'

'What time did you leave work?'

'It must have been about five thirty-five. I was going to catch…' she stopped as the policeman held up his hand and said, 'Please wait for the question.'

'What did you do when you left the office?'

'I walked down to Osaka station and got the Kyoto line to New Osaka station. Then I got the bullet train to Tokyo.'

'What time did your train to Tokyo leave?'

'Ten past six.'

'And what kind of train was it?' Josie hesitated and the policeman added, 'Nozomi, Hikari or Kodama?'

'Oh, I see. It was a Nozomi.'

The policeman looked down at a rail timetable in front of him and wrote Josie's name against the 18:10 Nozomi from New Osaka. Even upside down Josie could see that there were names against some of the other trains. She wondered which one Saburo had caught.

'Did you know Saburo Horii?'

'Not really. I only joined the Osaka branch last week and I'd hardly spoken to him.'

'Do you know of anyone who had quarrelled with Mr Horii?'

'No, I don't.'

'Did Mr Horii ever say anything to you that indicated he thought his life was in danger?'

'No, he didn't.'

'Do you have any other information that might be relevant to our investigation?'

'No, I don't think so.'

'Thank you for your cooperation. Please read through the notes of this interview and sign them to confirm they're correct.'

Rather hesitantly, the policeman handed her a copy of the notes, which had been made in tiny writing. Josie read through them slowly, wishing she'd done more work on getting her reading speed up. The two policemen didn't move a muscle but nevertheless managed to give a clear impression of impatience. At last Josie finished and signed at the bottom. The policemen stood up and Josie realised she was expected to leave the room.

Nobody looked up as she walked back into the office. Josie was glad, as she felt she must have a guilty look, as though she'd just been confessing all rather than just telling the police what train she'd been on.

After a few moments Mimi, the last interviewee, was called. As she walked past Josie's desk Josie looked up, meaning to give her an encouraging smile, to indicate to her that it wouldn't be as bad as she feared. But the expression on Mimi's face stopped her. She was white with fear and her hands shook so much she clenched them into tight balls. You would have thought she was going to the gallows rather than just a routine interview. Josie was shocked. Mimi had always seemed calm and self possessed – surely there was no reason for her to be worried now? Unless she knew more about Saburo's murder than she was letting on.

FIVE

Josie wrinkled her nose as a clash of expensive perfumes assaulted her senses. The street they were on, in the fashionable Azabu district of Tokyo, was crowded with stylish people wearing expensive casual wear from Emporio Armani or Max Mara. Beautifully pressed jeans in glowing spring colours were teamed with crisp shirts and cashmere sweaters thrown casually around the shoulders, a look Josie deeply envied but could never achieve herself. Dave, in his Gap sweatshirt and jeans, looked even more out of place than usual but for once Josie was oblivious to the reaction of people around her. She was trying to stop herself thinking about Saburo Horii and whether the police were any nearer catching the murderer. There had been nothing in the papers all week, just *enquiries are continuing*, which meant nothing.

The murder had been on her mind ever since Monday, though everyone in the office had studiously avoided mentioning it or giving any sign that they were thinking about it. Somehow that made it worse, as though Saburo had never existed at all. She wondered if her old friend Mr Tanaka, who they were on their way to visit, might know something about how the investigation was going, and what the reason was for the strange, nervous atmosphere in the AZT office. She hoped she'd get a chance to get him alone and ask him what he'd been doing that day when he'd pretended not to see her. Could it have something to do with Saburo's death?

The risk of an imminent collision with an expensively manicured woman carrying a tiny panting dog with a bow in its hair recalled her to reality. She linked her hand through Dave's arm, heedless of the problems of walking two abreast in such a sea of perfectly dressed humanity and, with an effort, brought her attention back to the present.

'I'm so glad you're going to meet Mr and Mrs Tanaka at last,' she said. 'It was nice of them to invite us round to meet Chiharu now she's back from America. I wonder what she'll be like?'

'How old is she?' said Dave, ducking to avoid a cyclist heading far too fast towards him.

'I think she must be about twenty three or twenty four by now. She did her degree over here, at Todai, and then went to do postgraduate work at Harvard.'

'Todai?' said Dave.

'Oh, sorry, that's Tokyo University. Their campus is not far from where Keiko and Yoshi live. They have a reputation for churning out civil servants. I wonder if that's what Chiharu is going to do.'

'That doesn't sound too promising. I suppose she'll be fabulously intellectual and wear thick glasses.'

'Don't jump to conclusions. Though I think she is pretty bright. And at least she'll speak some English which will make it much easier for you.'

'Much easier for you, you mean, not having to translate everything.'

'Much easier for both of us. Look, this is where we turn off.'

Josie swerved to the left, down a cul de sac that ended in a pathway she'd come to know well. She was a frequent visitor to the Tanaka house and the moment when she stepped onto the pathway and then entered the narrow tree-lined street beyond, leaving the fashionable crowds behind, was always a moment when her stresses and cares seemed to fall away. She glanced up at Dave, hoping he felt as she always did, that it was like entering another world, a quieter, more peaceful and slower moving one than the busy twenty-first century city they normally lived in. As they passed the weathered wayside shrine with its stone statue of some unidentified god, she promised herself for the hundredth time that she would ask Mr Tanaka about its inscription.

Beyond the shrine were the familiar little houses with curly tiled roofs. Their tiny gardens were filled with spring flowers interspersed with the hot pink of azaleas, the bushes clipped into tight roundels that were carefully arranged to resemble a careless scattering of boulders lapped by waves of forget-menots. Behind them were hydrangea bushes, already in bud and looking a little wilted in the sunshine. They were waiting for June when the rain would come sheeting down day after day and the hydrangeas' glossy green leaves would provide a gleaming backdrop to their bursting flowers.

'Did you know that in Japan hydrangea flowers change colour?' said Josie. 'They start off white, and then they turn pink and then blue. It's most peculiar.'

'What are you going on about?' said Dave. 'What hydrangeas?'

'Those ones over there. I know they're only in bud now. But I was thinking ahead.'

'While you were thinking ahead, did you happen to notice if we've reached the Tanaka's house yet?' said Dave.

'Oh, yes, we have. Actually we've walked past it. Sorry about that.'

Josie led the way back down the street to a worn nameplate that said *Tanaka*.

'Here we are,' she said, ringing the old-fashioned bell and waiting for the sound of barking that heralded the arrival of Mrs Tanaka and her little dog, Toto.

But when the door opened she got a surprise. Standing there with Toto held tightly under her arm was not the comfortable homely figure of Mrs Tanaka but a slim girl, dressed in skinny jeans and a Hollister T-shirt, with her hair in a fashionable gamine cut. She was smiling a smile that lit up her face and had one hand stretched out in welcome.

'Josie,' she said in American-accented English. 'You're Josie aren't you! I've heard so much about you, I just couldn't wait to meet you.'

She threw her arms around Josie and hugged her, almost squashing Toto, who didn't seem to mind, in the process.

'And you must be Dave,' she said to Dave, hugging him in turn. 'It's great to meet you.'

Dave smiled back.

'Nice to meet you too, Chiharu,' he said

'Oh, call me Cherie – that's what all my American friends call me. And I've told Mum and Dad to call me that now too.'

'Right, Cherie then,' said Dave, stepping into the entry hall and slipping off his outdoor shoes.

'I've given you the biggest pair of slippers I could find,' said Cherie, 'because Josie told my father you were a big guy. You certainly are – I hope the slippers are okay.'

'They're fine, just perfect,' said Dave.

'Then I'll take you along to the living room.'

Josie stepped unnoticed into her usual cherry blossom slippers and followed them down the corridor, feeling an irrational resentment towards Cherie, even towards her name. How could Mr and Mrs Tanaka's daughter be called Cherie? She wasn't American, even if she had spent the last year in the States. She was back in Japan now and ought to behave like a Japanese girl again, and not be so free and easy with... Josie caught where her train of thought was heading and stopped just in time. With

68

Dave, was how it had been going to end. As though she wasn't totally comfortable with pretty girls flirting with Dave. Heaven knew, enough of them had done it before without Josie being worried. She knew Dave would never fall for any of that stuff.

But this was different. This was Chiharu Tanaka, whose photos she had seen a million times. Chiharu as a little girl with straight black hair and serious brown eyes, Chiharu with her Girl's Festival dolls, Chiharu in her school uniform on her first day at school, Chiharu in a kimono on Coming of Age Day. How could she have turned into this frat girl called Cherie?

Josie pushed open the door to the living room to find Cherie introducing Dave to her parents.

'Oh, and here's Josie,' she said as Josie came in. 'Now, Dave, I want you to sit next to me at lunch so I can explain to you what everything is.'

'Dave's been to Japan before,' said Josie. 'He knows about Japanese food.'

'Oh, I didn't mean…,' said Cherie, as Dave looked at Josie in surprise.

'You usually have to explain things to me, you know, Josie,' he said. 'I know some things but not everything. If Cherie helps me out you'll be free to talk to Mr Tanaka.'

'Right, that's settled then,' said Cherie. 'And I can translate what they're saying for you so you don't feel left out. I know what it's like being the odd one out when everyone's talking a language you don't know. It's miserable.'

Josie managed to stop herself before a catty reply escaped her. If that was how it was going to be, well, fine. She would be quite happy talking to Mr Tanaka. He was her friend, after all.

'I hope Toto's better,' she said to Mrs Tanaka, switching into Japanese and deliberately turning her back on Dave and Cherie. 'He was a bit under the weather last time I was here.'

'Yes, he's fine again, thanks. The vet said it was just a tummy upset. Nothing serious.'

Josie turned to Mr Tanaka, who had stood up to greet her. He was wearing what Josie had come to think of as his weekend sweater, a faded beige jumper with a moth hole in the sleeve that looked as though one more wash would finish it off. It clung to his thin frame, making him look even bonier than usual.

'You must be excited to have Cherie home again,' said Josie, noticing how his eyes followed his daughter's every move.

'Yes, we are. We were very proud when she went to study in America, but it's good to have her home. It didn't feel right without her.'

He smiled at Cherie who felt his gaze and turned and smiled back. Josie felt ashamed of her jealousy. Of course it was wonderful that Cherie had come home. And she and Josie would be friends. Of course they would.

'Lunch is ready,' said Mrs Tanaka. 'It's just a simple family meal. Please excuse me for not giving you something more sophisticated.'

She ushered them through into the dining room where places had been set around the big mahogany dining table. The table was covered in little dishes of vegetables and fish, amongst which Josie recognised her favourite boiled tofu with curls of bonito flake and spring onion on top, and a salad of giant white radish and grated carrot. There was a gleaming plate of sashimi, the scales of mackerel glittering temptingly next to the deep red of sliced tuna, and little dishes of stewed beef with broad beans. Skewers of chicken and a plate of crunchy lotus root completed the feast. The rice cooker steamed quietly next to Mrs Tanaka's place.

Josie helped Mrs Tanaka hand round bowls of aromatic rice while trying not to listen to Cherie explaining to Dave what all the dishes were. And trying not to notice how flattered Dave looked.

'I hear you've just started working in Osaka,' said Cherie to Josie. 'I love the Kansai area. The people there are so much friendlier than they are in Tokyo. They'll strike up a conversation on the slightest pretext.'

'I hadn't really noticed,' said Josie, wishing Cherie hadn't spoken to her in English, forcing her to reply in the same language. 'But then, I'm only there during the week – I get the train back to Tokyo on Friday nights.'

'So you're on your own in Tokyo all week,' Cherie said to Dave. 'That must be hard for you. What do you do with yourself?'

'I manage to keep busy,' said Dave. 'But I must

admit, I'm getting a bit tired of microwaving readymeals from the convenience store.'

'I bet,' said Cherie. 'Tell you what, we could meet up and have dinner in some places I know. You could get something decent to eat for a change, and we can get to know each other better.'

'That would be great,' said Dave. 'It's really kind of you. Isn't it Josie?'

'Yes, said Josie. 'Really kind.'

She turned to Mr Tanaka and switched into Japanese.

'I expect you know about Saburo Horii,' she said.

'Yes. It was terribly sad news. I gather he was in the same section as you.'

'Yes, though I hadn't had a chance to get to know him. I'd spoken to him, but that was all. Did you ever meet him?'

'I did, though I didn't know him well.'

Josie wanted to ask if Mr Tanaka's visit to the Osaka office had had anything to do with Saburo but before she had a chance to do more than open her mouth, Cherie interrupted them.

'I was thinking I might go over to Osaka sometime soon,' she said, leaning across and switching into Japanese. 'I haven't been there in such a long time. We could meet up for lunch if you like.'

'Yes,' said Josie, trying not to grit her teeth. 'We could. But don't you have to work during the week?'

'Not at the moment. I'm looking around for something but it's not the standard recruitment time so there's not many companies looking for people.

I'm sure something will come up soon though.'

'Cherie has such good English,' said her mother fondly. 'It won't be long before someone snaps her up.'

'Well, let me know when you come over,' said Josie.

Cherie turned to Dave.

'Do you think you might find a reason to go over to Kansai one day? I could show you Kyoto and we could meet Josie for lunch.'

'I'm sure I can. To be honest, the work I've got at the moment isn't that demanding. I came here because it was a chance to be with Josie, but I'll be glad to get back to London and move on to something more challenging.'

'You're going back to London?' said Cherie.

'Yes, when my year here is up.'

'What about Josie?'

'That's up to her.'

Cherie turned to Josie with an enquiring look on her face. Josie racked her brains for something to distract her, but all she could come up with was Saburo Horii.

'You know the murder on the bullet train the other week? It turns out it was one of my work colleagues,' she blurted out before she could stop herself.

'Oh, I've heard you're a bit of a murder specialist,' said Cherie. 'Are you going to solve this one?'

'The police are investigating,' said Josie. 'I'm sure we can leave it to them.'

'Of course,' said Cherie. 'I expect you'd rather not get involved. Was it someone you knew?'

'Sort of,' said Josie. She hadn't been very frank with Dave about the fact that she'd spoken to Saburo. She'd just said it was someone who worked in the same section as her and given the impression she didn't know him. Dave wasn't in favour of Josie's getting involved in any more murder investigations so Josie preferred not to give him the idea there was another one in the offing. Because there wasn't. The murder was nothing to do with her.

Cherie turned back to Dave and said 'If you're interested I can get out some old photo albums to show you. You'll have to put up with a lot of photos of me, but they'll give you an idea of the sort of places we might visit. Places that are a bit off the beaten track, not the usual tourist haunts.'

'Sounds great. Josie's shown me the obvious places so I'm ready for a change.'

'I know lots of odd places. How about the tomb of the last samurai?'

'Who was the last samurai, and why was he the last?'

'Toshizo Hijikata. He was the leader of the *Shinsegumi*. They were a sort of private army in the nineteenth century, in the civil war when the Shogunate fell and the Meiji Emperor came to power. They were on the wrong side really – they supported the Shogun right to the end and they were all killed. That's why he was the last samurai, because they were abolished under the Meiji

Emperor. I used to be a big fan of the *Shinsengumi* when I was a kid.'

'Sounds great. Did you know about the *Shinsengumi*, Josie?'

'No,' said Josie.

'You should get Cherie to tell you about them,' said Dave. 'You could learn something.'

Josie wished she was sitting next to Dave so she could kick his ankle. She'd lived in Japan for years and didn't need Cherie to tell her about Japanese history.

'Come on, I'll show you the photos,' said Cherie, leading the way back into the living room and settling herself next to Dave on the sofa with a pile of photo albums. Mrs Tanaka vanished to the kitchen and Mr Tanaka sat in his usual worn armchair. Josie pulled up a stool to sit beside him, not without a longing glance down the corridor to the sliding door of the Japanese room, which was firmly closed. She wished she and Mr Tanaka could go there, and leave the sound of Cherie's chatter behind. The Japanese room was where they always talked when there was something serious to discuss. Its floor of straw *tatami* mats was cool in the summer and warm in the winter and gave off a faint aroma of summer meadows. The big sliding windows looked out onto a tiny Japanese garden where, at this time of year, the first irises would be coming into flower. She and Mr Tanaka would sit on the floor on either side of the low black lacquer table and he would gently probe until all her concerns and worries came tumbling out, and she could see clearly what she needed to do.

She wanted to talk some more about Saburo, somewhere where they wouldn't be disturbed and she could ask her question about whether Mr Tanaka's visit to the Osaka office had anything to do with Saburo's murder without Cherie interrupting. But Mr Tanaka made no move towards the *tatami* room. He sat in his armchair and let Toto jump onto his knee and settle with a little doggy sigh of contentment.

'How do you like working in Osaka?' he said, rubbing Toto's ear in an abstracted way.

'It's all right,' said Josie. 'I haven't been there long.'

'What kind of work do you do?'

'I check that the software upgrade has been properly installed on people's computers. It's a bit repetitive, but it means I get to go around all the different offices. So it's quite a good introduction really.'

'Yes,' said Mr Tanaka. 'I suppose it is. Do people talk much about the murder?'

'Not a lot. Not at all, in fact. We all avoid the subject.'

Mr Tanaka stopped rubbing Toto's ear and looked at her thoughtfully.

'Even you?' he said.

'Yes, even me.'

'That's unusual. Murder isn't a subject you normally avoid,' said Mr Tanaka.

'Well, this time is different,' said Josie.

'You're right,' said Mr Tanaka. 'Better not to get involved. Leave it to the police.'

Josie looked at him sharply. There was the suspicion of a twinkle in his eye.

'I do wonder about it, though,' she said.

'What do you wonder?' said Mr Tanaka.

'Well, I wonder how a murder could take place on a rush hour train without anybody seeing anything.'

Mr Tanaka nodded and waited for her to go on.

'Why commit a murder on a train at all?' Josie said. 'And why that particular train?'

'You think it was that particular train? Not just any train?'

'I don't know. It just seems like it should be important somehow.'

Josie hesitated and then went on, 'I wish I knew more about Saburo. If I'd been in the Osaka office longer I might have seen something that would give me an idea about why he was killed. As it is, I don't know anything. And I don't know who to ask. But I'm sure there's something going on, something people don't want to talk about.'

'There is something people don't want to talk about,' said Mr Tanaka. 'Or rather, they've been told not to talk about it.'

'I knew it. Was that why you were in the Osaka office that day when you pretended not to see me?'

'Yes. I was there because—'

He stopped abruptly as Toto leapt off his knee and raced after Cherie who had found a well-worn beanbag down the back of the sofa and thrown it across the room.

'Come on, Toto,' she cried. 'Let's see if you still know how to fetch!'

Toto barked and jumped as Cherie held the beanbag high out of his reach. Mrs Tanaka came to the door to see what the fuss was about and stood there smiling as Cherie threw the beanbag again and Toto scrambled after it.

Damn, thought Josie. Just when he was going to tell me.

Mr Tanaka got up.

'I have to be in Osaka next week,' he said to Josie. 'If you're free, perhaps we could have lunch and continue our conversation. There's something I want to tell you about Saburo.'

SIX

The trains, Josie thought, as she walked down from Osaka station to the office on Monday morning. Why were the police so interested in what train people got? Because whoever killed Saburo must have got the same train as him. So anyone who was still in the office when Saburo left couldn't have done it. That ruled out all the older workers who were still at their desks when she got back at five thirty. What time had Saburo left? She wasn't sure. She only knew that he wasn't there when she got back to the office. But the police had been interested in anything that happened before five o'clock, so presumably he'd left around then. He'd told her he was going to Shizuoka, so he couldn't have got one of the fast Nozomi bullet trains because they didn't stop there. He must have been aiming to get one of the slower Hikari trains. She decided to check the timetables when she got to work – it shouldn't be hard to spot what train he was on.

She tried to remember what had happened that afternoon but couldn't come up with much. All she could recall was that none of the boy wizards, as she'd started to think of them after Mimi called them that, had been at their desks, though that didn't mean they weren't around somewhere, and Mr Shiga hadn't been there, having left for his meeting in Nagoya straight after lunch. She'd seen him and Mr Ozawa heading off down the corridor together with Mr Shiga nodding anxiously as Mr Ozawa berated him about something.

She wondered about Koji, Taro and Mack and how well they'd known Saburo. It was odd that, although the four of them were of much the same age and must have joined the company from university at the same time, Saburo wasn't part of their group. Was it just that they had never hit it off, or had they been friends in the past and then quarrelled? Koji had said that Saburo had been 'too serious' for them. What did that mean? Was it just that Saburo didn't fancy pretending to be a character in a children's novel or was it more significant?

She thought back to her impressions of the three young men. Koji was the most open and accessible – bright, chatty and easy to like. Taro was more of a problem, slow witted with undercurrents of emotion that made Josie uneasy. And Mack, cool and supercilious, seemingly happy just to play the sidekick to Koji - Ron Weasley to Koji's Harry Potter - but always giving the impression that he was keeping things to himself.

The trouble was, she'd only just met them all. One lunch at Mrs Miyazaki's wasn't enough to reveal their characters. And she knew next to nothing about Saburo. There could be any number of things in his life that could have led someone to want to kill him.

And anyway, she reminded herself, it was nothing to do with her. The police were investigating and they would no doubt find the murderer without her help.

When she got to the office she found everybody was already there and hard at work. Mr Shiga nodded at her as she hung up her coat, though Josie wasn't sure whether he meant to be friendly or to point out that she was the last one to arrive. She switched on her computer and pulled up the bullet train timetables. It didn't take her long to find the train Saburo must have been on. The Hikari 478 left New Osaka at 5:40 and got into Shizuoka at 7:37. That seemed the most likely train, and it got into Tokyo, where Saburo's body had been found, at 8:40, a few minutes before Josie's faster Nozomi had arrived, which fitted with the timing of the discovery of the body.

Something was niggling at the back of her mind, something about who wasn't in the office on Friday afternoon, but she couldn't pin it down so she went down to the little kitchen to get a cup of tea. Mimi was there, as she always was, looking smart in her grey office suit, her lovely face carefully made up. Josie tried not to wince at the sight of Mimi's ears; however much she tried she couldn't manage to see them as an asset as everyone else did. But seeing Mimi in her little empire jogged Josie's memory.

Mimi hadn't been there when Josie came back to the office at half past five the afternoon Saburo was killed. Josie remembered because she'd taken her cup down to the kitchen and had had to wash it up herself. And the kitchen had been clean and tidy with everything put away, just as Mimi left it when she went home at night.

Josie took her cup of green tea back to her desk, deep in thought. She knew Mimi was much admired in the office. Even the older men simpered when Mimi handed them their tea, and Mr Ozawa's stern face softened when she came into the room. Mr Shiga was the one exception – he seemed to avoid looking at her as she put his tea down on his desk and never manufactured excuses to go down to the little kitchen as others did.

She wondered about Koji, Mack and Taro. As far as she could recall, Koji treated Mimi with the same jokey friendliness as he extended to everyone else. Taro seemed bashfully tongue-tied in her presence – Josie wouldn't be in the least surprised to find he was carrying a torch for her. And Mack didn't seem to take much notice of her at all.

But maybe Saburo had been closer to Mimi than any of them. Josie remembered Taro's innuendo about Saburo and Mimi at Mrs Miyazaki's and how Mack had slapped him down. Could that have been closer to the truth than she'd thought?

She jumped as someone tapped her on the shoulder.

'Sorry to disturb you,' said Mack. 'I just came to

say we're not going to Mrs Miyazaki's today. There's a big job on and lunch has been cancelled. But we're going to go out for a drink after work and you're welcome to join us.'

'Thanks,' said Josie, quickly minimising the train timetables on her screen before he saw them. She turned to him with her best smile, hoping he didn't suspect the way her thoughts had been running when he interrupted her. 'That'd be great. But will we be able to find anywhere still open that late?'

'Don't worry, Koji has a place. They know him there.'

Of course Koji has a place, thought Josie. I bet it was Koji who found Mrs Miyazaki's too. He has a knack for ferreting things out.

'Okay, then I'm in.'

'See you later, then,' said Mack. He strolled back over to his desk and nodded to the other two. Koji looked up and grinned across at Josie, who smiled back. Taro just kept his head down and got on with his work.

Josie brought up the train timetable again and looked at the list of tiny figures showing Saburo's train's progress. Saburo had been on his way to Shizuoka, he'd told her so, so why wasn't the body found until the train reached Tokyo? Either he'd been killed before Shizuoka and nobody had noticed the body for the next hour, which seemed highly unlikely, or Saburo had changed his mind about getting off at Shizuoka. Why would he have done that? Josie added the question to all the others she couldn't yet answer.

*

It was gone ten o'clock when Mr Shiga finally packed away his papers and turned off his computer. They all waited, glued to their seats, until he had shrugged on his coat and made his way across the room with his trademark puppet-like shuffle, muttering the ritual 'Thank you for all your hard work' as he went.

Josie switched off her computer and grabbed her coat. The other three were already heading for the door, followed by cross looks from the older men who looked like they would carry on for hours. Perhaps they never went home at all, Josie thought. Maybe their wives and children wouldn't even recognise them if they passed them in the street. Perhaps—. She stopped herself, feeling she was getting slightly hysterical. It must be the prospect of going out drinking on a weeknight with some guys she hardly knew, one of whom might be a murderer.

'Where are we going?' she asked Koji as they walked through Umeda station and took the escalator down two levels to the oddly named *Gourmet Museum*. When she'd first seen the signs, Josie half expected to find a display of desiccated desserts, but it turned out that *gourmet museum* meant a massive range of restaurants lining long convoluted passageways, all constantly filled with what looked like half the population of Osaka out to have a good time.

'Not here,' said Koji. 'It's too crowded, and anyway, all these places shut down soon. By eleven everyone will be gone.'

'We're going to Mama's place,' said Taro. 'Mama will take care of us.'

'Oh,' said Josie. 'I didn't realise we we're going to a Mama bar.' Mama bars were well known as the home-from-home of tired salarymen, and they weren't easy to penetrate – if you weren't introduced you could get a very frosty reception.

'It's Koji's Mama bar,' said Taro. 'But he takes us there sometimes.'

'You'll like it,' said Koji. 'Wait and see.'

They walked on, through a set of linking passages that Josie had never realised were there, into the underground retail paradise called Whitey. It stretched in all directions like a huge spider's web, its narrow passageways lined with little fashion shops, some still brightly lit and noisy with jingles, others already closed, their shutters down and lights off. Those that remained open had a tired air, as though they couldn't wait for the day to end, and the jostling crowds had an end-of-the-day feel as well. Noisy groups of slightly drunk girls carrying designer bags pushed past quiet couples as they all headed in the same direction, towards the two train stations, Osaka and Umeda, and the entrance to the underground.

Koji led the way, struggling against the flow of humanity heading in the opposite direction, into a five-way junction that made Josie's head spin. Mack saw her expression.

'Everyone gets lost in Whitey,' he said. 'It's part of the fun. But don't worry. Koji knows what he's doing.'

'I know this place like the back of my hand,' said Koji. 'Wherever you want to go at ground level, I can lead you to the right exit so you come up exactly where you want to be.'

'Couldn't we have got where we're going just as well through the streets without coming down here?' said Josie.

'Of course,' said Koji. 'But just you wait until summer arrives. When it's forty degrees outside you'll be glad to come down here. It's air conditioned and it leads to all the big department stores.'

'And it's warm in the winter,' said Taro. 'I bet our ancestors would have been glad of somewhere like this.'

Koji pressed on until the crowds thinned and the shops petered out, the passages got narrower and older and the buzz of commerce faded behind them. They reached a little enclave of old shuttered shops and tiny bars where lights could be dimly discerned inside. Koji stopped at one of them. It was made of dark wood turned almost black with age and had a little statue of a *tanuki* outside. A *tanuki* was an animal like a large raccoon that had the reputation for enjoying a party – a t*anuki* statue outside a bar meant a warm welcome within.

'Welcome to Mama's,' Koji said, ducking under a

half-curtain into a cosy little room lined with worn velvet banquettes with low tables in front of them. The air was permeated with blue smoke that caught at the back of Josie's throat. Behind an old fashioned bar that reminded Josie of an English pub stood a woman with a professionally friendly smile and sharp experienced eyes.

'Welcome back,' she said to Koji. 'I was beginning to think you'd deserted me, it's so long since I've seen you.'

'I wouldn't desert you, Mama,' said Koji. 'But I've been busy.'

'You boys work too hard,' said Mama. 'You should relax more.'

Her sharp eyes turned appraisingly to Josie, taking in her height, her sex, her messy hair and her undoubted foreignness in one practiced glance.

'Who's this you've brought with you?' she said, flicking her eyes back to Koji.

'This is Josie Clark. She's come to work in our office,' said Koji. 'So she's one of us now.'

Mama stretched her heavily lipsticked mouth into an exaggeratedly friendly smile.

'Welcome to our little home from home,' she said to Josie. 'Make yourself comfortable. That's what we're here for.'

She turned around and reached up to a high shelf to take down a bottle of whisky with Koji's name on it. All the shelves behind the bar were lined with whiskey bottles marked with customers' names, some of them expensive, others cheaper, all with their contents partly drunk.

'*Mizuwari*?' she said.

Koji looked round the group who all nodded, so Josie did too.

'*Mizuwari*,' said Koji.

They found an empty table next to a group of businessmen who looked as though they'd been there most of the evening. They leaned back against the faded velvet and stretched out their legs, arguing loudly and laughing as they drank whisky from cut glass tumblers. They were all smoking, the smoke from their cigarettes rising up and thickening the already smoky atmosphere. They nodded sociably as the little group sat down and frankly stared at Josie. She could see why – not only was she a foreigner, but the only woman in the place.

'Hey, Koji, introduce us to your friend,' said one of them. Sweat was trickling down his forehead and he mopped ineffectually at it with a large handkerchief.

'Miss Clark's a distinguished visitor from England,' said Koji. 'So mind your manners.'

'Pleased to meet you,' said Josie, and the businessmen chorused 'Pleased to meet you,' in return. After a long stare at Josie the man who had spoken turned back to his companions and their conversation resumed, much to Josie's relief.

'This isn't like anywhere I've been before,' she said.

'You've never been to a Mama bar then,' said Koji. 'But then, that's not surprising. Mama bars are meant to be private. That's the point.'

Mama arrived with Koji's bottle of whisky on a tray with a big jug of water, a bowl of ice and four whisky glasses.

She poured whisky into each of the glasses, topped them up with a liberal amount of water and ice and handed them round.

'*Kanpai*,' said Koji, raising his glass. They all chinked glasses and drank. Josie didn't really like whisky, but she found that it was so diluted with water that it was easy to drink. She'd have to remember to order *mizuwari* in future. Most of the men in the place seemed to be drinking the same thing, and each table had several bottles with names on them.

'In my opinion,' said Koji, leaning back and holding up his glass so the light sparkled through the cut glass. 'Suntory is the best whisky there is.'

'I like Suntory,' said Taro.

'Scotch whisky's the best,' said Mack.

'I like Scotch whisky,' said Taro.

'No, you can't beat Suntory,' said Koji. 'It's all in the water and Japanese water is the purest in the world.'

'Irish whisky is good too,' said Mack. 'It's got a special earthy flavour.'

'I like Irish whisky,' said Taro.

'But Suntory is refined,' said Koji. 'There's a lot of work gone into it.'

Josie drank some more of her whisky and stayed out of the debate, which looked as though it was going to get heated.

'I bought a bottle of Irish whisky on the way home the Friday Mr Shiga went to the Nagoya meeting,' Mack said, 'It was pricey but it had a real peaty flavour to it. You don't get that with Suntory.'

Josie pricked up her ears.

'Did you go off early that Friday?' she said. 'I didn't see you around when I got back from finishing my checks.'

'We all did,' said Mack, 'All three of us. We weren't going to sit around the office on a Friday night if we didn't have to.'

'Did you see what time Saburo left?' said Josie.

Mack gave her an odd look, and she realised she'd committed a faux pas.

'I wasn't looking at what Saburo was doing,' he said. 'It's nothing to do with me when he left work.'

Josie took a quick sip of her whisky, cross with herself for rushing into the conversation and putting her foot in it. But Koji came to her rescue.

'We all left around half past four,' he said, topping up their drinks. 'Taro and I went to New Osaka together and I got the five oh five to Okayama.'

'I waved him off,' said Taro. 'I ran along the platform beside the train, waving like he was Harry Potter going off to school.'

'You did,' said Koji. 'Everyone in my compartment stared at me.'

'I waited till he was out of sight,' said Taro, going pink with excitement, 'Then I had to run all the way down the escalator and up the other side to my platform to get my train. Everyone got out of my way. I was in Toyohashi by quarter to seven. My mum and dad were really surprised to see me.'

'I got to Okayama at twenty past six. It wasn't even dark. I was really happy – I haven't seen my home town in daylight on a Friday since last September,' said Koji.

'Saburo was still in the office when we left,' said Taro. 'I saw him. I said goodnight and he said goodnight back. I told the police and they wrote it down.'

'I didn't notice,' said Koji. 'How were we to know it was going to matter what time he left? The police asked me the same thing, but I couldn't remember seeing him.'

There was a heavy silence.

'Sorry,' said Josie. 'I didn't mean to bring everyone down.'

'I heard they've released the body so the funeral will be this week,' said Koji.

'Will you be going?' asked Josie.

'No, Mr Ozawa is going to represent the office. Saburo's family don't want a big fuss.'

Koji tossed back the last of the whisky in his glass and poured them all another, though Josie shook her head when he came to her. It was getting late and the men at other tables were starting to leave. Mama ranged their bottles of whisky back on the shelf again, ready to be taken down the next time they came in.

Koji got up rather unsteadily and made his way towards a door at the back which Josie assumed led to the toilets. After a moment Mack did the same, leaving Josie alone with Taro. Josie felt awkward. It was easy to talk when Koji was around but Taro on his own rather defeated her.

'I like whisky,' said Taro. 'I don't mind what kind it is. Hagrid drinks Scotch whisky, but I'd like to try Irish whisky.'

'Maybe Mack will let you try some of his,' said Josie.

'Mack's not likely to do that. He only goes around with me because Koji makes him. He and Saburo used to make fun of me but Koji made them stop.'

'Mack and Saburo? Were they friends then?'

'Yes, until they had a big fight.'

'What was the fight about, do you know?'

'I know, but I can't tell you. I promised not to tell anyone.'

'Who did you promise, Taro?'

'Not saying.'

'Why not? Why can't you tell me?'

'Not saying. It was a promise. I'll get into trouble if I tell you.'

Over Taro's shoulder Josie spotted Mack and Koji returning. The moment when Taro might have told her passed. But it left her with a strong desire to find out what Mack really did do the night Saburo died. And why he was being so evasive about it.

SEVEN

Josie didn't go to Osaka station much, except to get the train to New Osaka for the bullet train to Tokyo, and then she was in far too much of a hurry to look around. The station had been comprehensively rebuilt not long before and was now home to an eclectic mix of smart cafés and restaurants, none of which struck Josie as natural haunts for a plain man like Mr Tanaka. Terminus, where he'd suggested they meet, seemed like the least suitable of all. It had clearly been designed to appeal to the fickle youth of Osaka, those who wore the latest Comme des Garçons fashions and ate only the tiniest and most artistically designed cakes on the planet. They thronged Terminus when Josie arrived, the sound of their chatter so all-pervasive it blended into a single chirrupy hum. The sun shone in through large windows inset with coloured glass diamonds that twinkled like crystals and made glinting patterns on the floor. Josie felt large, awkward and out of date the minute she stepped inside.

Mr Tanaka waved to her from a corner table. He looked just as incongruous among the pretty pastel spring colours of the other patrons as she did. His old black work suit was shiny at the elbows and his tightly knotted navy blue tie showed signs of fraying. But he seemed oblivious to the oddity of his appearance in such a fashion-conscious place; Josie wished she could be so blasé about it. Trying not to meet the eyes of any of the delicately pretty girls in perfectly ironed dresses and tiny bolero cardigans who filled the tables she walked past, Josie smoothed her wrinkled grey skirt self consciously and made her way as unobtrusively as she could to his table.

They're not looking at me, she thought. I know I'm too tall and badly dressed and a foreigner to boot, but that doesn't mean they're taking any notice of me. It's just me being self-conscious, that's all.

She made it safely to Mr Tanaka's table and sat down.

'What will you have?' he said. 'I'm quite attracted by the Danish open sandwich.'

'Sounds good,' said Josie, seeing the waitress approaching and not wanting to look silly by dithering over the menu.

'Good, that's settled then,' said Mr Tanaka, giving the waitress their order.

'Would you like a juice with that?' said the waitress. 'We do pomegranate, guava or blood orange. Or maybe some coconut water?'

'Pomegranate,' said Josie. It sounded the least intimidating of the selection. Mr Tanaka just shook his head.

'Green tea, please,' he said, making Josie wish she'd had the courage to ask for that too.

Mr Tanaka reached across the table and pushed the narrow wicker basket of cutlery towards Josie. She took out a sealed plastic sachet, extracted the fresh wipe from inside and wiped her hands with it. Mr Tanaka did the same and then they both looked up simultaneously and their eyes met. Mr Tanaka's eyes were just as Josie remembered them; soft and kind with wrinkled laughter lines. Josie found herself smiling back at him.

The waitress arrived with their Danish sandwiches. Josie looked at hers in dismay. It consisted of a tiny crustless roundel of bread, a single perfect lettuce leaf, and a smattering of seafood. It would be gone in one bite, and she started to wish she'd ordered three or four. But, looking around, she could see that the pretty girls at the other tables seemed perfectly happy with their equally tiny portions.

I'll just have to pick up a meat dumpling at the hot dumpling stall on Umeda station as I go back to the office, Josie thought. Otherwise I'll be dead of hunger by the end of the day.

Mr Tanaka had taken a knife and fork from the cutlery basket and was cutting his tiny piece of bread into even tinier portions. Josie did the same – she could have just popped the whole thing in her mouth in one go, but she sensed that would be a faux pas. And she needed to make it last longer to fool her stomach into thinking it was getting a meal, not just a nibble. She drank some of her pomegranate juice, which was almost black and tasted bitter, envying Mr Tanaka his little stone cup of green tea.

She wondered if he would be up for a meat dumpling afterwards, but thought better of suggesting it. He was so thin, his wrists, which stuck out from his frayed cuffs, were half the size of Josie's. She had a sudden urge to take care of him, make him eat better, march him off to the Daimaru department store which occupied a good part of the station building and make him buy himself two or three new suits. But she knew it was impossible. There was an asceticism about his character, like a kind of secular monk, which meant that he took no interest in such fripperies as clothes and food. If there had been any way of persuading him to look after himself Mrs Tanaka would have found it long since. He was what he was, and Josie had to admit that deep down she admired him for it.

He looked up and caught her watching him. Unnervingly, he seemed to understand just what she was thinking. His eyes dropped to his frayed cuffs and he tucked them back inside his jacket sleeves.

'Mrs Tanaka bought me some new shirts just last week,' he said. 'But I keep forgetting to wear them. I like my old comfortable clothes. I'm not a fashionable person – I leave all that to Cherie.'

'How's she getting on with her job hunting?' said Josie, hoping to hear that she'd found something to keep her busy and out of Dave's way.

'There's no rush,' said Mr Tanaka. 'It's nice to have her home again so we're enjoying her having a bit of free time. She said she was planning a trip to Kyoto with Dave quite soon.'

'Oh, that's great,' said Josie, hoping Mr Tanaka would not detect her insincerity.

They'd both finished their sandwiches and the waitress had cleared their plates, leaving Josie with the rest of her glass of pomegranate juice to get through. She took a gulp, managed to avoid making a face, and said, 'You said you'd tell me what you were doing in Osaka that day I saw you. The day before Saburo was killed.'

Mr Tanaka looked down at the shiny glass table and unconsciously brushed a few crumbs into a neat pile.

'Before I tell you, I have to ask you to keep what I'm going to say to yourself,' he said.

'Of course,' said Josie. 'I'm surprised you even feel you have to ask.'

Mr Tanaka nodded but didn't look up.

'Normally I'd trust you with any information,' he said. 'But this time it isn't really mine to give, so I have to be careful.'

'I understand,' said Josie, wondering whose information it was.

'Right, well, it's to do with the Global Reinsurance section. Something's been worrying us for quite a while now. The margins in global reinsurance are wafer thin and we're pretty good at knowing where to get the best deals. But lately our competitors have been consistently undercutting us, and it seems like more than a coincidence. Plus there's been some odd activity going on in Osaka – as though someone unauthorised has been accessing our data. You can imagine how worried we've been.'

'And that's why you were here?'

'Yes, I came to discuss it with our Osaka people.'

'But surely, if you know it's happening you can trace where it's coming from? Identify the computer that's being used?'

'Yes, but it's not getting us anywhere. It's coming from different computers, some of them belonging to highly respectable people who couldn't possibly be involved in anything like this. Mr Muto, for example.'

Mr Muto was Mr Tanaka's oldest friend and the idea that he could be leaking information, or indeed had enough grasp of how a computer worked to do more than send the odd email, was laughable.

'So someone is getting access to other people's computers and stealing sensitive information?'

'Yes. That's what makes us think it might be someone in IT Support. They're the only ones with the capacity to do it.'

'Who do you suspect?'

'At the moment we just don't know. It could be anyone.'

'And does this have something to do with Saburo? Is it the reason he was killed?'

'I don't know, but it's not unreasonable to think it does after what happened to him.'

Josie paused, thinking about the warning Mr Ozawa had given her about data security when she had first arrived in Osaka, and the notices on everybody's desks saying *Data Security First*. Now she understood what that was all about.

'Do the people in IT Support know about this?'

'No, of course not. They just know there's been a big clampdown on security, and they probably suspect there's something up. But so far I think we've been able to keep it a secret. Only Mr Ozawa knows. We could hardly keep it from him, though—'

'Though he could actually be the one who's doing it,' Josie finished for him.

'Yes. We can't rule anyone out. He's running an investigation in Osaka, but we're also running a separate investigation from Tokyo which he doesn't know about.'

'Do the police know?'

'Obviously, when Saburo was killed we had to be absolutely frank with them, but they're not investigating the leak, just the murder.'

'Do you think it could have been Saburo who was doing it?'

'It could have been. Or he might have stumbled across the real culprit.'

'And then was killed to keep him from telling,' said Josie, her mind racing. Once more she wished she'd had a chance to get to know Saburo better before he was killed. Then she might have been able to judge which he was – criminal or innocent victim.

'Did anything happen the afternoon he was killed?

Anything out of the ordinary?' said Mr Tanaka.

'I'd only been in Osaka a week when it happened so I'm not sure I'd know what out of the ordinary looked like. But I did speak to Saburo and he seemed perfectly normal.'

Mr Tanaka looked disappointed. Josie wished she had paid more attention that afternoon, but how was she to know it would turn out to be important? All she'd been thinking of was going back to Tokyo to see Dave.

'I'll have a think about it and see what I can come up with,' she said. 'Maybe something will jog my memory.'

Mr Tanaka nodded and picked up the bill. At the door he paused.

'Will you be at Ken and Noriko's wedding next week?' he said.

'Yes, I'll be there with Dave.'

'We're going too. We can talk again then.'

He turned away and Josie watched his black suit merge with the others heading for the central gate and the train to New Osaka.

*

Josie could smell the enticing aroma of steamed minced pork long before the dumpling stall came into sight. It seemed to be calling to her and her disappointed stomach called back to it. She waited impatiently in the queue and when it came to her turn ordered two dumplings and took them to the quietest corner she could find to eat.

That wasn't saying much. Umeda station didn't have any quiet corners – it did extremely busy and marginally less busy and that was it. The constant roar, made up of a combination of passing footsteps and chattering voices, was occasionally interrupted by echoing announcements about departing and arriving trains and bursts of advertising jingles from the stands on the concourse, which today were selling luxury cars.

Josie wolfed down her dumplings, folded the greaseproof paper they'd been wrapped in and popped it in her bag to dispose of back at the office. Japan didn't do waste bins. There was no need; nobody ever threw any litter away – the mere thought would have horrified them. Their country, their environment, their responsibility.

She walked slowly away from the station, taking a moment to gaze up at the convoluted patterns of the bronze Art Nouveau windows of the Hankyu department store, which never failed to lift her spirits. She wondered whether to go in and do a little browsing among the brightly lit counters, but a glance at her watch told her she didn't have time for that. If she didn't get back to the office double quick she would be treated to one of Mr Shiga's best frowns.

She turned away, but as she did so caught sight of a hurrying figure on the other side of the passageway. Someone walking with bent head and a jerky gait like a badly controlled puppet. There was no mistaking that puppet-on-a-string awkwardness. It was how Mr Shiga walked and there surely couldn't be two of them like that in Osaka – not unless Mr Shiga had a twin brother.

Josie's first thought was a little flash of satisfaction that Mr Shiga wasn't at the office, so he couldn't tell her off for being late back from lunch. But then her curiosity was aroused. Why wasn't he at the office and where was he going? She had a sudden urge to find out. It wouldn't hurt if she took a bit more time and followed him, just to see where he was heading. She turned around and positioned herself just behind Mr Shiga, out of his line of sight. Not that he would have noticed her even if she'd walked alongside him – he was far too busy keeping his head down and not looking at people coming the other way, with the result that he bumped into them more often than not.

Josie felt as though she was in a not-very-well-made spy movie as she followed Mr Shiga down the passageway that ran alongside the department store towards the busy platforms of Umeda station. She wondered if he was going to get a train, but he turned away at the last minute into the Kinokuniya bookstore. Just a shopping trip then.

Kinokuniya was full of book browsers which made it hard for Josie to keep Mr Shiga in sight. He didn't behave like someone who had come to buy a book. He made his way purposefully through the shoppers and then out of the rear door, into the covered road where taxis queued to enter the station.

So far it had been easy to follow him, as he was busy negotiating his way through the crowds and never looked back. But when he crossed through the petrol-fume-filled bus station, where a noisy group was waiting for the bus to the hot springs at Arima, he suddenly turned around to look behind him and Josie had to duck into the waiting room to avoid being seen. Then she leapt out, pretending she had a bus to catch, as he headed on into the twisty old Kappa Passage, filled with tiny shops selling antique maps and old books. He slowed down, glanced in the window of one bookshop that had a display of prints of actresses from the 1930s, and spent so long studying the menu of a café that specialised in different kinds of omelettes that Josie decided he was just looking for somewhere to eat. But then he moved on again down the passage, past a busy Italian restaurant, until the passage ended in an echoing street under the railway tracks. He turned left along it and headed into a maze of little streets where Josie had never been before. Half way down one narrow street he stopped, looked around, and dived into a battered doorway.

Josie walked quietly past the nondescript door. There was a ramen shop next to it with a board outside advertising *kizune* udon, but the shop was grimy and unappetising and Josie didn't think anyone would go in unless they were desperate. The door seemed to lead to a stairway up to the first floor but there was nothing to suggest what might go on there. But as Josie passed, a sound came from the upper windows, a clacking sound like dominoes being spilled that Josie knew she had heard before somewhere.

The memory came flooding back. The time she had gone to Kabukicho, the Soho of Tokyo, with Ken, where from all the open upper windows came exactly that sound. The sound of Mah Jong players, gambling the nights and days away.

Was that what Mr Shiga was up to? Sneaking off to a dimly lit back street dive in working hours to play Mah Jong? Even Josie was shocked that conscientious Mr Shiga should be wasting his precious working hours in this unsuitable way. What had happened to the famous Japanese work ethic, which Mr Shiga had always seemed to exemplify in spades? It was enough to shake Josie's faith in the entire structure of Japanese society. He couldn't be doing that. And yet she'd seen him go in, and the sound of Mah Jong tiles reached her clearly from the window above. What else could he be doing?

The discovery would have worried Josie at any time, but following on as it did from Mr Tanaka's revelations about information going missing, it was frightening. How much did Mr Shiga gamble? How much did he lose? Enough to make him desperate for money, desperate to get more in any way he could, even if that meant doing something dishonest or, even worse, letting down the company? Enough to make him sell commercially sensitive information to rival companies?

Josie wished there was somewhere on the street to

sit down, as the awful thought overwhelmed her. Suppose Mr Shiga was stealing company information and Saburo had found out? What lengths would Mr Shiga go to to cover up his crime? Would he go as far as murder?

EIGHT

Back at the office, Josie sat at her desk and stared unseeingly at her computer screen, her mind still taken up with Mr Shiga and his Mah Jong habit. His empty desk seemed to shout out his guilt, but strangely no one else seemed at all bothered by it.

She wandered artlessly over towards his desk and mimed surprise when she got close and found he wasn't there.

'Oh, do you know where Mr Shiga is this afternoon?' she said to Mr Yamada, who sat at the next desk.

'Gone to visit a supplier. He won't be back until five o'clock,' said Mr Yamada, not looking up from what he was doing.

'Oh. Does he often do that?'

'Visit suppliers? About once a month.'

'Who's he visiting today?'

'I don't know. He doesn't tell me. If you want to know you can ask him.'

'Thanks,' said Josie, wandering back to her own

desk again.

She looked at her pile of checklists with distaste. She really couldn't concentrate on them this afternoon, not when she was bursting to tell someone what she'd found out about Mr Shiga. She wondered whether to phone Mr Tanaka but decided to wait until the weekend when she could talk to him in person. What she had found out was too important for a mere phone conversation.

In the meantime she had the afternoon to get through. She flipped through her pile of uncompleted checklists, pleased to see it was getting noticeably smaller. The number of blank sheets for the enormous domestic insurance section made her wince, and she quickly shuffled them back to the bottom. Not what she wanted to fill the afternoon. She wanted something more like a dainty snack than a full-course banquet. She turned to her little pile of missed computers, ones where she'd done most of the office but had failed to get access to one or two machines because the person was out of the office or engaged on some work they had to finish.

She flicked through the pile and was surprised to find one for the global insurance section. Mr Shiga had said that he'd done those himself, but he must have missed one. Josie thought of returning it to Mr Shiga to do, but then decided to cover it herself. She just felt like a peaceful hour on the comfortably furnished main floor. Besides, it would be interesting to see what the section was like.

She picked up her checklists and headed off to the

main floor. She hesitated outside the door of the global insurance section. She'd never actually been inside before. She wondered if Mr Tanaka's friend, Mr Muto, would be there and if he'd recognise her from the day they'd gone backstage at the Takarazuka Grand Theatre with Mr Tanaka. She wasn't sure he would. After all, she'd just been there in the guise of Mr Tanaka's assistant so there was no reason for him to take much notice of her. Except, she reminded herself, she was a foreigner. Everybody remembered foreigners.

She pushed the door open and went inside. It was larger than the IT Support office and had a view out through the pine trees to the street. There was an atmosphere of concentrated calm and Josie fancied she could almost hear the brains whirring as they calculated risk and how best to lay it off with other companies. She wondered if they enjoyed their work, or whether it was just something they did on automatic pilot while dreaming of something more exciting. Perhaps they were all frustrated artists or budding rock stars.

Fat chance, she thought, looking around the room at the dull faces and grey skin of the occupants. They all looked like heavy smokers who lived in company flats in the suburbs with wives who helped them on with their coats every morning and handed them a home made lunch in a little bento box. There wasn't any sign of Mr Muto and Josie felt a twinge of disappointment.

She found the computer she'd come to check. Its

owner was standing in front of it, deep in conversation with a colleague so Josie stood quietly at a respectful distance and waited for them to finish. Still talking, they walked away to look at some papers on another desk and then continued to the door and vanished from sight.

Bother, thought Josie. I'll have to leave it for another day. But then she realised the owner of the computer she'd come to check hadn't logged off before he left – he'd presumably been too engrossed in his conversation. Strictly speaking she shouldn't take advantage of his mistake but it seemed too good an opportunity to miss. She bowed to the man at the next desk, explained who she was and asked, in her best polite Japanese, if there would be problem if she started on her checks on the machine that had been left open. The man shrugged his shoulders, which Josie took to mean she'd been given permission. She sat down and quickly tapped the computer's keys before the automatic log-off kicked in.

She started to run her checks. She'd done them so often by this time she could have done it in her sleep. Time went by, and the silence grew heavier as Josie worked doggedly through the checks. Then suddenly she sat bolt upright. She hadn't been paying attention and she'd made a mistake with her last check, on whether the mailbox was properly set up. Instead of just checking the setup she'd accidentally accessed the mailbox. She reached quickly to close it again – she'd be in trouble if anyone found she'd been looking inside someone's mailbox. But then she stopped with her hand poised in mid air. If she could access someone's mailbox that easily, without them knowing she was using their computer, what was to stop her reading their emails and noting down any sensitive information she found there?

She glanced around the room; no one was paying any attention to her. Quickly she scanned the email list. There didn't seem to be any that were particularly interesting, but then she wasn't likely to strike gold on her first attempt. She picked an email at random and clicked on it.

It was from Mr Ozawa, asking for a meeting to discuss some request the computer's owner had made. Nothing important so far as Josie could see, but that wasn't the point. The point was that she had read it when she shouldn't have.

She looked round the room again, convinced that everyone must be staring at her. But they were all still bound up in their work. She looked at the email again and then, her hands damp with sweat, quickly closed it. She shut the computer down and hurried out of the room and back to her own desk, her heart thumping.

She couldn't believe it had only been a few hours earlier that Mr Tanaka had told her about sensitive information going missing from the global reinsurance section, given how much she'd found out since then.

Mr Shiga was at the bottom of everything. He had to be. He was the one who had easy access to all the computers in the building – until Josie arrived he'd had complete control of the checking process and could pick and choose which computers he accessed and when. It was no surprise that he'd checked all the global reinsurance machines already – that was where the information he was after was located. And there was no doubt about his motive, either. She'd just found that out. He was a gambler, which meant he must have a constant need for money to finance his gambling habit. Where better to get it than by selling commercially sensitive information? No wonder he went round looking as though he was hiding a terrible secret. He was not just a gambling addict but was defrauding his own company by selling their information to rivals. Josie wondered how that ranked on the scale of wickedness in Japan. Probably somewhere above murder.

Murder. Was Mr Shiga capable of murder on top of all his other crimes? She found it hard to believe. But if Saburo had found out about the gambling and the theft of information as she had done, then Mr Shiga had the strongest motive in the world for wanting Saburo dead.

Josie didn't know how long she'd sat at her desk revolving all this in her mind, but when she eventually looked up she saw it was gone five o'clock and the long evening stretched ahead. Suddenly feeling a desperate need for caffeine, she decided to brave the unattractive canteen for a strong coffee and a squishy white bread egg sandwich.

As she looked for a place to sit she noticed Mimi sitting by herself drinking a can of hot coffee from the vending machine in the corner.

'Can I join you?' she said, putting her tray down on the table before Mimi had a chance to reply.

Mimi nodded. 'Go ahead,' she said, in her high-pitched childlike voice.

'You must get tired of green tea,' said Josie, indicating the can of coffee.

'Of course not. You can't get tired of green tea,' said Mimi.

'Well, of making it then. Every time I see you, you seem to be making tea.'

'I love the taste of tea,' said Mimi. 'It's the taste of Japan.'

Josie wondered if Mimi meant that, or whether it was something they taught you to say in office lady school. For the first time it struck her that everything about Mimi was designed to give an impression of meekness and duty; her neat clothes, her careful makeup, her serene expression – nothing was the real Mimi except her ears, undisguisable and uniquely hers. And yet Josie was sure Mimi was not like that at all. Not at all meek and biddable, if you could only get to the real person behind the persona.

'I hear you have a taste for *mizuwari*,' said Mimi.

'How did you know about that?'

'News travels fast, or at least it does where Taro's concerned. He couldn't wait to tell me about going out with his new Hermione.'

Josie made a face.

'I'm not really into all that Harry Potter stuff,' she said.

'Aren't you? I am. I think Daniel Radcliffe is very good looking. He's going to come to Japan soon and I'm going down to the airport with my friends to see him. We're going to take a banner and hope he notices us so we can get a selfie with him.'

No you're not, thought Josie. Your friends might want that, but you just think that it's a girly thing to do. I wonder if there's anything I can do that will get you to come out from behind your mask?

'Mack and Koji shouldn't encourage Taro,' Josie said. 'It's not fair. It's just a game to them but he takes it seriously.'

'Taro can take care of himself. He's stronger than you think.'

'He doesn't seem the sort of person to… well, to get a job at a place like AZT.'

'Don't underestimate him. He's a genius on a computer, way better than the rest of them. It's just ordinary life that he struggles with.'

'What about Saburo? Was he interested in Harry Potter too?' said Josie.

'I wouldn't know,' said Mimi. 'I didn't have much to do with him.'

Not according to Taro, thought Josie. Taro thinks you and Saburo were an item, even though you pretend you weren't. That might explain why you were white with fear when the police interviewed you.

'But you knew him,' she said.

'Of course I did. He was in our section, wasn't he?'

'Do you think anyone might've had a grudge against him? Koji maybe? Or Mack?'

Mimi got up.

'I'm sorry to leave before you,' she said, using a formal phrase that told Josie she'd overstepped a line. 'But I have to get back to work. Please stay and finish your coffee.'

Finishing her coffee didn't take Josie long, though she lingered longer than necessary wondering about Mimi. She was a constant presence in the IT office, coming and going without anyone really paying any attention. She was a fixture, part of the furniture. Nobody thought about her. No, that wasn't true. According to Taro, Saburo had thought about her and Josie wasn't convinced by Mimi's denial that she knew Saburo as more than a work colleague. If Josie hadn't already established to her own satisfaction that Mr Shiga was at the bottom of all the trouble she might have asked a few questions about Mimi.

Back in the office she decided she ought to pop in on Mimi and apologise for having disturbed her coffee break with awkward questions about Saburo. But Mimi was in full office lady mode, her face blank, her slight bow when Josie gave her awkward apology giving nothing away. She silently handed Josie one of her endless cups of green tea and carried on with what she was doing, preparing some little delicacy for a visitor of Mr Ozawa's, the knife in her hand slicing expertly through the tiny vegetables she was cutting into decorative shapes.

The knife. It was, of course a *hōchō*, big and sharp

and shiny. A bit too shiny, like a brand new knife, and it didn't match the other knives in the set.

Mimi saw Josie stare at the knife and looked away.

'What happened to your old knife, Mimi?' said Josie, refusing to let her off the hook this time.

'I was told not to say,' said Mimi.

'Who told you?'

'The police. They came and checked everything the day after Saburo died and they noticed the knife was missing. They asked me all about it. How long it had been gone, whether I'd noticed anything suspicious, whether anyone had been in the kitchen late on Friday. And a lot more. They made it sound as though it was my fault the knife had gone. They made it sound as though—' Mimi stopped, leaving the unsaid words hanging in the air.

'Did the police tell you why they were interested in the knife?'

'They didn't have to. It went missing the afternoon Saburo was killed. And they found a knife like it on the train. So you don't have to be a genius to see why they're interested.'

Mimi's voice sounded strained, and Josie wasn't surprised. It isn't nice to find that the knife you used to use to chop vegetables had been used to kill someone. And even worse if the person who wielded the knife might be someone you knew. Or it could even be Mimi herself – she was the one best placed to take the knife. Josie wondered if that was what the police thought too.

NINE

'We're going to be late.'

'For the thousandth time, we're not going to be late. We've left plenty of time to get there, the train's only three minutes away and you assured me it's just a short walk at the other end. Stop panicking.'

Josie tried to take Dave's advice, but she found it impossible to be calm. She had a knack of arriving late for important events, and Ken and Noriko's wedding ranked pretty high in her book. For one thing, he was one of her best friends, someone with whom she'd shared adventures and discovered bodies, someone she trusted to come to her rescue in the disasters that seemed to pepper her life. For another, he was a former boyfriend, and what girl doesn't feel a twinge at least when an old boyfriend gets married?

She opened her mouth to say something cutting, but fortunately was drowned out by the announcer telling them to stand back as the train was approaching. At last, thought Josie, as they filed obediently into the carriage along with the rest of the Saturday afternoon crowd. Josie even managed to slide into one of the narrow seats that lined each side of the compartment ahead of a girl with a big bag from the Takashimaya department store. Serves her right, thought Josie smugly. If she'd spent as much time as I have commuting to work on the Tokyo Metro, she'd know how to get a seat ahead of the crowd too.

Dave strap-hanged, which wasn't too hard for him as his head nearly reached the ceiling anyway. Josie could see other commuters stealing surreptitious glances at his bulky frame, but Dave himself was oblivious. An older woman in a softly patterned jacket with lace-trimmed sleeves sitting at the end of the row of seats opposite stared at Dave and then caught Josie's eye and quickly looked down at the floor.

Josie was amused. Most people in Tokyo had got used to seeing foreigners and didn't stare at them any more, but this woman must be up from the country and not used to big city ways. And she had to admit that Dave, in his bow tie and tuxedo, was worth a second glance. Josie wondered if her dress was going to make the same favourable impression. She'd spent an age in Mitsukoshi's Occasion Wear department trying on dresses, but they all seemed too sweet, too girly, too, well, Japanese, for her. Plus they were all way too short. So she'd fallen back on an old wardrobe staple, a dress she'd bought at Zara in Shibuya one afternoon out shopping with Keiko. It had a wrap-around front with a belt that she could loosen if she ate too much, and a delicate pattern of lily of the valley. It looked dressy but not stiff – just the look Josie was aiming for.

The train slid smoothly onwards with none of the jolting and grinding of the London Underground, and Josie watched the names of the stations they passed light up in turn on the map over the door. Shin Otsuka, Myogadani, Korakuen, Hongo-sanchome...

'Next one's ours,' she said to Dave. 'Ochanomizu, that's it.'

The station was small, just two platforms and a ticket office. It was shallow enough not to need an escalator – they only had to walk up a short flight of stairs to find themselves in a street just wide enough for two lines of traffic. It was flanked on each side by tall buildings, trees just showing their early spring leaves, convenience stores, cafés and the inevitable vending machines stacked with canned and bottled drinks. Josie led the way down the street to where the sun shone dazzlingly on the curved glass window of a white fifteen-storey building.

'This is it,' she said. 'Hotel Orchid, Ochanomizu.'

They took the lift to the Heron Suite on the third floor where the reception for Ken and Noriko's wedding was taking place.

'Don't we get to go to the wedding then?' said Dave.

'No, that's at the Shinto shrine down the road and it's just for close relatives. Although, actually they're married already. Ken told me they submitted the documents to City Hall yesterday, and that's when the marriage legally takes place. But, obviously, it's the ceremony that people care about. We might get to see Noriko in her wedding kimono if we're lucky. That's why I didn't want to be late.'

As she finished speaking there was a rustle amongst the guests who were discreetly lingering in the foyer. Everyone turned to face the door as Ken and Noriko came in. Ken looked nothing like the work colleague Josie was used to. He wore a traditional black *haori*, a short coat with his family's crest embroidered on the front of each shoulder, and pleated grey trousers so voluminous they looked like a skirt. Noriko wore a heavy white silk kimono with long trailing sleeves and a stiff rounded white cap on her head that added at least thirty centimetres to her height. They both looked shy and happy. Everyone clapped.

'So, no veil, then?' said Dave.

'No veil. Just that big cap thing to hide her horns of jealousy,' said Josie. 'That's what the tradition is. Though I can't imagine why Noriko should suddenly have grown horns just because she's getting married.'

'Is she going to wear that thing on her head all through the reception?' said Dave.

'Of course not. They're doing the whole wedding thing, Ken's been telling me about it for months. Noriko's going to change into the most amazing kimono for the meal, and after that she's going to wear a meringue wedding dress and then a lovely dress from Hanae Mori to go away in.'

'This must be costing an arm and a leg,' said Dave.

'Yes, it is. But at least she doesn't have to buy the kimonos and dresses, they're all hired, along with someone to help her put the kimono on. Come on, let's leave our gift and go in.'

Josie felt like an old hand as she handed in her gift of money to the man behind the reception desk, all in brand new notes and in exactly the right kind of decorated envelope. She hoped Dave was impressed, and decided not to mention that Keiko had helped her out. But then, Dave probably knew that anyway.

The Heron Suite was filled with round tables, each big enough to seat a dozen people. They were decorated with trails of ivy and gold and silver ribbon, and by each plate was a little bouquet of violets. Josie could see colleagues from AZT dotted around the room, along with a lot of people she didn't recognise who must be Ken and Noriko's relations.

'Look, there's Cherie,' said Dave, waving. 'Nice to see someone we know.'

Cherie waved back from across the far side of the room and then came over to meet them.

'Hey, it's great to see you,' she said in English. 'We got here way too early so we've been having a look around. I checked and we're all on the same table. Look, that one over there by the window.'

Josie's heart sank. Ordinarily she'd be only too pleased to be sitting with Mr and Mrs Tanaka, but adding Cherie to the mix turned it sour. Try as she might she couldn't get over Cherie's breezy American manner and her friendliness towards Dave. Jealous, are we? said a voice inside Josie's head but she resolutely ignored it.

'Come on, Josie,' said Dave. 'Let's go and sit down.'

'I'll come with you,' said Cherie, linking her arm through Dave's and setting off with a cool disregard for whether Josie was following or not. Josie could hear her whisper something and then Dave's booming laugh rang out, making several of the people they passed turn around to see what was going on.

Go on then, make him laugh, Josie muttered under her breath. See if I care. I don't have anything to worry about. Dave's not going to be taken in by your free and easy American ways. He's a down to earth Londoner and proud of it.

She wondered if she'd get a chance to talk to Mr Tanaka about Mr Shiga and all that she'd found out about him, but it wasn't going to be easy, surrounded by wedding guests. She wished she'd rung him and told him sooner but it was too late now. She'd just have to try and get him on his own somehow.

Their table already had half a dozen people sitting at it, including Mr and Mrs Tanaka who both stood up at their approach and bowed formally. Josie never knew what to do when they did that. She could cope with bowing at work, but bowing from friends, especially friends who were a good deal older than her, always confused her. Though it wasn't as bad as friends who insisted on shaking her hand. That really freaked her out.

'This is your seat, by me,' said Mr Tanaka. 'Dave is opposite you with Cherie next to him. And might I introduce Mr and Mrs Suzuki who are friends of Noriko's family?'

A grey-haired couple, whose soft smiles and gentle demeanour reminded Josie of the emperor and his wife, stood up and bowed the full forty five degrees, which made Josie even less sure how to respond. In the end she simply chanted the standard phrase, 'I'm meeting you for the first time, please regard me with favour,' which made them bow even lower, and slid as silently as she could into her seat. There was a pretty menu card, written in Japanese and French, which promised a series of what Josie knew would be tiny but elegant courses.

The remaining seats at their table soon filled up with guests Josie didn't know and an air of expectancy filled the room. After a short wait the music system, which up until then had been trilling popular classics, began to play the wedding march from Lohengrin and Ken and Noriko entered. Josie almost gasped. Ken was still wearing his black *haori* but Noriko had changed into a spectacular wedding kimono of red and gold, embroidered with white cranes with spread wings entwined with green pine trees and fans embroidered in glittering gold thread. Her hair, released from the white cap she had worn earlier, now curled prettily, held in place by a shimmering gold and white comb trimmed with wisteria flowers that trembled as she walked. She looked shy and pretty while Ken looked more handsome than Josie had ever seen him, with an expression of pride on his face that turned to tenderness when he looked at Noriko.

'They're such a good match,' Josie said to Mr Tanaka. 'I'm so glad they found each other, even if it was the company matchmaker that introduced them.'

'Yes, they're well suited. Perhaps the old ways are still the best,' said Mr Tanaka.

'How did you and Mrs Tanaka meet?' said Josie.

'We were introduced by the local matchmaker,' said Mrs Tanaka. 'I didn't want to meet him at first as I wasn't ready to get married, but our parents arranged an evening at a restaurant for the two families so I was able to get a look at him without having to speak. And after that I told my mother I thought I was ready to get married after all.'

She laughed, but there was a soft glint in her eye as she looked fondly at Mr Tanaka.

Josie translated for Dave, who turned to Cherie.

'What about you, Cherie?' said Dave. 'Are you going to let a matchmaker find someone for you?'

'I don't know,' said Cherie. 'I'm not ready to get married yet either. What about you and Josie? When do you plan to get married?'

'Get married?' said Josie. 'We don't have any plans like that.'

'Why not?' said Cherie.

Josie stared at Dave, wondering what to say.

When you put it like that the question seemed unanswerable, and yet they'd never talked of marriage. Josie didn't even know how Dave felt about it.

She was saved from answering by the arrival of the first course, a little selection of vegetables dressed in different sauces. Josie turned to her neighbour on the other side, a woman who looked as though she'd only just fitted into her brocade suit and was now wondering how she was going to eat the meal without popping all the buttons of her jacket. She turned out, once she'd got over the initial shock of meeting a foreigner who spoke Japanese, to be both voluble and entertaining and Josie listened happily to her tales of the price reductions she'd managed to secure by her extraordinary bargaining skills, including a detailed rundown of how much her brocade suit had cost and how she had avoided paying full price for it.

Course succeeded course and her neighbour finally gave way to the mounting pressure and unbuttoned her jacket, revealing a lace blouse embroidered with pearls beneath. From time to time Josie glanced across the table at Dave and Cherie. The volume of conversation had risen so she couldn't hear what they were actually saying, but Cherie's body language said it all. She leaned close to Dave and whispered to him, then laughed, covering her mouth with her hand to hide her teeth as Japanese girls always did, but still managing to give off an air of American sophistication. Dave seemed fascinated, leaning towards her too and roaring with laughter at everything she said.

She's flirting with him, thought Josie indignantly. What does she think she's doing? One minute she's asking when we're going to get married, the next she's trying to get her hands on him herself. She felt herself grow hot, though that might have been the effect of the champagne being liberally poured by the assiduous wine waiter.

By the time the meal came to an end Josie felt decidedly squiffy. Her new friend in the brocade suit was clearly even more drunk than she was, staggering as she got to her feet to go to the Ladies. Josie joined her, and just got back to her seat in time to catch the start of the speeches. Well, some of them were speeches; in others, people sang or told jokes, or in the case of one rather frightened looking teenage boy, did surprisingly good magic tricks.

Then there was a lull while Noriko and Ken left the room again, until the music changed to Handel's wedding march and Ken and Noriko re-entered, this time with Ken in full morning dress and Noriko in the kind of huge white meringue wedding dress that Josie hoped she would never have to wear. Though she had to admit Noriko did look gorgeous in it, and the embroidery on the lace overskirt was astonishing.

The happy couple walked onto the dance floor, to the strains of the Blue Danube and began to dance, accompanied by a delicate patter of applause. After the first dance the music changed to disco and other couples started to take to the floor. Josie drank the last of her coffee and looked over at Dave, who was still engrossed in conversation with Cherie. Cherie caught Josie's eye and seemed to see something there. She came around the table to her father and took hold of his arm.

'Come and dance with me,' she said. 'You know you love it, even though you pretend you don't. Just one dance and then I'll let you off, I promise.'

Mr Tanaka stood up and followed Cherie onto the dance floor. Josie moved to sit next to Dave and slipped her arm through his.

'Do you want to dance?' she said.

'In a minute. Cherie told me about this great place to visit and I'm just going to look it up on my phone before she gets back.'

'A great place to visit with her, I suppose,' said Josie, trying and failing to keep the bitterness out of her voice.

'Considering you've decided to spend most of your time two hundred miles away, yes, I'm probably going to go with her. If you want me to go places with you, you need to stick around more.'

'That's unfair. It wasn't my fault I got sent to Osaka.'

'You could have said no.'

'But then I'd never have got anywhere at AZT. Once you've said no to something, you're out. They never ask you again.'

'And would that be so bad? If you come to London with me, what AZT does or doesn't think of you won't matter.'

'I know that. But I still want to do as well as I can while I'm here.'

'Or else you don't actually plan to leave at all.'

There was a moment of silence then Josie said, 'That's not true. You know I want to be with you. It's just that—'

She stopped. Both of them knew what she was going to say. She loved Japan. It had been her dream to live there, and she'd worked hard to make a go of it. It wasn't easy being a foreigner in Japan, but she'd got a good job with prospects, kind friends she loved, somewhere to live, a whole life in Tokyo. She fitted in; she understood the way of life, the little politenesses, the sense of community, the way people seemed to understand what you wanted even before you knew yourself. Even the bad things – the unthinking sexism, the hierarchy, the rigidity, had come to seem, if not natural, at least acceptable to her. She wasn't sure she could fit in in London any more. Where would she find a job and how could they afford a place of their own with London house prices going through the roof? It was all very well for Dave to be confident about going back; he hadn't been away as long as she had, and he already had a job with a good salary. Of course she would live with him, but she wanted it to be on equal terms. She didn't want to be a dependent, sponging off him. She wanted to make her own way, have her own career, be her own person. Dave didn't understand that. He thought just being together would be enough for her, but it wasn't. However much she loved him, she loved Japan more.

Just as the awful realisation crept over her that maybe she wasn't going to be able to sacrifice Japan for Dave, the music stopped and Cherie and Mr Tanaka came back.

'That's enough for me,' said Mr Tanaka. 'I can't keep up with this modern dancing.'

'If you're not dancing,' said Cherie, 'Can I borrow Dave for this number? It's my favourite.'

'I'd be glad to oblige,' said Dave, getting to his feet with a smile, not looking at Josie.

Josie watched their retreating backs as they headed for the dance floor. She hated Cherie for taking Dave away from her, but she hated herself more. She wanted to stay with Dave but if that meant going to London with him she wasn't sure she could bring herself to do it. Dave had made a lot of sacrifices to be with her – this year in Japan being the biggest. Once it was over, if they were going to stay together, she needed to do something for him. It was just that the thing he wanted her to do could turn out to be too much for her.

She looked across at Ken and Noriko dancing together, so happy, so certain that they'd done the right thing. Maybe that happiness wasn't for her. If she gave up on Dave she would never find anyone else that she wanted to spend her life with. She could keep Japan, if she wanted, but she would pay a heavy price for it.

She realised with a start that Mr Tanaka was watching her closely.

'Come for a little walk with me,' he said. 'It's quieter out in the foyer and we can talk.'

Josie got to her feet and they walked together into the foyer, which was almost deserted.

'You seem to be worried about something,' said Mr Tanaka. 'Can I help?'

'No, it's okay,' said Josie. 'It's just something Dave and I need to sort out. But I did want to talk to you about the Osaka office and what I've found out since we had lunch. I think it's important.'

Quickly she told him about how she had followed Mr Shiga and how she had been able to read the email.

'So you see, I think there's a strong chance that Mr Shiga is the culprit,' she said.

Mr Tanaka sat down at one of the little tables dotted around the foyer and Josie sat opposite him. His reaction wasn't exactly what she had hoped for. She had thought he would be impressed and enthusiastic, but instead he seemed thoughtful. She waited for him to speak.

'I've known Mr Shiga for some time,' he said eventually. 'I've never thought of him as being subtle enough to conceal something so exciting as a gambling habit.'

A wave of doubt swept over Josie. Could she have been wrong about what she'd seen?

'What about the email?' she said. 'He's the only one who had access to the Global Reinsurance computers.'

'Yes, I see that,' said Mr Tanaka. 'It's just that, to

be perfectly honest, I can't think of any information you could get just from an email that would be worth passing on. We are actually quite careful about things like that.'

'Oh,' said Josie, feeling deflated. 'You mean, someone would have to hack into the systems to get anything worthwhile?'

'Well yes, I rather think they would,' said Mr Tanaka. 'That's what's making it so difficult to track them down.'

Josie felt everything turn upside down. She'd been wrong. She had been so sure she had cracked the case, but now it was all unravelling in her hands. Just like her personal life. Through the open door of the ballroom she saw Cherie and Dave laughing together. Did Dave laugh like that when he was with her, or was that all over? Maybe it was time for them to part. This London business might be just what they needed to enable them to go their separate ways.

A wave of depression swept over her at the thought. Then she pulled herself together. I'm not done yet, she told herself. Not with Dave and not with Saburo's murderer either. So I've made a mistake – who doesn't? It doesn't mean I've screwed everything up. It just means I need to think it all through again, calmly this time. Like Mr Tanaka does.

She looked at her friend, who was watching her anxiously, and remembered all the times his peaceful certainty had held her together. This time was no different. She'd gone down the wrong path but now he'd put her straight and this time she was sure she wouldn't get it wrong.

'Come on,' she said. 'This isn't the time to be talking about murder. That can wait. Let's go and join the dancing.'

TEN

Monday morning found Josie back on the early train to Osaka feeling decidedly anticlimactic. She stared at the drizzly rain that ran down the window and told herself it was just a reaction to the excitement of the wedding and her lingering hangover. She'd drunk way too much and danced way too much and had altogether too good a time at the wedding to make a return to grim early morning reality anything other than a nasty shock. She'd be all right; she just needed something to give her a lift – starting with a good strong dose of caffeine.

She waited impatiently for the girl wheeling the little trolley dispensing life-giving hot coffee to appear in the doorway to the compartment and then trundle down the long aisle to her seat.

'Black coffee please,' she said. 'Make it two cups. And a danish pastry.'

She took the little cups of coffee, the tiny plastic pots of evaporated milk and a thin plastic stirrer that the girl handed her and fumbled in her purse for some change. Then she sat back, drank the first cup of coffee in one gulp and began munching on her danish. Time to do some hard thinking.

Problem number one: Dave. She feared losing Dave more than anything, and her extreme reaction to Cherie's no doubt innocent flirting was a symptom of that. But in order not to lose Dave she would have to give up Japan, and she was not sure that she could do that. It seemed insoluble. After a moment she decided to park problem number one and move onto problem number two: Saburo's murder.

She decided not to waste any time feeling foolish because she'd made up her mind on the basis of the flimsiest of evidence that Mr Shiga was stealing AZT's data and no doubt would turn out to be the murderer of Saburo into the bargain. Mr Tanaka had seen through that straight away, and quite rightly. Time to move on.

The first thing to do was to get a rational perspective on Mr Shiga. He wasn't much good as a boss, but then that was probably because he wasn't very good at personal interaction. It didn't mean he was a bad person. She vowed to get on better terms with him, and to start that very day.

Next: find out more about Saburo. How could she expect to work out who had killed him if she didn't know anything about him? She marshalled her meagre facts. He lived in Shizuoka, was the same age as Koji, Mack and Taro but didn't hang out with them, had probably been going out with Mimi at some point, though not necessarily just before he died, and had left the office around five p.m. that Friday to get the five forty Hikari bullet train from New Osaka station. He'd been going to Shizuoka but had stayed on the train for reasons unknown. Plenty of scope there to flesh out the picture. She decided to start as soon as she got to Osaka.

Having reached this conclusion she was able to relax and drink her second cup of coffee as the train flew along its now familiar track. A stop at New Yokohama, a fleeting view of Mount Fuji, mostly covered by cloud as it was ninety percent of the time in Josie's experience, the long ride to Nagoya, then Kyoto and New Osaka in rapid succession. A seasoned commuter now, she knew when to get up and queue for the exit, which direction to turn for the escalator as soon as she got off the train, the fastest route across the concourse to the escalator down to the Kyoto Line platforms. She stood waiting for the train at just the right place to be opposite the exit when it stopped at Osaka station with hardly a thought.

But when she emerged from the scrum around the ticket barriers at Osaka station central gate she didn't follow her autopilot and head down the street towards the office. Instead she walked through the internal station passages, past the café where she and Mr Tanaka had had lunch and emerged facing the pedestrian crossing that led to Umeda station next door. There she followed the passageway along the side of the Hankyu department store, closed and shuttered at this hour, then turned left and got the moving walkway to the Umeda station concourse, where she headed towards the Kinokuniya bookshop. That, too, was closed so she took the passageway that ran alongside it past the waiting taxis, down towards the familiar petrol smell of the bus station and the eerily silent shops of the Kappa Passage to the covered road where Mr Shiga had emerged from the station into the back streets. She remembered the route he'd taken well and soon reached the undistinguished door through which he had vanished. There was no sound of Mah Jong from the upper windows this early in the morning and no sign of life anywhere, so she felt able to linger and take a good look at the doorway. Which turned out to have a worn sign on it. Hoping nobody would see her, she stopped and peered at it. *Matsui Electronics* said the faded *kanji* lettering.

Josie went hot and cold. She knew Matsui Electronics. They supplied AZT with some of their less important kit like plugs and wiring. A lot of the old bits and pieces that lay around the IT office probably came from them. So Mr Shiga had been visiting a supplier after all.

Josie felt a flash of irritation. If he was doing something entirely innocent, why had he looked so furtive? But, as she headed despondently back to the office, she realised that Mr Shiga always looked like that. She was the one who had read something special into it, simply because she wanted to. She was excited about having met Mr Tanaka and keen to start investigating, so she'd simply invented a mystery that didn't exist.

She was so preoccupied with her thoughts she nearly jumped out of her skin when someone gently touched her elbow.

'I'm sorry,' said a familiar voice. 'I didn't mean to startle you.'

Josie brought herself back to reality and focused on a short figure standing hesitantly next to her.

'Koji,' she said. 'Sorry, I was miles away.'

'If you don't want to be disturbed I'll leave you alone,' said Koji. 'I just thought we could walk along to the office together.'

'Yes, of course. Sorry I didn't recognise you at first. I had something on my mind.'

'A work something or a personal something?'

Josie hesitated. She didn't want to discuss the Mr Shiga debacle with Koji.

'A personal something.'

'Then it's about love,' said Koji.

'Yes, I suppose it is,' said Josie, her mind flying back to Dave and Cherie.

'That's the worst kind of problem. Believe me, I know.'

Josie looked at Koji. Somehow she'd never thought of him having romantic problems. Or any kind of problem, really. He always seemed so confident, so on top of things.

'Oh, I've been through it, I can tell you,' Koji said, correctly interpreting her expression. 'There was this one girl, I really cared about her but she preferred someone else. I felt very bad about that for a long time, but you have to pull yourself together and get on with things, don't you?'

'Yes, I suppose so,' said Josie. 'My problem's different though. I've got this great guy but I may have to give him up.'

'Why would you do that?'

'Because staying with him would mean I'd have to leave Japan.'

Koji's clear brown eyes seemed to pour out sympathy and understanding. Josie felt he really did know what she was going through.

'Is this the boyfriend back in Tokyo?'

'Dave. Yes, it is.'

'It must have been tough when you got sent to Osaka.'

'It was. Maybe I should have turned it down, but it was everything I'd been working for since I joined AZT. I couldn't just give it up, could I?'

'Of course not. Though I suppose it hasn't turned out quite the way you thought.'

'It certainly hasn't,' said Josie. 'I thought it would be challenging and fun but it's just been a grind. And now this business with Saburo as well.'

Koji nodded. They were both silent for a moment and then Josie said, 'The worst thing is, whoever killed Saburo might be someone we know. Someone in IT Support.'

Koji stopped suddenly.

'What do you mean?' he said. 'Did the police say that?'

'No, of course not,' said Josie, realising she

should probably not go gossiping about the murder weapon having been a knife from Mimi's kitchen. 'Only, it has to be a possibility, doesn't it?'

Koji relaxed slightly.

'Anything could be a possibility,' he said. 'Saburo could have had all sorts of things going on in his life that we don't know anything about. Everyone has their secrets, especially at work.'

That's true, Josie thought. And if I want to find out who killed Saburo I'm going to have to find out what his secrets were – and what the murderer's secrets were too.

Koji was watching her closely and once again Josie had the feeling that he understood just what was going on in her mind. It made her nervous and she cast around for a way to change the subject. A sign over a glass-roofed alleyway lined with restaurants and 'slots' - places where you could play the slot machines - caught her eye. It showed the head of a woman, her hair done in traditional style, her expression sad and pensive, set in a circular plaque against an eye-catching black and orange background.

'I've always wondered about that sign,' she said. 'It seems so out of keeping with what's behind it. Who's the woman and what's she doing there?'

Koji looked up.

'That's Ohatsu,' he said. 'That sign is for the Ohatsu shopping arcade and it leads to the Ohatsu-tenjin shrine.'

'The Ohatsu-tenjin shrine?' said Josie. 'What's

that? I've never heard of it.'

'It's really called the Tsuyu no Tenjin Shrine,' said Koji. 'But people call it the Ohatsu-tenjin shrine because of the play. You know, *The Love Suicides at Sonezaki*.'

Josie looked blank so he went on, 'It's a famous *bunraku* puppet play by Chikamatsu. They call him the Japanese Shakespeare and *The Love Suicides at Sonezaki* is the Japanese *Romeo and Juliet*. I can't believe you don't know it. It's about a geisha, Ohatsu, and her lover Tokubei who works for a soy sauce maker and gets swindled out of some money. Things get so bad that they decide to commit suicide together at the shrine. Tokubei cuts Ohatsu's throat and she bleeds everywhere and then he cuts his own throat.'

Koji recounted this bloodthirsty story with relish.

'And this all happened at this shrine?' said Josie.

'Yes. The play's based on a true story.'

Josie made a face and Koji laughed.

'It's not scary. It's a place where lovers go to celebrate the undying love of Tokubei and Ohatsu and to pray for their love to be as strong. Come and have a look at it. It won't take long, and you could pray at the shrine for your relationship to succeed.'

'Alright,' said Josie. 'I'm not sure I want to end up like they did, but I don't mind praying at their shrine.'

They turned into the shopping arcade, which was decorated with banners depicting the lovers Ohatsu and Tokubei, she with her hair elaborately sculpted, he with a traditional samurai topknot. At that hour of the morning it was quiet, with just a few people using it as a shortcut, their footsteps sounding unnaturally loud on the chequered tile floor, but Josie could imagine how it would come to life at night, brightly lit and filled with noisy groups eating noodles and grilled chicken, or drinking in the *izakaya*, the Japanese equivalent of a pub, while the rattle and ching of slot machines filled the air.

The shrine at the end of the passage was smaller than Josie had expected, with a green tiled roof shaded by trees. It was guarded by two stone lions with blue scarves tied around their necks. Everywhere she looked there were reminders of the tragic lovers, including a little statue of them sitting on a stone bench, turned slightly towards each other with poignant sadness.

'Look,' said Koji. 'They're selling marriage charms with pictures of Ohatsu and Tokubei. One's pink and one's green. You keep one and give the other to your boyfriend and then you both carry them with you for good luck.'

Josie wasn't sure how Dave would react if she gave him a good luck charm with a picture of a soy sauce seller who killed himself on it, but she picked up a pair of charms anyway. It couldn't hurt.

'And you can leave a prayer to the gods on one of these,' said Koji, pointing out a selection of heart-shaped wooden plaques with the inevitable pictures of Ohatsu and Tokubei on them. 'You write your prayer on it and tie it to that board over there where all the other prayers are.'

Josie looked where he pointed and saw a forest of little prayer plaques rattling in the wind.

'Okay,' she said. 'But that's all.'

'I'm sure it will make all the difference,' said Koji. 'You wait and see.'

Josie felt a bit silly as she tied her prayer plaque up among the others. She didn't usually go in for prayers and superstitions but Koji had been so enthusiastic she hadn't liked to refuse. And maybe the star-crossed lovers would be able to help with her problem.

They were both thoughtful as they walked on towards the office. Josie stole a glance at Koji. He was frowning as he walked and his ever-restless fingers beat out a complex tattoo on his briefcase. Josie wondered what was on his mind.

'I'm not looking forward to another week at the office with all this hanging over us,' she said. 'I wish they'd hurry up and find out who killed Saburo so we can get back to normal.'

'Normal's not much fun either,' said Koji. 'To be honest, I can't wait to get out of here.'

'Are you planning a move?'

'Planning is putting it too strongly. There's a vacancy in the Tokyo office. It would be a promotion and I've been after it for a long time, but they never seem to make up their minds who to appoint.'

'I'm sure you'll get it in the end. Do you know who the other candidates are?'

'There's a couple in Tokyo. And a couple here. Or

at least there were.'

'Has someone dropped out?'

'You could put it like that.'

"Oh,' said Josie. 'You mean Saburo.'

'Yes. So you could say I had a motive for killing him, couldn't you?'

Koji stopped drumming his fingers and looked at her as though keen to see how she'd react.

Josie laughed uneasily.

'If that's a motive for murder, half of us would have killed the other half long ago,' she said.

Koji visibly relaxed.

'You're right,' he said. 'And anyway, Saburo and I were friends. We were in the same cohort and you know what that means.'

Josie did. It meant they'd been recruited at the same time and would move through the AZT hierarchy together and leave together when their careers were over. It was a bond almost as strong as brotherhood, and cohort members were obliged to look out for each other and help each other succeed.

'You must feel his loss very much,' said Josie.

Koji nodded.

'Yes,' he said, 'But on the other hand, Saburo's not being around does make things easier for me in a way. Or maybe not.'

'What do you mean?'

'Let's just say that Mr Ozawa doesn't always play fair. He always favoured Saburo over me, and I think he might have been planning to recommend Saburo for promotion. He had this idea I was less serious than Saburo. It's ridiculous, but I feel like that's still hanging over me. So maybe Mr Ozawa won't recommend me even now.'

'I don't have a lot of time for Mr Ozawa, but surely he'll recommend the best candidate,' said Josie, hoping to cheer Koji up. The thought of his damaged prospects seem to be weighing him down.

'I hope you're right. I really need this promotion. I've been stuck in Osaka too long.'

The grey bulk of the office building came into view and Koji turned and smiled at her.

'It's been good talking to you, Josie,' he said. 'I feel better now. It's just I've been really down about Saburo, and it's made me depressed about everything.'

'Of course,' said Josie. 'It's only natural. It's getting all of us down, especially not knowing who did it. But I'm sure the police will find the murderer soon.'

Koji nodded and pulled open the heavy door for her to go through into the foyer.

There was an odd atmosphere as they walked through the foyer and stood waiting for the lift. Josie glanced around. There seemed to be a lot more people there than usual and they were huddled together in little groups, whispering, as though they knew something she didn't. Even the granite-faced receptionist had unbent enough to speak to the security guard, who was leaning over her desk with a worried expression on his face.

She looked at Koji, who'd noticed the atmosphere

too.

'Something's going on,' he said. 'Let's go up to the IT office and see what they know.'

Josie nodded. She felt as though some sort of disaster was about to hit her but couldn't work out what it was going to be. Koji looked as though he felt the same – his fingers had begun their drumming again, setting Josie's nerves on edge. She wanted to tell him to stop but managed to restrain herself. They waited in silence for the lift to arrive.

When they walked into the IT office the atmosphere was even worse and Josie's feeling of unease intensified. Everyone was sitting huddled over their computers with glum faces. They all looked up as Josie and Koji came in, as though they were expecting someone else, then quickly ducked their heads back down again when they saw who it was. Mr Shiga was at his desk, frowning at his computer screen as though it was impossible to lift his eyes from it. The door to Mr Ozawa's office was closed.

'What's going on?' she whispered to Koji.

'No idea.'

He tapped Mack on the shoulder.

'What's up?' he said.

'Read your emails,' said Mack. 'There's an office meeting in half an hour. People are saying we're going to be shut down.'

ELEVEN

Josie sat down at her computer and opened up her inbox. There was an email from the Head of Branch, addressed to all staff.

As we enter the season of heat and humidity, I hope you all continue to find yourselves well, it began, in what Josie recognised to be a standard formal greeting for the time of year.

The purpose of this memo is to inform you of a special meeting which has been called for ten o'clock today in the conference room. It is a requirement that all staff attend. The meeting is expected to last half an hour and other commitments should be rearranged accordingly. We intend to make an important announcement of relevance to every member of staff. Directors and Section Heads are asked to ensure that all their staff are present at the meeting.

'All it says is that there's going to be a meeting and they're going to make an announcement,' she said to Koji, who was looking over her shoulder at the email.

'A meeting of all staff. That never happens. And it says an important announcement.'

'Maybe it's good news,' said Josie. 'You never know.'

'It's not good news,' said Koji.

'Maybe it's to do with Saburo. Maybe they've found the killer.'

Koji didn't answer, just turned away and went and sat down at his own desk, where he stared blankly at his computer screen just like everyone else.

Josie looked at the clock; three quarters of an hour to go until the meeting.

She went down to the kitchen to see if Mimi knew anything.

'I can't stop,' Mimi said. 'All the office ladies are going down to help set out the room for the meeting. Better head down there early if you want to get a seat. It's not big enough for everyone so if you're late you'll be squeezed in at the back.'

'Any idea what it's about? Is it to do with Saburo?'

'Nobody knows anything,' said Mimi, her face blank. 'And anyway, you'll find out soon enough.'

Josie helped herself to a cup of green tea and headed back to her desk. She couldn't see why Mack had been so sure they were to be closed down, nor why the people in the reception area had been so agitated. Unless it was to do with Saburo. But then, why call a special meeting like this?

She set off for the canteen a full twenty minutes

before the meeting was due to start and found when she got there that Mimi had been right. Though the room was filled with chairs, nearly all of them were already occupied and she had to squeeze along a crowded row to reach the last remaining seat, jammed hard against the wall.

People who arrived after her stood at the back, though the space there was limited and it looked uncomfortably crowded. Josie looked around for Koji and the others from her section, her height enabling her to see comfortably over the heads of the people near her. She couldn't see them in the seated area, but then she saw Mack and Taro come in and hesitate at the sight of the crowd. After a moment's consultation they squeezed their way around the wall and stood near the window that looked out over the main entrance to the building.

Mr Shiga was sitting near the front in an area reserved for section heads. He looked nervous, but then so did everyone else. Mimi was nowhere to be seen, and Koji came in just before the meeting started and stood at the back.

As the hands of the clock crept closer to ten an air of anticipation almost amounting to fear filled the room. The audience was a sea of black suits with flashes of white shirt, bringing home to Josie how few women there were. Presumably the office ladies were staying at their posts until the last minute, fielding phone calls and rounding up stragglers. And, apart from the office ladies, there weren't really any women on the staff. It struck Josie as odd; over

147

in Tokyo women were starting to make headway in AZT but Osaka seemed stuck in the past. Just like the ancient building they worked in; part of another era.

A few minutes before ten there was a stir at the front of the room. The directors and deputy directors filed in and took their seats at the front of the room, facing the audience. Josie looked at Mr Ozawa. As always his face was impassive but she thought she could see a film of sweat around his collar. Behind the directors a line of security guards took up position along the wall. Security guards? Josie thought. Seems a bit like overkill. What do they think we're going to do when they make their important announcement? Rise up in a body and storm the platform?

There was a pause during which everyone sat up straight without fidgeting. Then the door opened again and the Head of Branch came in, accompanied by a small entourage. Josie looked at him with interest. She'd only seen him once before, when she'd been taken into his office to be formally introduced as a new member of staff. He was tall and thin with a cold intellectual face but she knew he was well respected. Most people felt that he stood up for them when the high command in Tokyo criticised their performance.

When the Head of Branch reached the small platform with a single table and chair on it he paused and the whole room stood up. Josie, taken by surprise, scrambled to her feet a beat behind the rest. He motioned for them to sit down and the room fell silent as he cleared his throat and began to speak.

Josie listened closely at first, finding his unfamiliar voice difficult to grasp, but soon realised that he had begun with the usual elaborately expressed platitudes of appreciation that launched every speech she'd ever heard, and relaxed. Long, orotund phrases that reviewed the whole history of the Osaka office from its foundation in the nineteen sixties to the present day rolled past her ears. Everyone else seemed to concentrate hard on every word, as though to suck some special meaning from it.

But then he paused and said, 'And now I come to the reason why you have all been asked to attend today.' Josie pricked up her ears, while everyone else seemed to sit a little straighter. Those standing at the back positively stood to attention.

'I am delighted to tell you,' he went on, 'that our lengthy negotiations to obtain the freehold of our Osaka site have been successful, and our long held plans to rebuild can now go ahead. We are keen to make a start on this important work as quickly as possible.'

That doesn't sound too bad, thought Josie. I wonder why everyone is looking so glum about it.

'You will all want to know what this means for your future,' said the Head of Branch, with an agonising pause as he shuffled his papers. 'You will all be aware that it is company policy to concentrate functions in centres of excellence, many of which are located in Tokyo. It is the intention to set up a

149

functional centre of excellence in Osaka, but this cannot be done in the existing building. To expedite this important and necessary change, it has been decided to begin work on the new building without delay.'

Great, thought Josie. A centre of excellence here in Osaka would be brilliant. But where will we all go while the rebuilding happens? They'll have to rent somewhere. At least it will be in better condition than this place.

The Head of Branch paused, and his long face became even more solemn.

'I need hardly remind you,' he said, 'of the tragic event which struck one of our colleagues recently. The death of Saburo Horii has affected us all. The police investigation is continuing and I cannot say anything that would be prejudicial to that enquiry, but I have to tell you, with a heavy heart, that the police have been unable to rule out the possibility that his work was a factor in the terrible event which led to the loss of his life.'

That's a pretty roundabout way to put it, thought Josie. Is he saying someone here in the Osaka office killed Saburo or isn't he?

'I am confident that everyone here will strive to uphold the reputation of the Osaka office and that the police will soon resolve the issue of Mr Horii's death and absolve us all from blame. However—'

He looked up from his papers and there was another agonising pause.

'However,' he went on, 'this additional factor,

and the possible effect it might have on our good name in Osaka has led the Board to conclude that the Osaka office should make a complete new start once the new building is ready. It has therefore been decided that staff from this office will be dispersed to other offices as quickly as possible, both to facilitate the start of work on the new building and to enable us all to regain our good names. Accordingly, we have set in place a timetable for vacating the building and dispersing staff. As a specialist team from Tokyo will move in immediately to support the information technology aspects of the moves, the staff dispersal will begin with IT Support, which will close down forthwith. Your directors and section heads will give you more detail on how the moves will work immediately following this meeting. Thank you for your service and commitment. I wish you all the best in your future careers.'

There was silence in the room when he finished speaking and sat down. Everyone seemed as stunned as Josie was by the news.

After a pause, the Head of Branch gathered up his papers and left the room, followed by the directors. Clearly there was to be no opportunity for questions. The whole thing was a fait accompli.

Josie twisted around in her seat to look at the other members of IT Support, but they were already filing out of the door. Josie was trapped in her seat by the crowds, unable to get out until the whole row had moved.

She was late getting back to the office, having had

to struggle though crowds of people from other departments making their way slowly back as well. When she got there everyone else was already seated in an informal semicircle with Mr Ozawa at its centre.

'Ah, Miss Clark, there you are. Now we can start,' said Mr Ozawa, making it sound as though Josie had deliberately dawdled in order to inconvenience the maximum number of people.

Josie knew better than to protest. She slid into the only vacant seat trying hard not to look guilty. She could have saved herself the trouble as nobody looked at her. And anyway, she was still digesting the bombshell that had been dropped. Today? They were closing the office today? She was used, or at least she thought she was used, to Japanese decision making, where long periods of apparent inaction were followed by rapid change, but this was exceptional even for Japan.

Mr Ozawa cleared his throat and Josie turned her attention to him.

'As you have just heard,' he said. 'IT Support is to close forthwith. I have a list here of the offices to which you will all be transferred. As far as possible we have tried to ensure that you will be spread across a wide variety of locations so as to give you the best chance possible for a fresh start. Each of you will be called to my office individually immediately following this briefing to be told where you are to go. You will all commence work in your new postings on Monday. Until then, you will work with the incoming Tokyo team to ensure a smooth handover. I know I can rely on you to deal with this professionally in the best traditions of our office.'

I hope they send me back to Tokyo, Josie thought desperately. I hope they don't send me down to Hiroshima or somewhere in Kyushu. It's bad enough commuting to Osaka.

Mr Ozawa looked sternly at his staff.

'I want you to know that I have every faith in you,' he said. 'Are there any questions?'

There were no questions.

'In that case,' said Mr Ozawa, 'I will invite our Tokyo colleagues to join us.'

He nodded to Mr Shiga who opened the door. Half a dozen people, some of whom Josie recognised from the Tokyo office, came in looking sheepish.

Josie looked around as people paired up with their replacements. They looked stunned, unable to comprehend that they were soon to leave the office where some of them had worked for years and never come back. The building wouldn't even be there to come back to – the site would be surrounded by clean grey steel walls with a large printed notice giving details of the planned work and the timetable to completion. And then, one day not too far in the future, there would be a modern skyscraper and the battered old grey concrete building would be just another memory.

Josie was surprised to find herself feeling quite sad at the thought. She had begun to admire the old warhorse of a building, standing its ground when all around it fancy new buildings full of fashionable restaurants sprang up. She wondered what would happen to the old couple who ran the office canteen. She couldn't see a place for them in a shiny new skyscraper. And all the old bits of computer that littered the IT Support room, what would happen to them? Consigned to the scrap heap, no doubt, along with all the current equipment for which there would be no place in the shiny office of the future. It seemed a waste, but when they rebuilt in Japan they did it properly. Nothing old made it through to the brave new world.

The interviews with Mr Ozawa didn't last long. One after another Josie watched her colleagues knock at the door and enter Mr Ozawa's office until, surprisingly quickly, it was her turn. She hesitated before knocking, giving herself time to take a deep breath and summon up her courage. If he said she was being transferred to some far off location, what would she do? Take the transfer and ruin her year in Japan with Dave? Or turn it down and see her career, and quite possibly her job at AZT, vanish before her eyes? Not an easy choice, especially when it had been sprung on her so suddenly with no chance to think about what she really wanted.

She straightened her back. No point wimping around outside the door. Time to go in and face it.

Mr Ozawa's office, never tidy at the best of times, looked like the American Embassy just before they evacuated from Saigon. There were papers everywhere; on the desk, in teetering piles on chairs, on top of filing cabinets whose open drawers displayed more papers, on the floor in thick files with ancient webbing strips around them to keep them closed. For someone who ran an IT office Mr Ozawa seemed surprisingly wedded to old-fashioned ways of keeping track of his data.

He grunted when Josie appeared, and indicated the only chair in the room with no files piled on it, opposite his desk. Josie looked at him curiously. She'd never got much of an idea of what Mr Ozawa was like. He seemed like more of an absence than a presence, someone glimpsed in the distance at the end of a corridor, seen in conversation in the corner of the big IT Support room, caught whisking into his office and shutting the door firmly behind him. Josie had never had a conversation with him since her brief interview on her first day, and she couldn't recall seeing anyone in IT Support talking to him either, apart from Mr Shiga. He was an enigma.

Today he seemed as nervous as she was. It couldn't be easy for him, she thought, disbanding his whole office and scattering his staff to the four winds. And what did it mean for him? Would AZT give him a job somewhere he wanted to go or send him off to a distant outpost? Josie suddenly felt sorry for him. He'd got a wife and family somewhere whose lives were about to fall apart just like hers was, only they had even less say over what was about to happen to them.

Mr Ozawa shuffled through some of the papers on his desk. His face was as impassive as always, but the dampness around his collar had spread and there were dark circles at the armpits of his worn shirt. His jacket hung on an old-fashioned wooden coat rack with curled arms and a circle of wood near the base to hold umbrellas. Josie knew that if he was summoned by a superior he would grab the jacket and throw it on, but now, talking to a mere member of staff like her, he left it where it was, mute testimony to her lowly place in the hierarchy.

'Miss Clark,' he said in a voice so low she had to strain to hear it. 'Mr Shiga tells me that in your brief time here with us you have shown diligence and dedication to your work. I thank you for all your efforts on behalf of the company and IT Support.'

He bowed, and Josie found herself bowing back.

'It's a pity you haven't had more of a chance to gain experience with us, but I'm sure you'll make good use of all you've learnt while you've been here.'

He paused and Josie felt it was incumbent on her to say something.

'I've enjoyed working here, thank you,' she said, feeling her response was feeble but not able to think of anything more suitable.

'I am sure your experience will stand you in good stead in your future career,' said Mr Ozawa, while inwardly Josie screamed, get on with it, tell me where I'm going, put an end to all this suspense.

Mr Ozawa shuffled his papers some more.

'You were previously based in Tokyo,' he said, his eyes scanning though the list in front of him.

'Yes,' said Josie.

'Well, I'm pleased to tell you that you will, at least initially, be returning to the Tokyo office.'

Josie felt a sense of relief flood through her and then snag on that one awkward word.

'Initially?' she said.

'Yes, initially. Since your posting here was for training purposes, I imagine they'll want to consider sending you somewhere else to complete your training.'

'Can't I do that in Tokyo?'

'That's not for me to say. Talk to HR when you get to Tokyo. They'll let you know what's been decided.'

Mr Ozawa looked up, as though he considered the interview over. Josie was incensed. Was that it? All her Osaka hopes over in one bland sentence? Not the slightest attempt to think about how she felt or what would happen to her? Just *talk to HR when you get there*?

She started to say something she knew she would regret as soon as it was out of her mouth, but then stopped herself. This wasn't all about her. Everyone in IT Support was in the same boat, and soon the same thing would happen to everyone else in the Osaka office. A way of life was coming to an end, and a lot of people would be much more badly affected than she was. All that had happened to her was that a few inconvenient weeks away from Tokyo had come to an end and now she could go back to living with Dave and enjoying her life again. She had nothing to complain about. It was those people who had made their careers in Osaka she should be concerned about. Their lives were about to be turned upside down.

Josie knew how it worked in Japan. You went where the company sent you, no matter how far away it was or how inconvenient. Your family, on the other hand, stayed put. To move would disrupt that most important of things, the children's education. So wives and children stayed rooted where they were while husbands went to the other end of the country and lived in grim company flats with no friends around them and no chance to make any as they worked all the hours of the day for the company. Josie's anger subsided, and she looked at Mr Ozawa with sympathetic eyes. What would happen to him? He looked to be in his late fifties with not much of his career left to him. How would he tell his wife that he was going to be sent away?

Josie wondered what his home life was like. Did he have a close relationship with his family, or had putting the company first for so long left him estranged from them, an irrelevance who appeared at home only rarely to interrupt the lives his family had made for themselves without him? Did he feel a stranger in his own home?

Josie came to with a start as she realised Mr Ozawa was looking at her strangely, obviously wondering why she hadn't got up and left him to get on with the next task – telling yet another of his staff that they were to be sent somewhere unattractive.

Not everyone could go to Tokyo. Most people would be sent to more distant offices. Josie was one of the lucky ones.

'What will happen to you, Mr Ozawa?' she said, shocked at her boldness but unable to keep from trying to establish some form of human contact with the stiff man in front of her.

'To me?' he said, and Josie wondered if he would just refuse to answer her.

'Yes, where will you go? Will I see you in Tokyo?'

'I don't believe so,' he said. 'I gather I'll be going to one of the smaller offices where they need a man of my experience to give them a guiding hand.'

Exiled to the provinces, Josie thought sympathetically. To a 'smaller office' with fewer staff, less prestige and more work. A slow decline into old age and then thrown on the scrapheap.

She got up, bowed and left the office to go back to her desk and start clearing out her drawers.

As she piled her meagre possessions into a cardboard box the company had thoughtfully provided she felt a hesitant tap on her shoulder. She looked up to see Mr Shiga standing behind her.

'Can I talk to you?' he said.

TWELVE

'Not here,' Mr Shiga went on. 'Somewhere private.'

'It had better be outside the office then. There's nowhere private here today with everything in such chaos. We could go to a café,' said Josie.

Mr Shiga flinched as though she had bitten him.

'No, not a café. We can't be seen going to a café together,' he said. 'Meet me in the car park in half an hour. In the corner, where the trees form that little clump.'

'Okay. What's it about?' said Josie, but Mr Shiga had already headed back to his desk, his head bent as usual, not catching anyone's eye.

I can't imagine why I thought he was a computer hacker with a gambling habit, Josie thought. Anyone less likely to be doing something vaguely exciting or even mildly interesting I cannot imagine. I wonder what he wants to talk to me about that's so private?

As usual when she had something on her mind, she headed towards the little kitchen for a cup of green tea.

'So where are you being sent?' Mimi said, handing her a steaming cup.

'Back to Tokyo.'

'That's alright then. Better than most, in fact. I don't think there's many going to Tokyo apart from you.'

'Really?' said Josie, feeling flattered. 'I thought most people would get Tokyo.'

'I don't think Tokyo's very impressed with us lot,' said Mimi. 'I hear Mr Ozawa is off to Kyushu – some say Fukuoka, but my money's on Kumamoto.'

'Kumamoto? But that's right in the far west.'

'That's right. It's four hours from Osaka on the train. But at least you don't have to change at Hakata any more.'

'I've never got on with Mr Ozawa particularly, but you have to feel sorry for him,' said Josie.

Mimi's expression hardened.

'Serves him right. All this has happened on his watch.'

'What will you do, Mimi?' Josie said. 'Will you move somewhere else too?'

'I'll stay here as long as the office is open. Then I'll probably look for another job. Or maybe—.'

Mimi stopped and busied herself with the cups.

Hm, not going to tell me, thought Josie. I wonder what she's got planned. I bet it's something interesting.

'What about the others?' she said. 'Where are they going?'

'It's not for me to say. You'll have to ask them

yourself.'

Mimi picked up a tray of cups of green tea and moved towards the door. Josie held it open for her and followed her out.

Back at her desk she emailed Koji, even though he sat just across the room from her and she could easily have walked over to talk to him. But she had a feeling people wouldn't want to talk too openly about their moves just yet.

Where are you going? she typed and Koji emailed back, *Hiroshima. Could be worse. At least it's not that hard to get to from Okayama. What about you?*

Josie hesitated and then typed *Tokyo.*

Lucky you, came the reply. *I'll have to look you up when I'm in town.*

Anytime, Josie replied, feeling suddenly sad that she probably would never see Koji again.

*

Exactly thirty minutes after Mr Shiga had spoken to her she saw him get up and head for the door, looking so elaborately casual that he might just as well have held up a sign saying *I'm up to something.* Getting into the spirit of it, Josie waited until he'd left the room and then slid out of her seat as unobtrusively as she could. Nobody seemed to notice. Only Mr Yamada, who had the desk next to Mr Shiga's, glanced up briefly and then returned to his screen.

She didn't bother waiting for the lift but walked down the stairs, rather embarrassingly almost running into Mr Shiga in the foyer where the receptionist was asking him about the arrangements for a meeting later in the day. Josie walked past them without a glance, though she could tell that the sight of her made Mr Shiga stammer over his instructions.

It felt strange to be leaving the office during working hours, though she wasn't going far and would still be technically on the premises. But then it had been a strange day. Only four days left and then she would leave the Osaka office behind forever. Josie found it hard to believe that come Monday morning she wouldn't be getting up early to catch the bullet train but joining all the other commuters heading into Otemachi instead. She wondered what would be waiting for her back in Tokyo. A return to her old job at Corporate Support or a new posting somewhere in IT? Had she done enough in Osaka to justify the move or had it all been a waste of time?

She threaded her way between the lines of cars in the car park. The sun glinted off their windows and roofs and burned uncomfortably into the back of her head. Only a few more weeks and it would be summer and the rain would sweep in and turn June into a sodden, humid ordeal. And then the temperature would soar – thirty degrees, forty degrees, maybe more, and life outside an air-conditioned environment would be impossible. The patchy shade cast by the pine trees around the office would be a welcome relief then. She wondered whether they would leave the trees when construction work began, or whether their existence was about to come to an abrupt end just as Saburo's had done.

She waited behind the group of trees, which did quite an effective job of shielding her from the view of anyone looking out of the window of the IT office, and watched as Mr Shiga zigzagged towards her through the parked cars instead of just taking the direct route as she had done. This is getting very cloak and dagger, Josie thought, feeling a strong desire to giggle at the thought of Mr Shiga doing anything remotely swashbuckling.

He nodded when he saw her.

'Thank you for coming, Miss Clark, er, that is, Josie,' he said. 'I'm sorry to take up your time when I know everyone is so busy, but there's something I need to talk to you about. Several things, in point of fact. Several things that are, um, related. In a manner of speaking.'

He stopped and didn't seem to know how to go on.

'Is it to do with my work?' said Josie.

'No, not exactly. That is – well, it is about work in a way. Well, some of it is. And some of it is more about your er, um, work-related activities if I can put it like that.'

He glanced nervously up at the office windows and shrank back behind a tree trunk.

'They can't see us here, can they?' he said.

'Who do you mean?'

'Anyone. Anyone in the IT office.'

'I don't think so. And anyway, no one will be looking out of the window. They've got too much to do.'

'Yes, of course, you're right. I just don't want people to know we're having this conversation.'

What conversation? Josie thought. So far they didn't seem to be getting anywhere.

'So what's it about, Mr Shiga?' she said firmly.

'Well, firstly, it's about your reading emails which don't concern you.'

Josie could feel herself turning hot and cold. How did he know about that?

'You should have been more careful,' Mr Shiga said. 'You shouldn't have opened an unread email. Of course it got marked as read and then Mr Suzuki wondered why the computer thought he'd read an email which he hadn't read, and then he asked his neighbour whether he'd had the same problem and his neighbour said that you'd been using the computer. So it wasn't very hard to work out what had happened. Mr Suzuki came to see me and I have to say he was very reasonable about it and said no doubt you had made a mistake but he thought it would be a good idea if I ensured you didn't make any similar mistakes in future.'

'Yes,' said Josie, inwardly burning with embarrassment but determined not to admit it. 'I'm very sorry. It was just a mistake. I won't be doing anything like that again.'

'No, well, one advantage of what's happened is that you won't have a chance to, not while you're working for me, at any rate.'

'No, I suppose not. I really am very sorry.'

'Right, well, we don't need to say anything more about it,' said Mr Shiga, shuffling his feet as though trying to nerve himself to come out with the next thing that was on his mind.

'Was there anything else?' said Josie, to help him out.

'Yes, there was, actually.' Mr Shiga looked up and for once looked Josie full in the face. It was disconcerting. His eyes were much more penetrating than she had expected and seemed to bore into her in a way that made her feel distinctly uncomfortable.

'I'd be grateful,' Mr Shiga said, in a voice that had turned suddenly harsh, 'if you didn't follow me about the streets hoping that I won't see you. I don't know what you thought you were up to or what you hoped to find out, but I have to say that your ability to blend into the background is far less than you seem to believe.'

'Oh,' said Josie, startled into honesty. 'I really didn't think you'd seen me.'

'Of course I'd seen you. The whole of Umeda station must have seen you. It would be amusing if it wasn't so embarrassing.'

'I'm sorry,' said Josie again. It seemed that her main role in this conversation was to apologise.

'I accept your apology,' said Mr Shiga. 'I understand that the recent unfortunate death of our colleague Saburo has left us all a little on edge. I'm sure that's the reason for your strange behaviour.'

'I can explain,' said Josie, though as she said it she realised that any explanation would probably be

166

even worse than the original crime.

'I don't want you to explain,' said Mr Shiga. 'I just want to make sure you don't do it again.'

'Yes, I mean, of course not. Thank you,' said Josie.

'Well, that's what I wanted to say to you. I didn't want to do it in the office because I didn't want it to seem like a reprimand. Please think of it as more a piece of friendly advice.'

'Thank you, yes, I will,' said Josie, rapidly revising her opinion of Mr Shiga. Once she actually got to talk to him he turned out to be a lot stronger and more incisive than she'd given him credit for. Which made her wonder why his self-presentation was normally so weak.

She thought that would be the end of their strange conversation, but it seemed that Mr Shiga was still not finished. He looked up into the straggly branches of the pine above their heads and then gazed across the car park as though he had lost track of what he was there for.

'Did you want to tell me anything else?' said Josie.

Mr Shiga hesitated.

'You didn't know Saburo very well, did you?' he said.

'Saburo? No. I was only here a week before he got killed and we hardly spoke. So I didn't know him at all.'

Mr Shiga nodded.

'I feel responsible, in a way.'

'Responsible?'

'For what happened to him. I feel that if only I'd said something earlier, none of this would have happened.'

'Said what? And who to?'

Mr Shiga stared up into the tree again.

'Who to,' he said, as if talking to himself. 'Yes, who to was really the issue. I expect that's why I never did say anything.'

'But you want to tell me now,' said Josie encouragingly.

'You've been a breath of fresh air in our office,' said Mr Shiga. 'We've been stagnating here for longer than I care to remember, doing things the old way, thinking about things the old way. Not noticing what was happening under our noses. Saving face. Hiding things away. Keeping secrets. But you don't think like that. You're English and you think the way English people think. You would never let yourself drift into the kind of rut we've been in. That's why I want to tell you about Saburo.'

Josie waited in silence.

'They're sending me back to Shizuoka,' said Mr Shiga. 'It's kind of them, really. I can go back to living with my wife and my children, see them every day, watch them grow up. We've grown distant since I was moved to Osaka and I want to put that right.'

'Shizuoka,' said Josie. 'Isn't that where Saburo came from?'

'Yes. I've known him since he was a little boy. His parents live in the same street as us. I helped him get a job with AZT, though to be honest it was against my better judgement.'

'Why do you say that?'

'Not because he wasn't good enough. He was good alright. Too good. Too clever and too ambitious. I'm afraid his ambition may have led him into doing things he shouldn't have done.'

This time it was Josie who looked away and took time to gather her thoughts. Nobody had spoken to her as frankly as this since she'd come to Osaka, and she realised how superficial her knowledge of everyone around her was. Now Mr Shiga was tearing away the curtain and she was afraid she wouldn't like what he was going to reveal. She took a deep breath.

'I know about the stolen data,' she said.

'You know? How can you know?'

'Someone told me, it doesn't matter who. I haven't told anyone else.'

For one mad moment she thought of telling Mr Shiga she had suspected him but decided not to.

'I see,' said Mr Shiga, looking taken aback.

'Do you think it was Saburo who was stealing it?' she said.

'I don't know. I did wonder. It could have been him – it was well within his power. He was an extremely talented coder – he got into a lot of trouble at school for hacking into the website where the study aids were posted and changing some of the words to make rude phrases.'

Josie suppressed a giggle. Saburo sounded like fun.

'It's a long way from playing silly jokes on the school website to stealing commercially sensitive data,' she said. 'Why would he do such a thing?'

'I don't know. I don't think he was interested in money. He might have done it simply because he could. That was the kind of person he was.'

'So, if you knew him so well,' said Josie, a light dawning. 'Do the police suspect you of having something to do with his death?'

'The police suspect everyone at the moment.'

'But you were at a meeting in Nagoya that afternoon. I saw you leaving with Mr Ozawa, just after lunch.'

Mr Shiga looked uncomfortable.

'Yes, that's right,' he said. 'Mr Ozawa and I were both at the meeting all afternoon.'

'So you wouldn't have seen when Saburo left the office.'

'No, I didn't know what time he left. Or what train he got. Though there aren't many trains that stop at Shizuoka so I suppose I could have worked it out if I'd wanted to.'

'Have you any idea why Saburo didn't get off at Shizuoka like he was supposed to?'

'No idea at all. He must have changed his plans on the way as the police said the ticket in his pocket was only valid as far as Shizuoka, but I don't know why.'

A car drove into the car park and down the row of cars nearest to them, looking for a parking place. It seemed to bring Mr Shiga back to the present. He looked at his watch and then back at the office. His usual nervous manner came back and he bent his head away so Josie could no longer look into his face.

'I'm sorry, Miss Clark,' he said. 'I have to get back to work and so do you.'

'No, wait,' said Josie. 'I want to know more about Saburo. Who his friends were, what he was interested in, anything that might explain who would want to kill him.'

'I can't help you there. I don't know anything about his personal life. Just that he told his parents he had a girlfriend in Osaka, but he never took her home to meet them. And that he was in line to get the next promotion. That's all I know.'

Mr Shiga looked around the car park and, seeing it was deserted, made a sudden dash for the office entrance, leaving Josie on her own. She waited a few minutes, thinking about what Mr Shiga had said. Saburo was beginning to emerge as a distinct character, rather than just a murder victim; someone who had a home and parents, a history before he came to Osaka, talents, likes and dislikes. And a personality which was turning out to be rather different from what Josie had imagined from her brief acquaintance with him. Or at least it was different according to Mr Shiga. How far could she trust his story? Did he feel threatened by Saburo, the young genius from down the road who had moved into his sphere of work and been better at it than he was? Once again Josie's image of Mr Shiga turned on its head. He had been stronger and sharper in their little discussion than she had ever seen him before. Did his modest demeanour hide a steely interior?

Slowly she made her way back to the office. It was a hive of activity as the outgoing staff tried to pass on everything they knew to the incoming Tokyo team, with only four days in which to do it. Josie felt a little guilty, but the truth was it took her no time to tell her Tokyo colleague what she had been doing, and to pass her remaining checklists over to him with a sense of relief. He took them from her and put them in his bag.

'Actually,' he said, 'We won't need to finish the checking. All the computers here are going to be scrapped so it really doesn't matter any more.'

Josie nodded. It was a fitting end to her brief Osaka sojourn.

'So what shall I do for the rest of the week?' she said.

'If I were you I'd take some time off,' he said. 'I don't imagine anyone will mind.'

Josie thought about it. She had to stay in Osaka until the IT Support office closed for good on Friday, but it was unlikely that anyone would care what she did. It would be a relief to get away from the office. And it was her last chance to show Dave around the city. She could ring him and see if he could get away for a day.

The thought cheered her up and she reached for her mobile phone. But just as she was about to ring Dave's number a shadow fell over her desk. She looked up to see Taro looming over her with an agitated expression on his face.

'I need to talk to you,' he said. 'It can't wait. Come with me now.'

THIRTEEN

Not again, thought Josie. Why does everyone suddenly feel the need to tell me things? And why do they have to be so cloak and dagger about it instead of just sitting down and telling me? But she got up and followed Taro as he started off down the corridor at a fast lope. Anyone else would have had trouble keeping up with him, but Josie's long legs matched his stride for stride. At the end of the corridor there was a dead end where a sad looking fern drooped in a dry pot. Taro stopped and turned to face Josie.

'They're sending me to Sendai,' he said. 'It's awful.'

'Sendai? That's in the North East, isn't it? It'll be a long journey for you. Is that why you're upset?'

'The Tokaido bullet train doesn't even go there. You have to go to Tokyo and get the Tohoku bullet train from there. I won't be able to come home at the weekend. And I won't be able to come to Osaka any more.'

'Yes you will, just not as often. And you'll make

new friends in Sendai so after a bit you won't mind. Anyway, you can text Koji and Mack so it'll almost be like you're still seeing them.'

'No, that's not it. You don't understand.'

'It can't be missing Mrs Miyazaki's noodles that's bothering you,' said Josie, half laughing.

'I don't care about food. I can eat anything.'

'Well, what is it then?'

Taro stared at the sad neglected fern as though it had done him some terrible injury. Then he whispered, 'It's Mimi.'

'Mimi?' said Josie.

'I won't be able to see Mimi again,' said Taro. 'I love seeing Mimi. She's so pretty and bright and she has lucky ears. I've always wanted a girl with lucky ears. I thought she was getting to like me a little bit, but now there's no hope for me. I'll be far away and there'll be plenty of men around her. Koji's only going to Hiroshima – he can come back whenever he wants. And Mack's staying in Osaka.'

'How can Mack be staying in Osaka? The office is shutting down.'

'His family arranged it. They're rich and his father knows the Head of Branch. There'll be a small office here to look after Osaka clients so he'll be in charge of their IT systems. Those jobs always go to people with influence, not to ordinary guys like me. I'll be up in Sendai and I'll never see Mimi again.'

Josie felt bewildered. It had never occurred to her that Taro felt so strongly about Mimi. Certainly Mimi had never shown any sign of being interested in him. Though, thinking back, Josie realised that Mimi had always been kind to him, never laughed at him like the others and always listened patiently to his tales of his Harry Potter-style adventures and regular trips to Universal Studios.

'Well, you could stay in touch with Mimi too,' she said lamely.

'No,' said Taro. 'Mimi will forget me. She'll get married and she'll forget all about me.'

'Is Mimi planning to get married?' said Josie.

'Mimi could marry anyone she wants.'

'Yes, I'm sure she could, but that's not the same as actually getting married.'

'When Saburo was killed,' said Taro. 'I was happy. I thought there'd be a chance for me then.'

'Saburo? What's this got to do with him?'

'Him and Mimi. I saw them together. They thought I didn't know, but I used to follow them.'

'Saburo and Mimi were dating? Are you sure?'

'I saw them. Sneaking out at lunchtime, meeting up after work. They thought they were being clever but it was so obvious what was going on.'

'Did anyone else know about them?'

'Koji knew. And Mack. I told them what I'd seen. They said I should wait, that she'd find out what he was really like and then she wouldn't want to be with him any more. But she didn't get tired of him. She just went on.'

Josie looked down at Taro's hands. His fists were tightly clenched as though he wanted to hit someone. I wouldn't like to get on the wrong side of him, Josie thought. Let alone stand between him and his heart's desire, like Saburo apparently did.

'What can I do about it?' she said.

'Talk to her. She likes you. And you're a girl and girls talk about that stuff. Find out what she's going to do.'

'I've already asked her that and she wouldn't tell me.'

'Ask her again. Tell her I'll come back and see her. Tell her—' He broke off as someone walked down the corridor towards them.

'Please help me,' he whispered, and darted off back towards the IT office.

Josie lingered where she was for a moment, wondering whether to follow him. She decided instead to go to Mimi's little room and get some water for the sad fern. Her good deed for the day. Though it would probably be thrown on the scrapheap in a few weeks time when they cleared out the office and demolished it.

Mimi wasn't in the little kitchen, for which Josie was grateful, given the stories she had just been hearing. Could it be true about Mimi and Saburo? Were they in love? It seemed hard to believe, but Taro had no reason to lie about what he'd seen. Mimi was so hard to read – behind her perfect facade she could be thinking anything. Given longer to get to know each other Josie thought they might have become friends, but as it was their brief acquaintance would never rise above the superficial. When they all dispersed at the end of the week she and Mimi

177

wouldn't keep in touch. Josie was sorry to have missed the chance to get to know Mimi better, but that was how things went. Whatever Mimi had planned for her future, it had nothing to do with Josie.

She filled a jug with water and took it down to the fern. The water ran through the dry earth into the saucer beneath and Josie wondered whether it would do any good. But at least she'd tried.

Back in the IT office she was surprised to see the lights had been switched on and twilight darkened the windows. She'd been so busy she'd hardly noticed the passage of time. She picked up her phone to make her interrupted call to Dave but then hesitated. She felt strangely reluctant to tell him about the office closing. It seemed like a failure, and though it wasn't her fault she didn't want to admit that the grand career step she'd been so adamant about had turned out to be a damp squib. It's not the kind of news to break over the phone, she rationalised to herself, and anyway if he's still at work it might not be a good time. I'll suggest he comes over to Osaka. I can take some time off like that Tokyo guy said and show him around the sights, then I can tell him quite naturally before he goes back.

She felt reluctant to approach Mr Shiga directly after their odd conversation in the car park so she sent him an email asking if it would be okay to take a day off. He replied straight away to say that she could. But she didn't ring Dave right away. The fact

178

was, she didn't quite know what she was going to show him in Osaka. She'd never actually strayed outside the very small area between Osaka station, Umeda station, the office and a few of the back streets round about. There was the Ohatsu shrine, it would be nice to take him there. And Umeda Sky Building, of course. She'd seen that often, towering over the landscape with its weird double towers joined at the top by a bridge that made it look like a nutcracker made out of lego. There must be a great view from the top. And Osaka castle – she'd seen pictures of that and it looked very historic, though when she checked on Wiki it turned out it was a modern concrete replica. Never mind, it was set in parkland that looked attractive. And at least they could go to Osaka's main attraction, Dotonbori, where the whole of Japan went to eat. She was pretty sure she was on safe ground there.

Armed with the results of her research, she got out her phone and rang Dave's number. The phone pinged as he picked up.

'Hey, I was just thinking about you,' he said. 'And right away you rang. Must be fate.'

'It must be,' said Josie. 'Are you still at work?'

'No, I left hours ago. Work's really quiet. We've got to the end of a project and my boss is on a trip to the States so we can't start anything new. We're just twiddling our thumbs, so I rang Cherie and asked her to take me on that trip to Kyoto she promised me. She hasn't got anything on this week either so she jumped at it. I've just got off the phone with her and we're all set for Wednesday. I was just about to ring and tell you.'

I bet she jumped at it, thought Josie. Why does she always have to pop up and spoil things?

'Oh,' she said in a small voice. 'That's nice.'

'So what did you ring me about?'

'It's just, well, I've got a free day too.'

'That's great. We can all go to Kyoto together.'

'I've been to Kyoto,' said Josie, sounding sulky even to herself. 'I wanted you to come and see Osaka with me.'

'That's okay, I'm sure we can do both. Cherie and I will get the early train and take a look round Kyoto then we can come on and join you in Osaka. How about that?'

'When would you get here?'

'I don't know. How long does it take to get from Kyoto to Osaka?'

'About half an hour.'

'Well then, no problem. We'll see you for lunch.'

'Oh, I didn't mean—' said Josie but stopped herself. I didn't mean for you to bring Cherie with you, she'd been going to say.

'Actually,' said Dave. 'I've got something I want to tell you but I'll save it up until I see you.'

'Something to tell me?' said Josie, her mind instantly running on all sorts of disasters. 'Why can't you tell me now?'

'Hey, don't get excited. I'd just rather do it when we're together, that's all. It's only a couple of days away.'

'Okay,' said Josie reluctantly, her curiosity about what Dave's news could be making her forget to mention that she had something to tell Dave too. 'I'll meet you at New Osaka station at one o'clock then.'

She clicked off her phone and sat at her desk feeling cross with Cherie for getting in the way when she needed to talk to Dave alone. And for showing him Kyoto, historic capital of old Japan with its temples and palaces when all Josie had to show was Osaka. How could she take Dave to Osaka castle when Cherie had just shown him the Emperor's palace with its nightingale floors that squeaked when you walked on them so no intruder could creep in undetected? How could she take him to the tiny quaint Ohatsu Shrine when Cherie had just shown him the Golden Temple? It was as though Cherie set out deliberately to spoil her plans.

She stared crossly across the room towards the little enclave where Koji, Mack and Taro worked. She could see Koji explaining something to his Tokyo replacement, who nodded and asked questions. Taro was staring miserably at his screen, occasionally tapping a key on his keyboard. And Mack – Mack was nowhere to be seen.

That's odd, thought Josie. The Tokyo guy is working at Mack's computer, so where has Mack gone? She waited, and Mack reappeared a few minutes later sipping a cup of green tea.

Been to the kitchen then, thought Josie. I wonder if Mimi's there now. I could do with a cup myself. But she didn't get up to go and get herself one. She sat and let her thoughts run on, idly watching Mack as she did so. She didn't know much about him. He always seemed to be Koji's sidekick, not as clever as Koji, not as quirky as Taro, just there in the background, the Ron Weasley of their little group. But now, as she watched him from a distance without him being aware of her scrutiny, Josie realised that she'd got it wrong. She'd always been vaguely aware of his fashionable haircut and expensive suit, but she hadn't noticed until now that he moved differently from the other two. He walked with a quiet assurance that was in contrast to Koji's cocky strut, a confidence that didn't need to prove itself the way Koji constantly did. Koji talked fast, cut into conversations, brimmed with ideas. Josie could quite see why Taro had thought of him as Harry Potter. Mack was no Harry Potter, but he wasn't to be underestimated either. He was rich, Taro had said, and he had the assurance that came from having money. He was far too smooth to be a Ron Weasley. He was much more of a Draco Malfoy.

Josie sat quite still. Why had she thought that? Draco Malfoy was thoroughly unpleasant. Mack wasn't like that. He wasn't proud or sly. But all the same, once the thought had come into her head she couldn't get rid of it. She knew so little about him. He never talked about himself, and his manner gave nothing away.

She thought back over her limited acquaintance with him. The noodle lunch at Mrs Miyazaki's – he'd been quiet then, playing the perfect sidekick, which enabled him to avoid responding to her question about whether Saburo hung out with them, leaving it to Koji to answer. But he'd reacted strongly when Taro had suggested there had been something between Saburo and Mimi. Too strongly, as though it mattered to him more than he wanted to show. Josie wondered what that meant.

Then they'd gone out drinking together at that Mama bar of Koji's, and Mack had been evasive about his whereabouts on the afternoon that Saburo had been killed. Of course, as he lived in Osaka, there was no need for him to do anything so precise as catch a train the way Koji and Taro had, but all the same, Josie'd got the distinct impression that he didn't want to say what he'd been doing. But why not? What did he have to be secretive about?

Appalled at her growing suspicions Josie looked away, and then back across the room at Mack. He was explaining something to his Tokyo colleague, and though Josie couldn't hear what he was saying she could tell that he was doing it well; his colleague was nodding and looking thoughtful, occasionally asking a question and writing down the answer. Mack was good at IT too, just as good as the others. As good as Saburo had been? Or better? Good enough to be the mystery hacker, or to be the one who discovered who the hacker was?

Josie felt her frustration mount. She was pretty effective with technology, but she knew that her skills were too limited to allow her to delve into how the sensitive information had been stolen, and she didn't dare ask anyone else to help her for fear they might turn out to be the hacker themselves. There must be some other way to find out.

It was growing late, and some of the IT workers were shutting down their machines and shrugging into their coats. Mr Shiga had been called into Mr Ozawa's office for a consultation so his desk stood empty. There was a palpable feeling of a long and difficult day reaching its end. Josie supposed she'd better head back to the grim hostel and tell them she wouldn't be staying there any longer. She didn't think it would make much difference to them. It wouldn't take her long to pack up her things and send them back to Tokyo so she could leave straight from the office on Friday. They'd probably finish early that day – there'd be nothing left to do by then.

Across the room Koji and Taro stood up and walked into Mr Ozawa's office with their Tokyo opposite numbers. Mack was left on his own and Josie could see him shutting down his computer and preparing to leave. She did the same and found herself walking down the corridor behind him and getting the same lift.

'I hear you're staying in Osaka,' she said as the lift descended.

'Who told you that?' said Mack sharply.

'Oh, sorry, wasn't I supposed to know? I just heard it somewhere.'

'It's not a secret,' said Mack. 'But we're not supposed to discuss it. I'm sure you understand.'

'Of course,' said Josie, though she didn't see why

at all.

'Goodnight, then,' said Mack striding out ahead of her when the lift reached the ground floor.

Josie walked slowly after him, not wanting to catch him up and find themselves walking down to the station together when he so clearly didn't want her company. But instead of heading towards the station as she'd expected, Mack turned in the opposite direction and walked rapidly away. Unthinkingly, Josie did the same. There was no reason why Mack shouldn't walk in that direction – he was a free agent and didn't have to go straight back home after work. But all the same, Josie had a funny feeling about it. There was something odd about the set of Mack's retreating back. He was up to something, she was sure of it. And she was going to find out what.

FOURTEEN

Mack walked so quickly that Josie found it hard to keep up with him. Remembering how scathing Mr Shiga had been about her shadowing skills, she was careful to keep well back, though that had the disadvantage that when he turned sharply down a side street she had to run to catch up. She turned the corner just in time to see him vanish into a little café. Josie slowed down and walked casually down the opposite side of the road, trying to pretend she was just window shopping.

There wasn't much to look at; the road was hardly wide enough for one lane of traffic in each direction and the few shops were older and less fashionable than the ones nearer to the station. Josie's eye was caught by a shop selling hats, great piles of them in every conceivable shade, but none of them seemed very new and there was a forlorn look to its dimly lit windows. The only shop that was open at that hour was a brash new convenience store but there didn't seem to be anyone in it except the bored assistant checking his phone behind the counter.

She managed to get a surreptitious look at the café where Mack had gone in as she went by. It didn't look a very prosperous place. The outside was painted a dull brown and the gold lettering on the window promising coffee and English tea was faded. There was no sign of Mack – he must have taken a table at the back, out of sight.

Josie stopped at the next corner, wondering what to do. Should she risk going into the café and running into Mack or wait out here to see what developed? As she hesitated she saw something that made up her mind. In the distance a figure was walking towards her, too far away to make out clearly, but silhouetted against the light from the main street the prominent ears were unmissable. Mimi!

Hurriedly Josie retreated around the corner, out of sight. She peeped around and saw that Mimi, too, vanished into the little café. That settled it. She was going in. She walked back down the street and pushed open the café door.

The place had an air of having been left behind by the march of time. The yellowing walls were painted with a barely discernible pattern of trailing ivy; battered green rattan chairs encircled oilcloth-covered tables. The lights were dim and there was a vague odour of fermented soya lurking in the background. In a tired-looking glass showcase sagged a few leftover French patisseries while behind it a sallow faced girl sat perched on a high stool with her back to the room, counting the takings. There was no sign of Mack or Mimi. The only other customer was a woman with a pile of heavy bags at her feet, sitting at the front of the café staring out into the street with a blank expression.

Baffled, Josie sat down at a table in the corner and stared at the menu. The girl behind the counter left off her counting and ambled over.

'Milk tea,' said Josie and the girl wandered away and returned with Josie's tea in a flowered china cup. Josie looked around as unobtrusively as she could, wondering where Mack and Mimi could have got to, and eventually spotted that the room was not square, as she had thought, but had an extra piece that extended behind the back wall where the counter was. Josie could just make out that there were tables there too, and at the far one, out of sight of anyone unless they deliberately walked round the back, were Mack and Mimi.

Josie hastily turned away and picked up her cup of tea, hoping they hadn't spotted her. She strained her ears, trying to make out what they were saying, but they were too far away and speaking too quietly for her to make anything out. Anyway, she scolded herself, there's no reason to think they're saying anything more interesting than *how was your day?*

She wondered whether to go over to their table but couldn't work out what she would say if she did. *Fancy meeting you here* wasn't going to be very convincing given the lengths they'd gone to to avoid being seen on the way there. It would be obvious she'd followed one of them and how was she going to explain that?

The woman by the window gathered up her bags and slowly made her way out, the door giving a forlorn ting as she left. The girl behind the counter finished counting the cash, plugged in the earphones of her mobile phone and gave herself up to the bubblegum rhythms of J-pops. Josie mechanically drank her tea and let her mind drift back over the events of the day. It had been the longest day of her life, starting with catching the early train at Shinagawa, then meeting Koji and visiting the Ohatsu shrine, and then the shock news that the office was closing and the revelations from Mr Shiga and Taro. It all started to jumble together in her mind, so that she couldn't separate out Mr Shiga from Taro, both their voices echoing together in her head in a weird duet. Her head dropped forward on her chest and she jerked it back up again. No sense getting this far and then falling asleep on the job. But what job? What on earth did she think she was trying to do? So Mimi and Mack had met up secretly, so what? If they were an item they might well want to keep it secret from their AZT colleagues. She felt her head beginning to droop again and fervently wished she'd gone straight home when work finished, not followed Mack. She wasn't going to learn anything here.

Her head jerked back up again as she felt a touch on her arm.

'Hey, Josie,' said Mimi. 'What brings you here? I didn't think anyone from AZT ever came here.'

Josie sat up and tried to look as though she had a reason to be there and hadn't been falling asleep.

'I just came in for a cup of tea,' she said. She peered over Mimi's shoulder and saw Mack sitting at the table in the corner, gesturing for her to bring her cup over and join them. He smiled and nodded at her, and she smiled weakly back.

'You look really tired,' said Mimi, picking up Josie's cup and bag. 'Come and sit with us for a bit before you go home. It'll give you a chance to put yourself back together.'

Josie stood up and followed Mimi back to their table.

'This is a surprise,' she said. 'I didn't expect to run into you two here.'

'No,' said Mimi. 'It's a pretty out of the way place.'

'I hope I'm not disturbing you,' said Josie. 'You know, if you've got something private to discuss.'

'Of course not,' said Mack. 'We were just talking about what happened today. What it means for everybody.'

'It's a big change,' said Josie cautiously.

'You'll be alright,' said Mimi. 'But some of the older guys will be hit hard.'

Josie had the odd sensation that their conversation was taking place in a dream and that underneath their exchange of platitudes something more significant was going on, but she was too tired to work out what it was.

'There's going to be a farewell party on Friday,'

said Mimi. 'We were just talking about it. It's going to be in the office and Mr Ozawa's asked me to organise it. It'll be a big do. What do you think we should have to eat?'

'I don't know,' said Josie. 'What do you think?'

'I think it's best to keep it simple,' said Mimi. 'People won't want to stay too late. They'll all want to pick up their luggage and get their trains.'

'What do you think?' said Josie to Mack.

'Mimi's right. Best to keep it simple.'

'I think so too,' said Josie.

There was a pause and Josie saw Mimi and Mack exchange a glance. Then Mack said, 'It's getting pretty late and they want to shut this place up. I'm heading back to the station. Do you want to walk along with me, Josie?'

'What about Mimi?'

'Her place is in the other direction.'

'I'll come with you, then,' said Josie. 'What time is it?'

'Gone eleven.'

Josie reached for her bag, a wave of tiredness engulfing her. Mimi helped her into her coat, which she somehow found hard to manage by herself.

'You look worn out,' said Mimi. 'It's a long way back to your hostel and I'm not sure you'll manage to stay awake long enough to get there. Why don't you come back to my place and stay the night instead? It's a bit small but there's room for two and it's close by.'

'Well,' said Josie hesitantly. But she had to admit

she didn't much fancy the long journey back to the hostel late at night when she was already tired. The trains would be full of sleeping drunks, not noisy or aggressive as they would be in London, but slumped in unattractive heaps and Josie was afraid that Mimi was right and she, too, would fall asleep and be carried past her stop.

'Okay then, thanks,' she said. 'If you're sure I won't be a nuisance.'

'No problem,' said Mimi. 'I'll be glad of the company.'

'Then I'll be off,' said Mack. Josie could see he couldn't wait to get away and leave her with Mimi.

The girl at the counter watched them leave impassively but pulled down the blinds the minute they were out of the door. Josie wondered how Mimi and Mack would say goodbye, but in fact they just said *see you* as though it was the end of an ordinary evening, and Mack immediately turned and strode away towards the station, taking a lot of the tension that had pervaded the atmosphere with him. It made Josie realise that Mack and Mimi had been a lot more disturbed than they'd let on to find that she had turned up in their secret meeting place, and also that they'd gone to a lot of trouble to stop her suspecting how disconcerted they'd been.

It was odd – it was the first time she'd ever seen the two of them talking together for any length of time. They'd never seemed particularly friendly at work, never stopped to chat to each other and Mack hardly ever went into the little kitchen when Mimi was there. It had never struck her before, but now she could see that they had been deliberately avoiding each other, making sure that no one saw them together and started to draw conclusions. She wondered how long it had been going on. Since before Saburo died? Or had it started afterwards? Had Mimi moved rapidly from one conquest to the next?

Josie glanced at Mimi's calm face and immediately felt guilty. Mimi had only ever been kind to her and yet here she was coming up with the most alarming suspicions. And just when Mimi was kindly putting her up for the night too. Josie felt ashamed of herself.

It was only a short walk from the café to Mimi's flat, which was in a large old concrete block with old-fashioned external walkways. The breeze blew a gentle scent of wisteria over them from a gnarled old tree in the courtyard. It was covered in blossom that waved soft tendrils over the balconies and draped itself along the edge of the walkways.

Mimi saw Josie drinking in the scent and smiled.

'My namesake,' she said.

'What is your name? I've only ever heard people call you Mimi.'

'Yes, that nickname has really stuck. My real name is Miyu Fujii.'

Fuji was the Japanese word for wisteria. Fujii meant a wisteria-covered well.

'Such a pretty name,' said Josie. 'Is the Mi in Miyu for beauty?'

'Yes, it is,' said Mimi. 'The yu is for grace.'

'Beauty and grace, and wisteria,' said Josie. 'You have such a lovely name, it's a shame no one uses it.'

'I prefer it that way,' said Mimi. 'I don't feel it's the real me that works at AZT. It's just someone playing a part. So having a different name helps.'

She opened one of an identical row of doors on the first floor and ushered Josie in with an apology for living in such a humble space. The flat was tiny – just one small square room, immaculately tidy, a mini kitchen in what in London would have been the entrance hall and a little folding door that led to a toilet and shower.

'It's just like my old flat in Ichikawa,' said Josie, looking round at the polished wooden floor, the neat pile of bedding in the corner, and the tiny table with a laptop computer on it.

'It's all I can afford, I'm afraid,' said Mimi. 'It's not a very good area but it's close to the office. A lot of single girls live here.'

She went into the kitchen and poured out two cups of green tea from the dispenser standing next to the sink. Trust Mimi to have green tea on the go at all times, thought Josie, accepting a cup gratefully and sinking down onto the battered sofa.

'I've got a spare futon you can use,' said Mimi. 'My sister sometimes stays over so I keep it for her.'

'How old is your sister?'

'She's eighteen. She still lives at home, but I wanted to be independent.'

'And where is home?'

'It's in Wakayama. It's not that far from Osaka. My parents work in the *kamaboko* factory there.'

'I've never thought about *kamaboko* being made in a factory,' said Josie, who was fond of the pink and white roundels of *kamaboko* that turned up in miso soup.

Mimi laughed. 'I'll take you there sometime and show you how it's done,' she said. 'It's only a little place. They use locally caught fish so it's very fresh. Drink your tea and then I'll make up the beds. You're obviously exhausted.'

'It's okay. I think the walk has revived me,' said Josie, her curiosity about Mimi and her life overcoming her tiredness. 'What made you get a job at AZT?'

'It was a stroke of luck. I went to Wakayama Women's College but I wanted to come to Osaka to work as there's much more going on here. I'd come over at the weekend to go out with my friends, and then I met…' she hesitated and went on '…someone who told me there was a job going at AZT. So here I am.'

'But don't you find it frustrating being an office lady?'

'Not really. I'm not ambitious and there isn't anything I particularly want to do, apart from getting married, of course.'

'Why do you want to get married? I thought Japanese women nowadays liked to stay single.'

'Not me. I want to be settled, to have someone to look after me. Don't you?'

Josie decided to pass on that question.

'Do you think you'll marry Mack?' she said.

'I don't know. It's too soon to tell.'

'You haven't been together long then?'

Mimi's expression changed to one of wary caution.

'Not that long,' she said.

'How did you get together?'

'Oh, I don't know.' Mimi got up and began sorting through the pile of bedding in the corner. 'He just asked me out one day, I think. I don't really remember.'

Josie wished she could see Mimi's face, but Mimi kept it resolutely turned away. She's lying to me, Josie thought. I wonder why.

'Do you go to his place much?'

'No, I've never been there,' said Mimi, and then, realising how strange that sounded added, 'His flat's in Namba so it's easier for him to come here.'

'What about Saburo?' said Josie.

'Saburo?' said Mimi, dropping the pillows she was holding and whirling around to face Josie. 'What do you mean? What's this got to do with Saburo?'

'I thought you and Saburo were going out. Or have I got that wrong?'

'Me and Saburo?' Mimi hesitated. 'Well, yes, I suppose I did go out with Saburo. But that was all over before I got together with Mack.'

'What happened? I mean, why did you break up?'

'We didn't, exactly. I can't really explain. Shall I show where everything is in the bathroom? Then you can have a shower while I make the beds.'

'Okay, thanks,' said Josie.

'There's shampoo and soap here that you can use, and there's a clean toothbrush in the medicine cabinet,' said Mimi, 'And there's clean towels in the cupboard and a cotton *yukata* you can wear. It's only an old one but it will do for tonight.'

'Thanks. It's really good of you.'

'Not at all. I'm glad we've got a chance to get to know each other better,' said Mimi, making Josie feel thoroughly ashamed of her probing. So Mimi had a complicated love life – so what? She wasn't the only one.

Josie showered quickly and wrapped herself in Mimi's pretty *yukata*, patterned with goldfish swimming sinuously among stylised swirls of blue water. It smelled very clean, with a slight echo of the scent of wisteria Josie had caught outside. It was familiar and Josie recognised it as Mimi's scent, that hung in the air when she brought green tea and comforting words at work. No wonder all the young men were in love with her. And probably a lot of the older ones too. She was so pretty, and Josie was even starting to get used to her lucky ears.

When Josie came back the room had been transformed with two futons laid out on the floor side by side, each with a spotless white pillow and a soft fluffy quilt decorated with wisteria flowers.

'I'm done in the shower,' she said.

'I won't be long,' said Mimi. 'You go to sleep. I'll be as quiet as I can.'

197

Josie got into bed and lay listening to the splash of water as Mimi had her shower. The noise lulled her into a half sleep in which the events of the day seemed to swirl around her in a confusing hotchpotch where everyone seemed to wear two faces. Was Mr Shiga the weak work-obsessed salaryman he appeared to be or the decisive boss who had spoken to her in the car park? Was Taro charmingly simple or simply dangerous? And was Mack Mimi's romantic prince who would carry her away to a brighter future or something much more sinister? She hoped he was the former. Mimi deserved a break. But then her thoughts swirled on again, to Mimi and Saburo. What had their relationship been, and how could Mimi have moved on to Mack so quickly? And why had she been so scared before the police interviewed her? Had Saburo been the one who stole the data or not?

A double ding from her phone jerked Josie back to consciousness. Cursing herself for forgetting to set it to silent, she reached for her bag and stared groggily at the screen. It showed a message from Koji.

I've got something to tell you, it said. *Meet me tomorrow morning before work at the Ohatsu shrine. It changes everything.*

FIFTEEN

Josie woke the next morning to the smell of coffee. Mimi was already up and dressed, though it was a good deal earlier than Josie usually liked to greet the new day.

'Sorry I can't offer you anything to eat,' said Mimi. 'I don't generally have anything in the mornings.'

'Just coffee is fine, thanks. I need to go out early anyway and I can pick something up at a coffee shop before work,' said Josie, scrambling out of bed and hurrying to the bathroom to dress.

By the time she re-emerged Mimi had tidied the futons away and the room was back to the pristine state in which Josie had first seen it. The polished surface of the little table positively gleamed in the early morning sun and probing sunbeams failed to discover the least trace of dust in the corners of the room. Whatever else might be going on in Mimi's life, she was clearly an ace housekeeper.

They walked down towards the office together in

a slightly awkward silence. Mimi seemed to be back in work mode, all formality and deference, while Josie was worried about what it was that Koji had to tell her. She felt she'd had enough of being told things by her colleagues but couldn't think of a way to stem the tide of revelations that seemed to be coming her way. Except for Mimi, of course, whose secrets remained hidden.

When they reached the AZT building Mimi went in while Josie carried on down the street towards the Ohatsu shrine. She was early for her meeting with Koji but was happy to sit and wait for him in the peace and quiet of the shrine and get her thoughts in order for the day ahead. So she was disappointed to see that she didn't have the place all to herself. There was a couple there ahead of her, reading through the prayer plaques that hung from the wooden board. They weren't the kind of sweet young couple she had imagined would come to the shrine; they were middle aged, the man in a salaryman's black suit, obviously stopping off on his way to work, his wife (Josie could tell from the way they talked to each other that they'd been married a while) in an old-fashioned trying-to-be-smart dress with too much powder on her careworn face.

Josie stood in the shadow of the trees watching them for a few moments. They seemed to be having an earnest discussion about the wishes written on the prayer plaques, perhaps searching for ideas that would be suitable for them. Josie wondered what they were going to wish for. Were they having problems, arguing all the time and getting angry? Or maybe they never saw each other as he worked long hours to help his company out of the recession and she stayed at home, bringing up the children and making him a bento lunch to take to work. Maybe they never talked and felt like strangers.

The husband pointed to a prayer plaque and his wife peered at it carefully, then smiled and nodded. They headed towards to the kiosk to buy a plaque. Josie wondered what they had found that suited them so well. They seemed happy now, united as they wrote their plaque. Not like her and Dave, breaking up, getting back together and still unable to decide whether they wanted to spend their lives together. Or even what country they wanted to live in.

Josie watched the couple hang their plaque on the board. She should bring Dave here, she thought. It was no good praying for your relationship on your own – you had to do it together.

She was so busy watching the couple she didn't notice Koji walking towards her, and jumped when he spoke.

'You're very tense,' he said. 'Didn't you hear me call to you?'

'No, sorry, I was off in a dream,' said Josie.

The couple she'd been watching walked slowly back to the arcade leading to Umeda and the bustle of real life. Josie turned to Koji.

'Let's go to Doutor,' she said. 'I haven't had any breakfast yet and I'm absolutely ravenous.'

They walked along the little shopping arcade,

where Josie was disappointed not to catch another glimpse of the couple from the shrine, to the main road where there was a tiny branch of the huge coffee chain Doutor, tucked in between a mobile phone shop and a Family Mart convenience store. Koji settled for a cup of Doutor's fiercely strong black coffee while Josie ordered the ham and egg salad morning set with toast and a cappuccino. They found a couple of round red plastic stools at the counter by the window, the only places left. All around them workers on their way to the office drank coffee, munched ham rolls, smoked and stared at their mobile phones as if the answers to all the problems of the universe were there. The atmosphere was already thick with smoke and noisy with the clatter of trays and the shouts of the servers telling customers their orders were ready. Josie felt the smoke catch at the back of her throat. In theory the café had a non-smoking section, but the place was so small it was a meaningless distinction.

One day I'll wake up and find that Japan has gone non-smoking overnight, Josie thought. It can't come soon enough.

Koji drank his coffee quickly and lit a cigarette, adding his plume of smoke to the general fug, then moved his stool closer to Josie's so he could whisper confidentially in her ear.

'I've found something out,' he said. 'About Mr Shiga.'

Oh no, thought Josie, not Mr Shiga again. Out loud she said, 'Tell me.'

'Well, you know the day Saburo died? Mr Shiga was at a meeting in Nagoya.'

Josie nodded, her mouth full of egg.

'He left the office about two o'clock and didn't come back. He said the meeting was going to run late.'

Josie nodded again, taking a big slurp of her cappuccino. It was too hot and she swallowed it with an effort, afraid of burning her throat.

'Except it didn't run late. It finished early. It was over by six o'clock.'

Koji sat back in his chair triumphantly and stared at Josie, waiting for her response. Her mind still on her too-hot coffee, Josie struggled to see the point.

'It was over by six o'clock?' she said. 'What does that prove?'

'It proves that he could have been at Nagoya station by six thirty easily. And guess what time Saburo's train stopped at Nagoya?'

'I don't know.'

'Six thirty four. Look I've got the timetable here.'

Koji pulled out his laptop and balanced it on the counter.

'See,' he said. 'Here's Saburo's train, the Hikari 478. It left New Osaka at five forty, stopped at Kyoto at five fifty six and then Nagoya at six thirty four.'

Josie wondered briefly how Koji knew what train Saburo had been on, but then realised he must have worked it out the same way she had, based on when Saburo had left the office. But she still struggled to follow Koji's point. It was too early in the morning for her brain to work the way it should.

'So what are you saying? That Mr Shiga could have got Saburo's train? I suppose he might have, if he was going home for the weekend too.'

Koji looked exasperated.

'Isn't it obvious? If Mr Shiga got that train, he could have been the one that killed Saburo.'

Josie felt the light dawning but, having suspected Mr Shiga herself before and turned out to have got it wrong, she was reluctant to put him back in the frame again without a good reason.

'On that basis, it could equally well be Mr Ozawa. He was at the same meeting so he could have got Saburo's train too,' she said, taking a cautious sip of her coffee and finding it was now cool enough to drink.

'No, you don't understand. I've got another reason for thinking it could be Mr Shiga.'

Koji paused and looked around the café. It was beginning to thin out as people headed off to work so there was nobody within earshot. He stubbed out his cigarette, leaned over and almost whispered in Josie's ear, 'Have you heard anyone say anything about data having gone missing?'

Josie froze. She wasn't supposed to know anything about that. Koji took her response as a sign of surprise.

'Not many people know about it,' he said. 'But someone's been selling our confidential data and Saburo and I had thought for a long time that it was Mr Shiga.'

'Saburo and you?' said Josie. 'You talked about this?'

'Yes. Both of us had spotted some suspicious activity and we were on the trail of the person who was doing it when Saburo was killed.'

'Did you tell the police about this?'

'They didn't ask me. Anyway, it's private company business. It wouldn't do for it to get out.'

'I think you should tell them, you know. Obviously it's going to be relevant to the investigation.'

'The point is,' said Koji. 'Saburo was very close to identifying who it was. He told me so. I think he must have cracked it just before he died. And I think it was Mr Shiga.'

'And on the basis of that and the fact that Mr Shiga's meeting ended early you think he's the one who killed Saburo?' said Josie, finding herself still oddly reluctant to suspect Mr Shiga all over again.

'Don't you?'

'I don't know. I've thought so many different things over the last few days I've lost track. Anyway, how would Mr Shiga know what train Saburo was getting?'

'Maybe he asked him before he went to Nagoya. Maybe Saburo told him he was about to find out who was stealing the data and Mr Shiga wanted to stop him. Maybe he lied about the meeting finishing late to put Saburo off his guard.'

'Surely the police must have checked up on all this? People's alibis and so on?'

'If they have, it doesn't seem to have got them anywhere. There's no sign of an arrest. Maybe we know more than they do. Don't you think it would be good if we could solve it before the police do? Harry Potter and Hermione would.'

'That's Taro's line,' said Josie. 'Come on, it's time to go to work.'

*

By the time they got to the office everyone else had already arrived and got down to work, but the room hummed with a tension that didn't come from the routine tasks they were all engaged in. Something was going on.

Josie sat down at her computer. The first email she saw was headed *Further visit by the police*. She read it slowly.

As you are aware, it said, *the police investigation into the unfortunate death of our colleague, Saburo Horii, is continuing. The police are committed to identifying the killer and bringing them to justice. In pursuit of that aim, they wish to further interview the following people. They will be visiting the office this morning and interviews will take place in Meeting Room Seven in the order listed below.*

Below was a short list of names, beginning with Mr Ozawa and Mr Shiga. None of the older workers were included, but Mack, Koji, Taro and Mimi were all listed. As was Josie herself. She felt an odd little frisson of fear. Of course she had nothing to do with

Saburo's death and she was happy to help the police in any way she could, but it felt odd to be on a list of people who were presumably under suspicion. Or something. The police hadn't said why they wanted to interview this group again. Josie tried to think what the connection was. All she could think of was that, apart from her, they were all friends or close colleagues of Saburo. Mr Ozawa and Mr Shiga were directly above him in the hierarchy; Koji belonged to the same cohort, a relationship closer than friendship; Mack and Taro were from the cohort below so could reasonably be assumed to be recipients of his help and advice. While Mimi – Mimi had been his girlfriend. It hadn't exactly been common knowledge, but it was well enough known for the police to have picked up on it and to take an interest in her as a result. I wonder what the Japanese for *cherchez la femme* is, Josie thought, with a mental nervous giggle. And not just the woman in the case, but the men around her who might have reason to feel jealous of Saburo, like Mack, her present boyfriend or Taro her frustrated suitor. Or Koji, Josie suddenly realised, as she remembered Koji's talk of the girlfriend he had lost. What if Koji came before Saburo? Even Mr Ozawa and Mr Shiga might have taken more of an interest in her than was suitable to their positions.

I wonder who has an alibi and who doesn't, Josie thought, remembering her conversation with Koji that morning. It all depends on the trains. Anyone who couldn't possibly have got the train Saburo was on is in the clear, and anyone who could have got it, either in Osaka or somewhere else, must be under suspicion.

She glanced around the room. Everyone was busy, and the Tokyo team had clearly decided to concentrate their efforts where they could do most good and leave her out of things. She called up the timetable for the bullet trains that ran on the Tokaido line between Osaka and Tokyo and studied it carefully.

Saburo had caught the Hikari 478, leaving New Osaka station at 17:40 and due to get into Shizuoka at 19:37. But he hadn't got off at Shizuoka, he'd stayed on until his train reached Tokyo at 20:40. Why had he done that? Was he already dead, or had he changed his plans for some reason? It was unlikely that he'd been killed so early – in the hour between the train stopping at Shizuoka and reaching Tokyo the body must have been discovered, especially as the train stopped at Mishima, New Yokohama and Shinagawa before it got to Tokyo.

As Koji had pointed out, Saburo's train had stopped at Nagoya at 18:34, so anyone who got to Nagoya before then could have transferred to Saburo's train.

An awful thought struck her – she'd got a later train than Saburo but it had been a Nozomi with fewer stops and a faster journey. Could her train have caught up with Saburo's? Was that why the police wanted to interview her? She checked the timetable. The train she'd got, the Nozomi 250, was a fast train that only stopped at at Kyoto, Nagoya, New Yokohama, Shinagawa and Tokyo. It had got her into Tokyo at 20:43. Although it was a fast train and Saburo's train had been a slow one, her train had started so much later than his, leaving Osaka at 18:10, that it hadn't caught it up at any of the intermediate stations, and it hadn't got into Tokyo until three minutes after the Hikari 478 that Saburo was on. So Josie couldn't have made the transfer to Saburo's train anywhere on the journey. That was reassuring. But what about the others?

Taro had said he'd had to rush for his train after he saw Koji off. So he must have got the Hikari 530 which left Osaka at 17:16. It was the only train that stopped at Toyohashi and it would have got him there at 18:47. But the stop before Toyohashi was Nagoya, and the train stopped there at 18:27 – seven minutes before Saburo's train arrived. So Taro would have to go on the suspects list.

Koji had got the Hikari 475 at 17:05, but he'd been going in the opposite direction to Saburo – west to Okayama, not east to Tokyo. His train got into Okayama at 18:20 – far too late for him to have come back again and caught Saburo's train. Unless he got off somewhere on the way? Josie checked the timetable. The next station from Osaka going west was New Kobe. Koji's train had stopped there at 17:19. And Saburo's train had stopped there too, at 17:25, on its way to Osaka. So Koji could have made the transfer too.

Mack and Mimi were easier to understand. They

were both based in Osaka so shouldn't have been getting any trains at all. But suppose one of them did? Boarded Saburo's train at Osaka perhaps, or got an earlier train to Nagoya and changed trains there? It was perfectly doable.

Josie looked at the long columns of stations and times on her screen, each one representing a bullet train, sixteen carriages long, each carriage seating a hundred people. All of them full to bursting at that time of day. All those people travelling at more than two hundred miles an hour, rushing home from work, looking forward to the weekend. Except that one of them had never got there. And one of them had ended up a murderer.

A frisson of excitement running around the room made her look up. Two policemen in full uniform had just gone into Mr Ozawa's room. The interviews had begun.

Though Josie tried to concentrate on clearing out her emails - there seemed to be an awful lot that she should have deleted weeks ago - she couldn't help her attention slipping and her eyes drifting towards the door of Mr Ozawa's office. Were the police asking him about that meeting in Nagoya that had ended earlier than planned? Presumably he'd come back to Osaka when it ended, but could he prove it? Did he know what Mr Shiga had done? Josie wished she could be a fly on the wall – it would be so much easier if she could get the answers to her questions instead of just speculating about them.

She jumped as Mr Ozawa's door opened and the

police came out. Josie watched as Mimi led them down the corridor to Meeting Room Seven, wondering if the other interviewees were feeling as nervous as she was. Especially Mimi. Since she'd spent the night at Mimi's flat she'd developed a fellow feeling for her that she'd never felt when they were simply work colleagues. She was pretty sure Mimi wasn't telling her the truth about Saburo and Mack and what happened on the afternoon Saburo died, but all the same she felt sympathetic towards her. Maybe it was just a feeling that, as the only two women in the office, they should stick together, but Josie found herself worrying more about Mimi's interview than her own. Mimi had seemed frightened before her last police interview. What did she have to be frightened about?

The interviews seemed to move quite quickly - they obviously weren't in-depth interrogations - and Josie's turn came quicker than she'd expected, just before lunch. Once again she went into the interview room, once again she was confronted by the same two policemen. They nodded at her in a slightly more friendly way than before.

'We're just checking some of the details of what you told us in your last interview,' said the one behind the desk, turning over a pile of papers in front of him until he reached the one he wanted. Josie craned her neck trying to read what it said. It seemed to be a list of some sort.

'In your last interview you said you left the office at half past five on the Friday that Mr Horii was

211

killed. Is that correct?'

'More or less,' said Josie. 'It was around half past five.'

'How close?'

'Not more than five minutes either way.'

The officer taking notes made a small amendment to his typed sheet.

'And Mr Horii was not in the office at that time.'

'That's right,' said Josie, wondering what they were getting at. If Saburo had got the five forty train from New Osaka he couldn't possibly have been in the office at five thirty.

'Please take a look at this list,' said the policeman, passing his sheet of paper across to Josie. 'It shows all the members of IT Support. Please identify any names of people who were not in the office when you left.'

Josie ran her eye down the list. 'Mr Ozawa, Mr Shiga, Mack, Koji and Taro weren't in the office,' she said.

'And the office lady?'

'I don't know,' said Josie. 'I didn't see her.'

Guiltily, Josie remembered her visit to the kitchen before she left, and its neatness, that suggested Mimi had already gone. But that was mere inference, nothing more, so she didn't feel honour bound to mention it.

'Did you go into the kitchen that day?'

'Yes, a couple of times.'

'Do you recall whether all the knives were in their proper places?'

'I didn't notice the knives,' said Josie.

'Did you see anyone else go into the kitchen that day?'

'I don't think so. But then, I wasn't here most of the time. I was out working on computers in other offices.'

The policeman glanced at his colleague who nodded.

'Thank you, Miss Clark,' he said. 'That's all we wanted to ask.'

Josie walked slowly back to her desk, trying to imagine what was going on in the collective police mind. They already knew who was in the office and who wasn't. Presumably they'd checked the train timetables as carefully as she had. The next thing was to go over the alibis, or lack of them, of the people who'd left the office early that day. They'd all had access to the knives in the kitchen but which of them had a motive to kill Saburo? That was what Josie still didn't know. At the moment it looked as though all of them did. Even Mimi.

SIXTEEN

The concourse between the bullet train platforms and the JR platforms at New Osaka station gleamed in the early afternoon sun, shiny and spotless. Josie dodged across it, through the uncaring hordes hurrying from one set of platforms to the other or queuing to exit through the long line of automatic barriers, and then stopped as the sight of them sparked off a new thought. She'd hardly ever used those exits, not since the first time she came to Osaka when she'd made the beginner's mistake of transferring to the underground to get from New Osaka to the Osaka main station. She'd soon learned that the fastest way was by the JR Kyoto line and she'd never used the underground again. Which was what made her pause now.

It was only three stops to Umeda on the underground, less if you got off at Nakatsu which was just a short walk from the AZT office. And if you wanted to go the other way, from the office to New Osaka station, without anyone seeing you, getting the underground from Nakatsu would be a very effective way to do it. A short walk through the back streets, keeping away from the route most people took towards Osaka station and then the anonymity of the underground in the rush hour. Perfect camouflage. Mack could have done that, that Friday afternoon. Or Mimi, with a hat pulled down to cover her all-too-recognisable ears. Either of them could have blended into the rush hour crowds and caught Saburo's train.

Stop it, Josie told herself as a wave of people emerging from the bullet train platforms swept past her and forced her to the edge of the concourse. Leave it alone just for one day. Concentrate on Dave and having a good time. Saburo can wait.

She waited for the wave to die down and then headed for the bullet train ticket barrier and took up a position from which she could see the bottom of the escalators leading down from the platforms. A new train had just come in and a new crowd spilled off the escalators and through the barriers, making Josie feel grateful she'd found herself a place of relative safety. It didn't take her long to spot Dave, towering head and shoulders over the rest, walking at a measured pace like Gulliver taking care not to crush any Lilliputians as he stepped among them.

'Here,' she shouted. 'Dave, I'm here!' But he couldn't hear her over the hum of the crowd, the clatter of their feet and the echoing announcements. She jumped up and down, waving, causing people around her to edge away from the crazy foreigner,

215

which luckily had the effect of making her more visible. Dave spotted her, nodded, and made his way towards the corner where she stood. At the barrier he stopped.

'How do I get out of here?' he said, looking at the complicated instructions on the barrier in bafflement.

'Put both your tickets in the slot at once,' said Josie. 'The ordinary ticket and the bullet train ticket together.'

Dave did as he was told and the barrier thudded open. He walked through and enveloped Josie in a big bear hug.

'Not here,' she said. 'Everyone can see.'

'Of course they can. What's wrong with that? You're getting far too Japanese about things.'

'Where's Cherie?' said Josie.

'She got stuck behind a big group of schoolkids. She'll be along in a minute. Kyoto was amazing, you should have come with us.'

I should have gone with them, thought Josie. Why didn't I? Just because Cherie makes me feel jealous. It's silly.

Just then Cherie joined them. She was wearing Comme des Garçons jeans and a sweatshirt with a sequinned picture of Pokemon on the front. She looked effortlessly slim and chic. Josie tried not to resent her and succeeded better than she'd hoped.

'Hey, Josie,' Cherie said. 'It's great to see you. We're starving. We didn't eat anything in Kyoto because the food in Osaka is so good we wanted to wait. I've been telling Dave about the crab at Kani

Doraku all the way from Kyoto.'

'I really am starving,' said Dave. 'We left Tokyo at six o'clock and we've been walking around Kyoto all morning. Take me to the crab before I faint.'

'Follow me,' said Josie. 'Dotonbori here we come.'

Josie didn't like to admit it, but she was as excited as the other two to be eating in Dotonbori at last. She'd heard so much about it, she'd have been gutted if she'd left Osaka without ever having been there. If Osaka was the kitchen of Japan, Dotonbori was its fiery oven, home to an unimaginable number of restaurants all vying to outdo each other with the quality of their cooking. Thousands of people went there every day to eat Osaka specialities cooked as only Dotonbori could cook. And, if you couldn't wait to get inside a restaurant to eat, you could fill up on tasty snacks from the street stalls that filled the air with fragrant smoke and irresistible aromas of fried octopus, boiled noodles and sweet golden biscuits shaped like fishes.

Dotonbori didn't disappoint them. The atmosphere was like a carnival, the streets packed with locals and tourists, the stallholders calling out their wares and finding no shortage of takers. The main Dotonbori street ran alongside the canal, so you could look down at the reflections of the gaudy neon lights or stand on the bridges to gaze down at the water and take the perfect souvenir photo. Even Josie, who didn't usually remember to get her phone out for a photo until it was too late, managed to get some shots, and Cherie took endless photos of Dave and Josie together, promising to email them as soon as she got back to Tokyo.

'Look,' said Josie, pointing to the neon signs, 'There's Dotonbori Taro playing his drum. I must get a picture of that. And the Glico Running Man too.'

'Focus,' said Dave. 'Crab, remember?'

'There's Kani Doraku,' said Cherie. 'Can you see the giant crab?'

'Wow,' said Dave. 'It must be six metres across. And the legs are moving.'

'So are the eyestalks,' said Josie. 'Which is a bit creepy. Come on, let's get inside where we can't see it.'

'I don't like the look of the queue,' said Dave. 'I don't want other people getting between me and my crab.'

'It's moving pretty fast,' said Josie. 'We should get in soon. And we can get some *takoyaki*, you know, those octopus dough balls you like, to eat while we wait.'

They stopped at the *takoyaki* stall, where a cheery girl constantly turned little balls of dough in iron moulds, their colour ranging from pale cream for the freshly poured moulds through to golden brown for the ones that were ready to eat. The hot balls with their hidden centre of chewy octopus kept them quiet until they found themselves at the head of the queue and were ushered up to the first floor and into a pale wooden booth.

'Are we having the crab medley?' said Cherie.

'Whatever you recommend,' said Dave and Josie nodded agreement. 'And don't forget the beer.'

The waiter came and Chiharu gave their order rapidly in Japanese. They were soon supplied with several large brown bottles of Kirin beer, rapidly followed by lots of colourful little dishes of artistically arranged crab legs, some of them cooked as tempura, others de-shelled and rolled into sushi. They tasted as fresh as though they had been pulled from the sea the second before.

For a while the only sound was the snap of crab legs and the glug of beer being poured as they gave their full attention to the feast, but eventually, having turned the prettily arranged dishes into the remains of battlefield with crab shells littered across them, they sat back and wiped their hands on the hot towels the waiter brought. As he cleared the plates and replaced them with little dishes of ice cream, Josie decided it was a good moment to take the plunge and tell Dave about what had happened to the Osaka office.

'So, I've got some news,' she said, rushing into it before her courage deserted her. 'It turns out I won't be staying in Osaka after all. The office is being redeveloped so they're closing it down.'

'Closing it down?' said Dave. 'What do you mean? How can they be closing it down?'

Josie tried to look unconcerned, as though offices closed down all the time. She reached for the beer bottle and poured the last of the beer into their glasses.

'They've been wanting to redevelop for ages,' she

said, trying to sound casual. 'But they couldn't because of some problem about getting the freehold. But now that's settled so they've decided to get on with it.'

'So how much longer will you be working here?'

This was the hard bit.

'Just until the end of the week,' she said. 'IT Support is being shut down first, then they'll move on to the rest.'

She clearly hadn't managed to make it sound as routine as she'd hoped, as both Dave and Cherie stopped with their spoons halfway to their mouths and stared at her.

'That's very fast, even for Japan,' said Cherie. 'Still, it's not unknown for things to move quickly once a problem's unblocked. If they've been ready to go for a while and just needed the final decision, then I suppose it makes sense.'

Josie felt a wave of gratitude. Maybe Cherie wasn't so bad after all.

'Yes, that's it,' she said. 'So you see, it's quite normal.'

She risked a glance at Dave. He didn't look convinced. In fact, he looked as though a suspicion was dawning.

'Hang on a minute, Josie,' he said. 'You're not telling us everything here. There's got to be more behind it than just negotiations over the freehold. This is about that guy that got killed, isn't it?'

'Of course not. Nobody said anything about him.'

'They don't have to – it's obvious. And that

means the murder has something to do with your office.'

'Oh, do you think so?' said Josie.

'Don't play the innocent with me. I know you can't stay away from the slightest sniff of murder. I bet you've been finding out all about it, getting yourself involved and putting yourself in danger.'

Dave glared at her, and Josie shrank back in her seat.

'Of course not. Well, I have found out one or two things, but I'm not in any danger. It's a police investigation, it's nothing to do with me.'

'And are the police anywhere near catching the killer?'

'I don't know. They don't tell us, just turn up and ask more questions when they feel like it.'

'So the police have been around to the office asking more questions,' said Dave. 'I rest my case.'

Cherie, looking uncomfortable, signalled to the waiter to bring them tea. They all waited as he poured it into little stone cups. Josie sipped hers, and said quietly, 'I thought you'd be pleased. I thought you wanted me back in Tokyo.'

'Of course I do,' said Dave. 'But I worry about you – about what you're getting yourself into.'

'I'm not getting myself into anything,' said Josie. 'And if I do, I'll tell you.'

'I suppose that's the best I can hope for,' said Dave. 'And at least this makes it easier to tell you my news.'

Josie kicked herself. Of course, he had something

to tell her and she'd jumped in and got her revelation in first. She should have waited – it would all have gone much better then.

'Yes, please tell me,' said Josie, putting all the enthusiasm she could into her voice. 'I've been wondering about it ever since we spoke on the phone.'

Now it was Dave's turn to look awkward.

'I've been a bit nervous about telling you this,' he said. 'But your news makes it much simpler.'

'How does it make it simpler?' said Josie. 'What's going on?'

'Just this.' Dave paused and took a deep breath. 'My company's having a major structural rethink.'

'You haven't lost your job!' Josie exclaimed, her mind running wildly over how they would pay the rent on their pricey flat in Tokyo if Dave wasn't earning.

'No, I haven't lost my job. I'm shocked you have so little faith in me. In fact, I've been offered a promotion, one that I've always wanted. I'd be in charge of my own projects, I'd make way more money and I'd have a chance to influence the decisions that are made about where the company goes next and the kind of projects it takes on in future.'

'It sounds brilliant,' said Josie. 'Well done.' She reached across and gave him an awkward hug, rather impeded by the table between them.

'Thanks. But it's not all jammy. They want me to do some things in return.'

'Oh,' said Josie. 'What things?'

'Well, they want me to move into the new job pretty quickly. And since I'll be more senior they want me to have a place where I can entertain. They're willing to lend me quite a lot to buy somewhere.'

Josie felt her heart grow cold. She could see where this was going.

'This place. Where would it be?'

'In London, of course. That's where my company's based. And anyway, part of the restructuring involves pulling out of markets where we're less successful. Japan for instance.'

'So what happens to the year we were going to have together in Japan?'

'I'm sorry Josie, truly I am. But I can't stay on. My job is being wound up and I've been offered a great chance back home. I'd be a fool to turn it down.'

'Yes, of course, I see that,' said Josie. 'Well, we've managed in different countries before, I suppose we can do it again.'

'I knew you'd say that. That was why I'd been putting off telling you. But now you're leaving Osaka it's a perfect time for us to go back to London together. It couldn't have worked out better.'

'Now just a moment,' said Josie. 'That wasn't our deal. A year in Japan first is what we said.'

'Don't you love me, Josie?'

'Of course I do but—'

'Then come with me.'

223

Josie was silent and Dave went on, 'You know we've been here before. Last time we hit the crunch point it was about you going to Japan, and it broke us apart. You got what you wanted and I tried to make my life work without you, but I couldn't. This time I want it to end differently. You know we're no good apart. We need to be together, and that means that for once in my life I'm going to ask you to do something for me. Come back to England, to London. You know it's your real home. We could be very happy there. If we don't take this chance, there won't be another one.'

Still Josie couldn't reply. She thought back over their relationship, over all the times she had wanted something and Dave had compromised, given up what he wanted, made sacrifices so she could have her way. This time, she knew, he wasn't going to do that. It was an ultimatum, but also an offer that no girl in her right mind would refuse. A new life, prosperity, being with the one she loved. What could be more important than that? Japan, she thought miserably. Last time she'd had to choose between Dave and Japan she'd chosen Japan.

In the silence Cherie shifted in her seat and coughed tactfully. Both Dave and Josie had forgotten she was there and Josie was suddenly uncomfortably aware that they'd inadvertently exposed the central flaw in their relationship to a comparative stranger.

'Can I say something?' said Cherie.

'Why not?' said Josie. 'I don't think either Dave or I have anything more to say.'

'I don't want to interfere,' said Cherie. 'I know this is something for the two of you to work out. But I just want to say something that might help you make up your mind. You see, I understand more than you think about your problem. I've had to make the same decision myself.'

'You?' said Josie.

'You're not the only one who's left her home and her family, gone to live in a strange country and found themselves feeling surprisingly at home. It was the same for me when I went to the States. Suddenly I was free of all the restrictions and formality of Japanese life, free to do and say what I wanted, become who I wanted, without any limits being placed on me because I was a girl. I loved it. I felt like I wanted to stay forever. Especially when I met someone who became very important to me.'

'I didn't know...' Josie began.

'Of course you didn't. I haven't said anything to you about it, though Dave knows. He's been great helping me get over it.'

'But why didn't you stay in the States with this guy, er...'

'Paul. His name's Paul.'

Why didn't you stay there with him if it's what you really want?'

Cherie smiled sadly.

'You're very fond of my parents, aren't you?' she said.

'Of course I am. They've been so good to me and they're such lovely people.'

'Yes, and I'm their daughter, their only child. I'm all they've got to take care of them when they get old. That's my duty. I'm a good Japanese daughter and I know I have to put them first. I can't afford to go off and live in another country and have a life that doesn't include them. I have to stay here.'

'Can't this Paul come to Japan?'

'He doesn't speak the language. He can't get any work here. And he has a family in the States that he doesn't want to leave.'

'That's tough,' said Josie. She could see that Cherie's eyes were beginning to fill with tears.

'Yes, it's tough. But I know it's the right thing for me to do. You're luckier than I am. You're being offered the chance to go back to your own country, to see your family and take care of them and still have the man you love. Why are you hesitating?'

Because it's not what I want, Josie wanted to say, but she couldn't bring herself to hurt Dave so badly. And she wasn't sure that, if it actually came to it, she could bear to see Dave go back to the UK and leave her behind. She'd made that decision once before and hadn't been able to stick to it. What made her think it would be any different this time?

She looked at Dave. He was staring down into his tea, avoiding her eyes.

With an effort she tried to lighten the mood.

'Let's not talk about this now,' she said. 'You're here to see Osaka, so that's what we're going to do. Next stop, the Umeda Sky Building. It's two skyscrapers joined together with an observation platform so they look like a giant nutcracker, and escalators with transparent walls at the top. I'm sure you'll love it.'

She looked anxiously at Dave. After a moment he looked up at her and smiled.

'Okay,' he said. 'I won't push you for an answer now. Take some time to think about it. But you're going to have to make your mind up soon. And, whatever you decide, it's final.'

Cherie stood up and picked up the bill.

'I'd love to see the Sky Building,' she said. 'I haven't been to Osaka since it was built. It will be the perfect contrast to all that history in Kyoto.'

Dave nodded. 'We've come to Osaka to see the sights, so let's see them,' he said, taking the bill out of Cherie's hand. 'After all, it may be our last chance.'

Josie stood up too and followed them to the till. Cherie was right – the only thing was to forget all about their conversation and have fun while they could. Because, one way or another, she and Dave wouldn't be going sightseeing in Osaka together again soon.

Then her phone rang.

'If that's someone from your office, don't answer it,' said Dave.

'It's Mimi,' said Josie. 'But it's not from the office. It's her private phone.'

Josie hesitated, wondering what to do. The phone stopped ringing and then started again.

'I can't just ignore it,' said Josie. 'She may be in

trouble.'

Dave shrugged and turned away as Josie hit the answer button.

'Josie?' said Mimi's voice at the other end. 'Josie, I need your help. Something awful has happened. I don't know what to do or who to talk to. Please say you'll help me.'

'Where are you?' said Josie.

'I'm at my flat.'

'Stay there. I'll be with you in half an hour.'

SEVENTEEN

'What did she say?' said Dave.

'She's in trouble. She needs help. I have to go,' said Josie. 'I'm really sorry. You two go to the Sky Building. I'll try and join you later.'

'We'll go with you,' said Cherie. 'Maybe we can help.'

'No, I don't think that's a good idea. I think it would just frighten her if we all turned up. Let me go on my own.'

'Okay,' said Dave. 'You know your friend better than we do. But if you need reinforcements, you know where we'll be.'

'Thanks,' said Josie, grateful for the instant understanding that Dave always seemed to supply. 'I hope it won't come to that. I'll get in touch as soon as I can.'

It seemed strange to walk out of the restaurant and find Dotonbori was just the same, full of cheery crowds and enticing smells. Somehow Josie felt that everything should have changed, just as the mood of her little party had. It wasn't just the discussion with Dave and his news that had made the difference. It was Mimi's call. Something was seriously wrong, Josie could tell. Something had happened, something bad. She'd never known anything to upset Mimi before, but her voice on the phone had been full of fear.

Josie looked up at Dave, who put his arm around her and drew her close while Cherie tactfully walked on ahead.

'Don't worry,' said Dave. 'It'll all work out. It always does. You've got a knack of solving problems and you'll solve this one too.'

'I'm sorry I haven't told you much about what's been going on,' said Josie. 'It all seems to have got out of hand the past couple of days. Ever since they said they were closing down the office, people have been telling me things but none of them add up to anything that makes sense. I think Mimi could be the key to it. That's why I'm so worried about her. There's a murderer still out there and I'm sure they're watching Mimi and seeing what she does. So far she's held her nerve but I think she's starting to lose it. And if she does there's no telling what might happen.'

They reached Namba station and took the Midosuji line to Umeda. It was late in the afternoon and the rush hour was beginning to build; Cherie and Josie managed to get seats but Dave had to strap hang. Josie stared unseeingly at the adverts for English language schools and new flats in developments somewhere far from the centre of the city, while the station announcements echoed through her head. Shinsaibashi, Hommachi, Yodobashi passed by, people alighted and more people got on until the train was jam-packed.

At Umeda they said their goodbyes, Dave and Cherie heading off towards the Sky Building while Josie walked the familiar route to the office, feeling conspicuous as she fought her way through the crowds of people heading towards the station. She was afraid of running into someone from the office and being asked what she was doing, so she ducked down a side street and continued on past the café where she'd seen Mack and Mimi talking. Its drab window looked just the same and Josie found it hard to believe it was only the previous day that she'd seen it for the first time; it felt like she'd known it for years.

She reached the little back street where Mimi lived and climbed the stairs to her flat. The blind was drawn and it looked like nobody was home, but when Josie tapped softly on the door and called, 'Mimi, it's Josie,' the door opened a crack and then widened until there was just enough space for Josie to slip through.

It was dark inside as the drawn blinds shut out the afternoon sun. Josie followed Mimi into the living room, stumbling as her eyes adjusted to the lack of light. Mimi sat on the sofa, motioning Josie to sit beside her. Then she reached across and raised the blind.

Josie recoiled in shock. There was a gash across Mimi's forehead and stains on the front of her jumper where blood from the wound had dripped.

'My God, Mimi, what's happened? Did you have an accident?'

'Not exactly,' said Mimi. Her eyes were unfocused and Josie could see that she was in shock.

'Did someone do this to you?'

Mimi nodded. Tears began to spill from her eyes and she wiped them away with the edge of her sleeve.

'Oh, Josie, it was awful. I was so frightened.'

'What happened? Who was it? Tell me everything. No, wait, I'll get you some tea first. You look like you could do with it.'

Mimi nodded and Josie went to the kitchen where the ever-warm pot sat on the counter, waiting to dispense tea as though everything was normal. She poured a cup and took it back to Mimi.

'There, drink this slowly and then, when you're ready, tell me what happened. There's no rush. Just take it easy.'

Mimi nodded and gulped at her tea gratefully. Josie went back into the kitchen, found some ice in the fridge and wrapped it in a tea towel.

'Here,' she said. 'Put this on your head, it will make you feel better. I don't think the cut is actually too bad but you're getting quite a lump. Maybe you should see a doctor.'

'No, no doctors,' said Mimi. 'I don't want anyone to know. It's not as bad as it looks. The bump will go down soon and there'll be nothing to see by tomorrow. I can pretend it never happened.'

'You're not planning on going into work tomorrow are you?'

'Of course I am. Otherwise people will know something's wrong. And then the police—' She stopped and shuddered.

'Why are you so afraid of the police? You looked terrified that day they interviewed you.'

Mimi didn't answer, but tears welled up in her eyes again.

'Okay, sorry I asked,' said Josie. 'Just tell me what happened this afternoon, alright?'

Mimi nodded and took another gulp of her tea.

'I came home from work early,' she said. 'Nobody works late any more. It's all finished. There's nothing to do. We're all just waiting for Friday. I was getting myself something to eat when the phone rang. It was Mack. He said he was just leaving work and he needed to talk to me, so I agreed he could come round here.'

Mack, thought Josie. Of course it was him. I've had my suspicions about Mimi and his so-called relationship.

'He wanted to talk to me about the police interviews. I expect you know, they were checking up on everyone's alibis.'

Josie nodded.

'They did that with me too,' she said. 'Luckily it was pretty clear I couldn't have got Saburo's train.'

'I told them what I told them before,' said Mimi.

'That Mack and I had spent the whole evening together here in my flat so neither of us could have got Saburo's train. I'm not sure whether they believed me or not.'

'Why shouldn't they believe you?'

'Because it wasn't true.'

Tears spilled from her eyes again and Josie went and got a box of tissues from the desk and handed it to her. Mimi blew her nose and took another gulp of tea.

'I'd better start at the beginning,' she said. 'I need to explain about me and Mack.'

'I think you need to start further back than that,' said Josie. 'Before you explain about Mack, tell me about you and Saburo. And you and Koji come to that.'

Mimi looked startled.

'Koji? What do you know about Koji?'

'Nothing really. I just knew there'd been a girl in his life and I took a guess it was you. Looks like I struck lucky.'

Mimi stared at her hands twisting in her lap and took a deep breath.

'Koji,' she said, 'was my first boyfriend. From before I came to AZT. He was the one who told me about the job. I thought he was fun to be with and he took me out to interesting places, but he was never anything special. More of a friend really. It was different when I met Saburo. With him it was serious from the word go.'

'When did you meet him?'

'When I started work at AZT. He used to help me out, teach me about how things worked. Koji used to go out drinking a lot after work – he likes his whisky, you know.'

'I do know,' said Josie, thinking of the bottle of whisky with Koji's name on it at the Mama bar.

'Well, that wasn't much fun for me. Saburo was different. He took me to the cinema and out to nice places for dinner. He was kind and considerate and we just hit it off together. I even went to Shizuoka with him once, though we kept away from his parent's house. He showed me around, we had such a good time.'

Josie nodded and waited for Mimi to go on.

'And then it all went sour,' said Mimi. 'Koji started to take little digs at me, insinuating things without actually saying them. And Taro started acting funny and even Mr Shiga treated me differently. I told Saburo I thought we should tell people we were in a relationship. That way there wouldn't be any misunderstandings.'

'You mean, people didn't know?'

'Not generally. Taro found out of course and told Koji and Mack but that was about it.'

'And what did Saburo say?'

'He said we had to keep it secret. He was in line for a promotion and he thought having a girlfriend at work would count against him. And he said he was doing some special work that was going to pay off in a big way, but he couldn't tell me about it because it was too sensitive.'

Mimi pulled some more tissues from the box, and balled them up in her hand.

'We had a big row about it. Here, in my flat. He was furious, and then he walked out. It was awful.'

'When did this happen?'

'A few weeks before he died.'

'And then what did you do?'

'Nothing. I just went on going into work and trying to avoid him as much as possible.'

'Do you think anyone else noticed?'

'Mack did. That's when he started being friendly. And I thought, why not? He's rich and he said he'd look after me. And then this happened.'

She paused, and in the silence they both heard a noise from outside. A kind of shuffling noise, as though someone in an uncomfortable position was trying to ease the strain.

'There's someone there,' said Mimi, panic in her voice.

Josie said nothing but leapt up and was out the door in a moment, almost falling over Taro who was crouched on the outside landing, trying to fold himself up as small as possible under the window.

'Taro,' said Josie. 'What are you doing here?'

'I came for Mimi,' he said. 'I often come here. I like to know she's alright.'

'Were you listening at the window?'

'No. I wouldn't do that. Couldn't hear anything anyway.'

'Well go away. And don't come back.'

Taro nodded, stood up, stretched his legs and

ambled down the stairs. Josie watched him until he was out of sight then went back into the flat.

'It was only Taro,' she said. 'He's gone now.'

'Taro tries to look after me,' said Mimi. 'But he has a funny way of doing it.'

'Do you think Taro knows about you and Mack?'

'Taro knows everything. He knew about me and Saburo so why not about me and Mack?'

'And you and Koji?'

'Maybe that too. I don't know.'

Poor Taro, Josie thought. Mimi and Saburo, Mimi and Koji, Mimi and Mack, but never Mimi and Taro.

Finding Taro outside seemed to have stopped Mimi crying, so Josie seized her chance.

'Tell me what happened here this afternoon,' she said. 'You and Mack had a row and he hit you. But why? What did it have to do with the police interviews?'

'I told the police that Mack and I had been together the whole evening, so he couldn't possibly have got Saburo's train. But I lied – he wasn't here.'

Josie took a minute to digest this information. Not only did Mack (and Mimi for that matter) not have an alibi for the time of the murder, they had actually lied to the police about it. That didn't look good.

'Why did you tell them that if it wasn't true?' she said, as gently as she could.

'Mack told me to. He said he'd gone out and bought a bottle of whisky, taken it back to his flat and got drunk that evening and he was sure the police would never believe him. He said that, since we were both on our own, it was simpler to say that we were together. That it would just make it easier for the police to catch the murderer because they wouldn't be distracted by us not having alibi's. It made sense at the time and I didn't want to get involved with the police so I said I would do it. That's why I was so nervous before the first police interview – because I knew I was going to tell them a lie. And then today, when they came back again and asked me more questions I was so frightened. Mack could see I was in a state. That was why he came round.'

'And then he threatened you?'

'Yes, he said if I said anything he'd tell them it was all my idea to lie to them. He said I'd go to jail. He shouted and he hit me, then he left. I don't know where he went.'

'I always thought there was something creepy about Mack. You're well free of him.'

'But what am I going to do now? Suppose he tells the police it was all my idea?'

'He won't do that. He thinks he's frightened you enough to make you stick to your story.'

'So you think I should just go on lying like he wants?'

'Hang on a minute. I didn't say that.'

'So what then?'

'Couldn't you go to the police and tell them everything?'

Mimi recoiled.

'I can't do that. I've lied to them. I've committed a crime.'

'But they'd go easy on you if you go to them voluntarily.'

'No, I can't. It would bring shame on my family.'

Josie recognised she was beaten. To do something that might bring shame on one's family was a complete impossibility in Japan. Even she, a mere foreigner, understood that.

There was a ting from Josie's phone. A plaintive text from Dave: *We've been up the Sky Tower and now we're having a coffee at Osaka station. We'll need to get the train back to Tokyo soon. Can you come and see us before we go or is it all too complicated?*

Josie looked at Mimi.

'I need to go to the station to see my boyfriend,' she said. 'And you could do with some fresh air. Walk along with me and we'll think as we go.'

'Okay,' said Mimi and Josie texted *On my way* to Dave.

It was just at that point in the evening when twilight turns to darkness. The air still held the warmth of the day, and the scent of the wisteria on Mimi's balcony was strong. Josie looked at Mimi's lovely face silhouetted against the softly waving tendrils of the wisteria and felt for the first time that her lucky ears were an asset that enhanced rather than detracted from her beauty. Without her ears Mimi would be pretty but ordinary; with them she was remarkable. No wonder all the young men in the office circled around her like bees around their queen. But would any of them murder for her? Or was there another reason for Saburo's death?

On an impulse she said, 'Have you ever heard anything about information being stolen from AZT? Commercially sensitive information?'

'Not really,' said Mimi. 'Just the odd whisper. But it would explain a lot about how people have been behaving recently.'

'You don't think that could have been what Saburo was working on?'

'Maybe.There were some odd things he said sometimes that would fit with that.'

'Saburo wasn't well off, was he?'

'No, none of them are, only Mack.'

'So he might have wanted money. Wanted it enough to steal for it?'

'No, of course not. Saburo would never do that.'

'But he might have found out that someone else had stolen it?'

'He might have. I don't know. He was very secretive about what he was working on.'

They were walking past the battered old café again. Mimi shrank back behind Josie though the chances that Mack was in the café were very low. Josie looked in as they went by. Sitting in the window, just behind the faded gold lettering, was Taro. He saw her and raised a hand in greeting. Josie didn't respond.

Mimi and Josie walked on, past the AZT office where the tall pines stood guard over the entrance. Josie suddenly felt violently protective of them. She wondered if there was any system in Japan for stopping trees from being cut down as you could in the UK, of forcing the developers to preserve them to stand guard over the next building. But she knew it was a forlorn hope. The next building would be a skyscraper that would dwarf the tall pines. They would not survive, and there was nothing she could do to save them.

But she could do something about Mimi, and, looking at the pines, she realised what it was.

'I've got it,' she said. 'I've got a plan. If it works, it won't just put you in the clear, it will bring Saburo's killer to justice as well. Just give me until Friday. I promise I'll sort it by then and you won't be involved.'

EIGHTEEN

Josie could feel her heart thudding. Don't be silly, she said herself. Nothing awful's going to happen. It's perfectly straightforward and all planned out. It's fine.

Somehow, telling herself this didn't seem to make much difference. Her heart went on thumping and a little voice inside her head said, stupid plan, what a stupid plan, whatever made you think it would work? If it all goes wrong, which it probably will, you could quite easily end up dead. You should have thought about the risks a bit more before shooting your mouth off. You only came up with this idea to look good in front of Mimi, but how do you think she's going to feel when it all goes wrong? There's still time to back out. Nobody would blame you.

Shut up, she said savagely to the inner voice, which stopped abruptly. She put a calm expression on her face and took a deep breath. Focus, she thought, then pushed open the door and walked into the IT office.

It was unrecognisable as the cluttered place she'd encountered just a few weeks before. The old bits of kit that had littered the floor were gone, the desks were clear and the computers switched off. Most of the desks had been pushed back against the walls but a half dozen had been assembled in the middle of the room and covered with a white cloth. In the centre of the tables were serried ranks of bottles; mainly sake but with some whisky and a substantial group of big brown beer bottles. This was going to be some party. Josie was glad to see that Mimi's trusty green tea dispenser had been moved out of the little kitchen onto the table, and a pile of cups waited next to it. At any other time Josie would have headed straight for the sake, but today she needed to keep a clear head.

Her colleagues were huddled in an awkward group near the window, making conversation in a stilted way as people do when a party hasn't quite got started. They seemed to be discussing the likely fate of the pine trees, as they were looking out and pointing towards the clump of trees where Josie'd had her conversation with Mr Shiga. Josie ran her eyes over the group. All her suspects were there – Mr Shiga, his head bent, his eyes fixed on the floor; Taro, looking longingly at the drinks table; Koji, looking twitchy and bored; and Mack with a sulky look on his face that Josie had come to realise was his habitual expression. Even Mimi, for once, was released from her kitchen. She stood on the edge of the group, an expression of polite interest on her face, and gave Josie a nervous smile as she approached. Josie smiled back but didn't go over to talk to her. Not today.

She looked around the group again. She felt as though she knew them well, as though she had worked with them for years. She had to remind herself that she had only met them a few weeks before, that her knowledge was superficial at best and, at the worst, could be dangerously mistaken. One of her colleagues was a murderer and she didn't know which. Well, today was the day she would find out. Assuming all went according to plan. And if it doesn't? said the little voice, surfacing gleefully inside her head. She pushed it back down below the surface of her consciousness and joined the group.

'Ah, Josie,' said Mr Shiga, stepping back to make room for her. 'We were just discussing what will happen to our pine trees. We've all got quite fond of them over the years.'

'I remember when they only reached the top of the ground floor windows,' said Mr Yamada. 'And look at them now.'

Everyone turned to look at the trees again, their faces serious. Except for Taro, who nodded and winked at Josie as though sharing a joke only the two of them understood. She frowned back at him. She could do without Taro's odd sense of humour right now.

'My uncle has a red pine in his garden,' said Mack. 'He's been pruning it for years. It's a lovely shape.'

'There's one in the grounds of our local temple,'

said Mr Yamada. 'And the temple buildings are made of red pine wood too.'

'Maybe our trees could be used for something like that when they're cut down,' said Mr Shiga. 'It would be nice to think of them serving a useful function when we're gone.'

Taro's eyes wandered away to the drinks table again.

'I think we're all here now, Mr Shiga,' said Mimi, who had also noticed Taro's impatience to start. 'Shall I let Mr Ozawa know the speeches can begin?'

Speeches, Josie thought. I should have known there'd be speeches.

'Yes, of course,' said Mr Shiga. 'Time for the speeches. Please tell Mr Ozawa we're ready for him to join us.'

'We need to get our drinks first,' said Taro. 'We can't drink the toasts if we haven't got any drinks.'

'Quite right,' said Mr Shiga. 'Taro, will you please open up the beer and pour us all a glass?'

Taro didn't need telling twice. He rushed over to the table and began sloshing beer into glasses with more enthusiasm than skill. Josie saw Mimi wince as beer foamed up in the glasses and over the sides to drip down onto the clean tablecloth.

Taro took no notice, handing out glasses of beer to everyone. Josie noticed Mr Shiga take out his handkerchief and wipe the beer from the outside of his glass and wished she could do the same as Taro thrust a dripping glass into her hand. She remembered her intention to stay on soft drinks and tried to refuse, but Taro wasn't listening. It's only beer, she thought, and I'll need something to drink the toasts. So long as I steer clear of the sake I'll be alright.

Mimi reappeared with Mr Ozawa and, to Josie's surprise, the Head of Branch. The sight of him immediately silenced the slight buzz of conversation. Everyone stood in respectful silence while he thanked them for all their efforts and recalled some of the supposedly amusing incidents that had occurred over the years. Everyone laughed politely at his feeble jokes and clapped enthusiastically when he finished. Then they all drank a toast to the company and the Head of Branch left, to a noticeable lightening of the atmosphere.

Taro rushed around refilling everyone's glasses and then Mr Ozawa gave a really quite funny speech about the personalities and interests of each one of his staff which showed that, contrary to Josie's private belief, he had been paying attention all along. At the end he lifted his arms high and called out 'Osaka AZT IT Support!' three times in a ringing voice. Each time the whole company shouted '*Banzai*!' and raised both hands high in the air. At the end they all drank down their beer and burst out laughing.

With perfect timing, Mimi and a whole team of office ladies emerged from the kitchen and covered the white tablecloth with steaming dishes. Josie was amazed. There were towering heaps of white and fried rice, steaming bowls of noodles, glistening piles of chicken on skewers and countless little dishes of vegetables and pickles. The air filled with an irresistible aroma of fried chicken, and Josie, who had skipped breakfast, felt her stomach leap in response. Then came the pièce de résistance – sixteen whole crabs, fat and pink, one for every member of the section. It was a feast the like of which Josie had never seen before and her respect for Mimi, who had organised the whole thing, rose to new heights.

There was an agonising delay as everyone found themselves chairs and arranged them around the tables, then the feasting began. Josie wished she could relax and enjoy it more, and that the butterflies in her stomach didn't mix uncomfortably with the crab, but she did her best and managed to eat a surprising amount. After all, she told herself, I'm going to need the energy later on.

Mimi didn't sit down to eat with the rest until all the food had been served and everyone issued with a set of chopsticks and a bowl, and even then not until Mr Yamada called out 'Where's our beautiful office lady? Why isn't she here celebrating with us?'

Then Mimi emerged bashfully from the kitchen to a round of applause and sat down across the table from Josie. Their eyes met and a flash of shared knowledge passed between them, then Mimi looked away. I wonder if she's as nervous as I am, Josie thought. More, probably, but she hides it well. And she's covered up that gash on her head very well too. You'd never guess it was there.

Thinking about Mimi's injury, Josie involuntarily

turned to look at Mack. He was sitting at the far end of the table dealing very efficiently with a crab claw and taking no notice when Mimi came round with plates of food. It was as if they didn't know each other. Josie wondered what Mack thought was going to happen about their supposed engagement now that he had attacked her violently. Did he think that she was just going to accept it as part of the price she had to pay for marriage to a rich man? It wouldn't be surprising. Men in Japan had treated women as chattels throughout history and not much had changed in the twenty-first century. Women still weren't able to stand up for their rights. Except Josie was pretty sure that Mimi was different. Whatever happened later that day when they carried out Josie's plan, Mack was going to be toast.

People had finished their crab and had begun swopping places to sit next to other people or reach for plates that hadn't come their way. Koji came and sat in the seat next to Josie, helping them both to a refill of sake as he did so.

'I thought you might be avoiding me,' he said. 'Why didn't you come and sit down our end with me and Taro and Mack? You're supposed to be our Hermione, aren't you?'

'Even Hermione needs some time on her own to work on her spells,' said Josie. 'And I'm not sure Taro is so keen on me being Hermione now.'

'Why, what have you done?'

'Nothing. Just caught him spying on Mimi.'

To Josie's surprise, Koji laughed.

'He's been spying on Mimi for months. She knows all about it and she doesn't care. I think she finds it flattering.'

'I'm not so sure about that. Nobody likes being spied on.'

Koji caught Josie's sharp tone and immediately became contrite.

'Of course not. I'm sorry. I wasn't thinking. But Taro's harmless, you know. And he really does love Mimi.'

'He's not the only one, is he? You used to go out with her, didn't you?'

'Who told you that?'

'She did.'

Koji's habitual smile vanished.

'Did she tell you how she dumped me for Saburo too?'

'Yes, she did as a matter of fact. Though she didn't put it like that.'

A flash of anger passed across Koji's face and was gone, replaced by a bland smile.

'I'm over it,' he said. 'I don't have time for girls anyway. I've got my career to think about.'

Josie tried to stay calm, or at least to look as though she was. This was her chance to start putting her plan into action.

'Yes, me too,' she said. 'And I'm going to give my career a real boost when I get to Tokyo.'

'Really? How?'

'You know someone here has been stealing commercially sensitive data. I've been working on replicating how they did it, and I've found the answer. As soon as I get into work on Monday I'm going to tell them everything I know. Once they know how it was done they'll be able to trace who did it. Somebody is going to be in big trouble.'

She didn't dare look Koji in the face as she said it. But he took the revelation calmly.

'Good for you,' he said. 'It's nice to see someone from our section getting on in the world. Think of me slaving away in Hiroshima teaching idiots to use a computer while you're scaling the corporate heights.'

'Thanks, I will,' said Josie.

'Another drink?'

'No thanks, I'm not staying long. I'm getting the seven thirty seven back to Tokyo.'

'That's a shame. I was thinking of going on to Mama's when the party winds down.'

'Count me out.'

Josie looked at Koji to see how was taking the information she had so carefully given him, but his expression was blank and he was staring at something over her shoulder. She turned to see Mr Shiga hovering awkwardly nearby as though he wanted to join them. Or perhaps hoping to overhear what they were saying, Josie thought. Well, he needn't have worried. She was going to make sure he got the message too.

'Oh, Mr Shiga,' she said. 'I was just telling Koji I'm going to have to leave soon. I'm booked on the seven thirty seven Nozomi to Tokyo.'

'That's a shame,' said Mr Shiga, as Koji, never

one to spend time in Mr Shiga's company if he could help it, moved off to rejoin Mack and Taro. 'But I expect you have plans for the weekend.'

Josie sighed theatrically.

'I'll be working all weekend. I've got some important research results to write up before Monday. I think the Tokyo office will be very interested in them. You see, I've worked out how the missing data was accessed.'

'Really?' said Mr Shiga. 'Does that mean you know who the culprit is?'

'Not yet,' said Josie. 'But once I get onto an AZT computer in Tokyo it shouldn't take long to trace it back.'

Did an expression of panic flit across Mr Shiga's face? Josie wondered. Or was it more one of relief?

'But we must tell Mr Ozawa straight away,' said Mr Shiga.

'I thought of that,' said Josie, 'But with the situation here I think it's better to let Tokyo handle it.'

'Yes, I see what you mean,' said Mr Shiga. 'Well, in that case I'll say my goodbyes now. I hope your career in Tokyo goes well and I look forward to hearing of your future success.'

'Thank you,' said Josie. 'And thank you for all your help while I've been here.'

Mr Shiga nodded and turned away as someone else claimed his attention.

Two down, two to go, thought Josie. She headed back to the table for another drink. Intrigue was thirsty work.

With a glass of sake in her hand she surveyed the scene. Mr Shiga was working his way around the little groups dotted around the room, talking briefly to each of the people there, no doubt expressing his formal thanks for their work as he had done to Josie. Mr Ozawa had stationed himself by the sake and was pouring it liberally for anyone who came near. Taro was one of his most frequent visitors, Josie noticed, so she headed that way and lingered nearby as unobtrusively as she could. She didn't have to wait long; Taro gulped down his glass of sake and came back for more.

'Hey, Taro,' Josie called. 'Go easy on the sake or you'll never get home tonight.'

Taro turned a resentful look in her direction.

'I can hold my drink,' he said. 'You leave me alone. I haven't done anything.'

'You mean, apart from hanging around Mimi's flat all the time trying to spy on her?'

'I wasn't spying. I was making sure she was alright.'

'Whatever you say,' said Josie. 'Anyway, it's not going to matter after today. At least, not to me. I'm off to Tokyo tonight on the seven thirty seven Nozomi and I don't expect I'll be coming back to Osaka again soon.'

'I'm getting the seven forty three Hikari to Toyohashi, said Taro. 'We could walk down to the station together, if you like.'

'Oh,' said Josie. She wondered if Taro had an

ulterior motive for wanting to leave with her. But if he did, it didn't affect her plan, and anyway, nothing could happen in the crowded streets between the office and the station. It was the train that was dangerous.

'Okay,' she said. 'Let's do that.'

Taro nodded and reached for another drink. Josie began to move away but then realised she'd only shared half of her information with him.

'By the way,' she said. 'Did you know that someone has been stealing confidential data and selling it?'

'Of course I knew,' said Taro proudly. 'Taro knows everything.'

'Oh. So maybe you know who it was, then,' said Josie.

'No, I don't,' said Taro. 'Nobody knows, and they're not going to find out. Whoever's doing it is too clever for them.'

'So far,' said Josie. 'But I think you'll find that's about to change.'

'What do you mean?' said Taro, an expression of alarm on his face. Interesting, thought Josie. He's never been much good at hiding his feelings, but I don't see why he should be so obviously upset by what I said. Unless, of course, it's him. Let's see what happens if I prod him a bit more.

'Well, I've been doing a bit of work on it and I know how it was done,' she said, watching Taro's reaction intently. 'I'm going to tell them about it when I get to the Tokyo office on Monday and then they'll be able to trace who did it. So if I was the person responsible I'd be getting pretty worried right now.'

Taro practically reeled back from her.

'You can't have found out,' he said in a panicky voice. 'You're no good at IT. You're a girl and girls can't ever be good at IT.'

'You're in for a big surprise,' said Josie. 'But don't take my word for it. Wait until Monday. Then you'll see.'

'No, I won't. You don't really know anything. You're just trying to scare me,' said Taro, his expression changing to one of simple-minded cunning.

'Have it your own way,' said Josie. 'But I don't see why you should be so bothered. It wasn't you, was it?'

'No, it wasn't me,' said Taro. 'But I know who it was. Taro knows everything.'

He drew himself up to his full height, making him only a couple of inches shorter than Josie, and walked away with what was clearly intended to be dignified indifference but which looked to Josie much more like a fit of pique.

Josie didn't waste much time worrying about Taro and what he did or didn't know. She checked her watch – time was running out and she still had one more person to tell about her plans. Mack would be the most difficult to approach naturally after their awkward encounter with Mimi at the café, but Josie consoled herself with the thought that he didn't know how much Mimi had told her after that about their relationship and what he was forcing her to do.

Mack was in a little group near the door who were sharing a bottle of sake and discussing the latest Apple launch. Josie hung around the outside of the group until someone noticed her and made room for her to join the little circle.

'I hear you've been transferred to Tokyo,' one of them said to her. 'Perhaps we'll run into each other. I'm moving to the domestic insurance office there.'

'I'm hoping for the IT office,' said Josie. 'But I'll have to wait and see where they send me on Monday.'

'You live in Tokyo don't you? That makes things a lot easier. I'll have to look out for somewhere.'

'Yes,' said Josie, deliberately raising her voice to make sure Mack heard her. 'My boyfriend and I have a flat there. He can't wait for me to get back. I've sent all my things on ahead and I'm catching the seven thirty seven Nozomi tonight.'

'Then I'll say goodbye and good luck,' said her companion, moving away just as Mack stepped closer.

'With you leaving tonight, I don't suppose we'll see each other again,' he said. 'Goodbye and good luck.'

'Thanks,' said Josie. 'Same to you. I'm sure you'll do well. Staying in Osaka will leave you well placed for a job when the new centre of excellence opens. They'll be glad to have someone with your skills and experience.'

Mack looked flattered.

'I hope it goes well for you in Tokyo too,' he said.

'I'm pretty sure it will. In fact, I'm confident I'll get the job I want in the IT office in Tokyo when I tell them what I've been able to find out here.'

'Find out?' said Mack. 'What do you mean?'

Josie took a deep breath and repeated yet again her story about knowing how the theft of the data had been carried out and planning to find out who the culprit was on Monday. If Mack was worried by it, he didn't show it. But then, he had never shown much emotion. Josie could easily imagine him as a cold, silent killer.

'Well, it sounds like you're all set up then,' said Mack. 'Here's to your brilliant career.'

He tossed back the sake in his glass and walked away.

Josie checked her watch again. It was nearly half past six. If her plan was going to work she needed to catch the seven thirty seven just as she'd said.

A wave of fear washed over her at the thought. Now the time had come she wasn't sure she could face it. She dreaded sitting on the train as it sped towards Tokyo, waiting to see if her guess was right as the minutes ticked by. If the killer was one of the people at the party, they now knew that they couldn't afford to let her reach Tokyo with her supposed information. So the chances were they'd use the same method to silence her as they'd used to silence Saburo. Or try to, she reminded herself. Unlike Saburo, she knew what was coming. She hoped that would be enough to save her.

The sight of Taro making his way towards her steadied her. The time had come to leave the warmth of the party behind and go out into the dark to catch a murderer. She squared her shoulders. She was ready.

NINETEEN

She took a last look around the room. The party had moved through the classic stages of any gathering where there's alcohol, from nervous chill at the start through polite conversation over the meal to loud conversation and laughter after it. A good time to slip away. But first she needed to speak to Mimi.

She found Mimi, as she had expected, in the kitchen, presiding over a scene of organised chaos as the big table in the IT room was cleared of its remnants of food and order was gradually restored. Everything they'd used for the party was being washed up and put into boxes ready to be moved on to their next home, wherever that might be. Josie glanced at the block that normally held the painfully sharp chopping knives. It had one or two of the smaller knives in it but the larger ones were nowhere to be seen.

Mimi's eyes followed Josie's.

'We used the knives to dismember the crabs,' said Mimi. 'They're still out on the table somewhere.'

There was a pause while they looked at each other and an unspoken thought passed between them. Both of them knew that when the knives were collected in there would be one missing.

'I'm heading off now,' said Josie, in what she hoped was a calm voice. 'Got to catch the seven thirty seven.'

Mimi nodded.

'It's been good working with you,' she said. 'Take care.'

Impulsively Josie gave her a hug. Mimi didn't respond, just stood there impassively with a blank look on her face. Doesn't want to give anything away, thought Josie. She's right, we've got to play our parts now. She deliberately made her own face blank as she turned and left the kitchen. She found Taro waiting outside with her coat.

'Thanks, Taro,' said Josie, taking her coat from him and putting it on. 'You must be sad to leave.'

Taro nodded.

'It's hard to leave a place where you've been happy,' he said.

'Have you been happy here?'

'Oh yes. I had friends here. That made me happy.'

'Koji and Mack, you mean?'

'And Saburo.'

'Was he your friend?'

'He was always nice to me. I was sorry when he died, but I think he brought it on himself.'

Josie was startled.

'Brought it on himself?' she echoed.

Taro held the door open for her and followed her out into the corridor before replying.

'Saburo would never just let things take their course,' he said. 'He always wanted to hurry them up. Hurrying things up is pointless. You just end up in the same place only with more trouble and effort. He should have waited.'

'What things did he try to hurry up, Taro?'

'Promotion, money. They were all things that would have come to him in time, but he couldn't wait. And Mimi. He tried to hurry Mimi. That was a big mistake.'

Josie was startled.

'What do you mean, Taro?' she said. 'How did he try to hurry her?'

'You're our Hermione,' said Taro. 'You should be able to work it out.'

The lift came and took them down to the foyer. They walked past the icy receptionist and out into the street. It was dark but still warm, though a light breeze made Josie shiver and draw her coat around her. She tried to think what Taro meant but nothing came. She shook her head.

'You'll have to help me out, Taro,' she said. 'I can't see what you're getting at.'

'Where did Mimi get that cut on her forehead?'

'I can't tell you that. It's Mimi's private business.' Taro nodded.

'There's a lot that's Mimi's private business.'

Josie stared at him but his face gave nothing away. She turned away to look at the shops they passed, shops she'd probably never see again – there'd be no reason for her to walk down this street in future. And suddenly she realised what Taro was getting at.

'Mimi broke it off with Saburo, didn't she?' she said. 'Before he was killed. He wasn't the great love of her life. He was just someone who'd do until something better came along. And the something better was Mack.'

'Mack's rich,' said Taro.

Yes, thought Josie, Mack's rich. And that's what it's been about all along as far as Mimi's concerned. To end up with the richest one. She's a tougher cookie than I've given her credit for.

She suddenly wished that Saburo hadn't been killed, that the office wasn't being closed and that she could go back to her first day in Osaka and see people as they really were, not how she'd decided they must be. But she knew that was just a fantasy. She would do no better given a second chance than she had the first time. There was too much going on under the surface in the Osaka office for that ever to work. Too much that she'd failed to understand.

Above all she'd failed to understand Saburo, what he had done and why he had been killed. She thought she knew some things. She was sure he had tracked down the person who stole the data and had warned them that he was going to expose them. Warned them just as she had just done, on a Friday afternoon before getting the train home. But he'd done more than that. Out of all of the young men who circled around Mimi like flies around a honey pot, he had seemingly been the successful one. The one who would get the promotion, secure the beautiful girl with lucky ears. It must have been intolerable for someone, but for who?

It was strange to be spending her last hour in Osaka with Taro, the person she'd made the least effort to get to know while she'd been there. She'd hit it off with Koji from the first, taken, she now realised, an instant dislike to Mack and thoroughly misunderstood Mr Shiga. But Taro had been an enigma and she hadn't bothered to unravel it. Even though people kept telling her that Taro knew everything, she hadn't bothered to find the key to unlock his knowledge. Well, it was too late now.

The familiar sight of Osaka station brought her thoughts back to the present. She wondered if the person who needed to stop her reaching Tokyo would take the same route to the station, or if they'd decide on the anonymity of the backstreet walk to Nakatsu and the underground to New Osaka. As she and Taro joined one of the queues of people lined up for their turn to pass through the barriers of the central gate she felt a terrible desire to look around to see if there was someone behind them that she knew, someone who would not wish to be spotted, but she resisted. For all she knew the person she was waiting for was already there, at her side.

'This way,' said Taro, mistaking her hesitation for uncertainty about the way to go. 'It's this escalator to the Kyoto line platforms.'

'Yes, of course,' said Josie, kicking herself for being so silly. She had a job to do and she needed to get on with it. It would never do if she missed her train.

At New Osaka she felt a pang of nostalgia as they crossed the concourse to the bullet train platforms. Only two days before she'd waited here for Dave and Cherie, thinking they were going to have a pleasant day out. Instead she'd found herself precipitated into a sequence of events that had led her here – about to get on a train with a murderer who had a very good reason to ensure she never made it to Tokyo. And a sharp knife hidden in their coat that had recently been used to sever crab's legs.

She shuddered, wondering what on earth had made her come up with so stupid a plan. Taro was right; all she was doing was hurrying things. If she'd waited, the police would have got there in the end, slowly ground through the alibis until they found the one that didn't stand up. And then got a confession, however long it took. That was how justice worked in Japan; the police found a suspect and got them to confess. They always confessed in the end, even the innocent ones.

She looked up to see Taro looking at her strangely.

'Sorry,' she said. 'I was miles away. What platform is my train?'

'Twenty six,' said Taro. 'I'll come with you shall I?'

'No need,' said Josie. 'I'm fine on my own.'

'I've got time before my train leaves,' said Taro. 'I might as well see you all the way.'

And see exactly where I sit, too, thought Josie. If he's the one I'm after that would make things simpler later on. Like walking down to the station with me instead of trying to follow me and not be seen. If he's the one, that is.

Josie wanted to refuse him, but felt that he wasn't going to be deterred - and anyway, what did it matter if he knew from the start where her seat was? - so she let him lead the way up the escalator to the platform and along to the sign showing where compartment seven would stop. They didn't have long to wait – her train glided into the station, its graceful shape and shining white flanks looking as though it wouldn't hurt a fly, let alone give house room to a murderer.

'I'm fine now, Taro,' said Josie as the doors slid open. 'You go and get your train. Thanks for coming with me, and all the best in the future.'

'All the best, Josie,' said Taro. 'I hope your plans work out the way you want.'

For a moment Josie was startled, but then she realised he was referring to her supposed plan to get promotion in Tokyo with the information about who stole the data.

'Thanks,' she said. 'Best of luck with your career too.'

The person in front of her in the queue got on the train and Josie followed, her heart thumping. She had to wait while a family in front of her found their seats and stowed their luggage in the overhead rack but then she reached her seat, an aisle seat at the end of a row of three. She settled down and put her bottle of green tea in the netting bag on the back of the seat in front of her, and then realised that Taro was still standing on the platform watching her. She waved to him and tapped her watch. He nodded and moved away, and Josie felt an odd sense of relief. She liked Taro, but there was something about him that made her nervous and she was glad to be on her own.

The compartment she was in wasn't completely full. People were dotted around and, though there was a salaryman engrossed in a huge pile of papers in the window seat, the middle seat of her block of three remained empty. She hoped it would stay that way. She sat back and closed her eyes, feeling her head starting to ache from all the sake she'd drunk.

Someone jogged her elbow and she nearly jumped out of her skin. Her heart pounded and her mind raced in confusion. Then she realised that it was the salaryman in the window seat. He was pointing towards the window where someone standing on the platform was tapping on the glass and mouthing something she couldn't hear. She peered out and finally made out from the jerky movements that it was Mr Shiga.

She got up hurriedly and went back to the door, where Mr Shiga met her.

'Thank goodness I've caught you,' he said. 'I couldn't let you leave Osaka without giving you this.'

He held out a roll of cardboard.

'What is it?' said Josie.

'It's your certificate. To say that you satisfactorily completed your work experience with us and are ready to move on to become a fully fledged IT Support worker. I know you're hoping to join the Tokyo IT office and I thought it would help you when you go into work on Monday. I tried to catch you before you left but I got caught up with Mr Ozawa and couldn't get to you.'

'Thank you,' said Josie, taking the cardboard roll from him with a sense of unreality. Her thoughts had been focused on murder, while Mr Shiga had been thinking about a roll of paper.

Or had he? This certificate could be the perfect excuse to check that she was genuinely on the train and to find out where she was sitting. Mr Shiga could have deliberately not given it to her earlier to provide himself with an excuse to go after her, and maybe to get the train himself after he'd seen that she was really on it.

She looked at him, hoping to see something in his face that would tell her if he had terrible plans in his mind. But his head, as always, was bent and he wouldn't look her in the eye. She would just have to wait and see.

The urgent voice of the announcer called to them to stand back as the train was leaving. Mr Shiga turned away and Josie went back to her seat, managing to restrain herself from looking back along the platform to see what Mr Shiga did. If it was him she was after there was no point in catching him out now – it would prove nothing. She must wait until later, until whoever it was came to silence her with the knife from Mimi's kitchen.

TWENTY

The train slid out of the station and gathered speed. Josie's pounding heart slowed. It would be a long time to Tokyo – two and half hours, with stops at Kyoto and Nagoya, and then a long straight run to New Yokohama, Shinagawa and finally Tokyo. If the murderer followed the same plan he'd used with Saburo, as she was sure he would, then nothing would happen until they got past New Yokohama.

It had worried her that the murderer had persuaded Saburo to stay on the train instead of getting off at Shizuoka – it seemed an unnecessary complication. But then she'd realised it was crucial. It gave the killer time to get clear, as the passengers slowly left the train and the doors were closed behind them. And then the delay while the cleaners worked their way through the train to the disabled toilet. Seven minutes, that's how long it took them to turn a train around. In seven minutes the murderer could be far away – could even have got straight onto another train and be on their way back to Osaka.

She was sure that was how it would work this time too. But the long journey stretched intimidatingly ahead and her confidence in her plan began to ebb away as the train glided through the darkness. She began to wish she'd told Dave what she was planning and asked him to be on the train in case something went wrong. Or that she had a Plan B. Plan A was beginning to look increasingly scary.

The train slowed down as it came into Kyoto. Josie tried to see out the window but the darkness outside made it hard to make out the platform. The salaryman next to her stuffed his papers into his briefcase, gathered up his coat and made his way past her to the exit. A surprising number of people seemed to be leaving the train, and less than usual joining it. Of course, she thought, the train's come all the way from Hakata down in Kyushu, so a lot of people must be ending their journey here, not going on to Tokyo And the rush hour's over now.

The train moved off again. Josie felt curiously exposed with two empty seats next to her, as though the presence of the salaryman had offered some protection. She stood up in her seat and peered over the high back of the seat in front of her at the rest of the compartment. It was only half full, and many of the occupants were asleep or engrossed in their mobile phones. Nobody was paying any attention to her. It was as if she was all alone on the train.

Stop it, she told herself. Nothing is going to happen before New Yokohama. You're just frightening yourself for no reason.

She took out her phone and tried to occupy herself with Facebook and Twitter. But neither of them held her attention. She peered down the aisle, wondering where the girl with the trolley was. She was desperate for a coffee and for the sound of another voice, even if all it said was, *do you want milk and sugar?*

She sat back again and half closed her eyes, hoping to doze her way through the next couple of hours, and succeeding in calming her racing mind. Which meant it came as an even greater shock when someone walked down the aisle and stopped next to her seat.

For a moment she didn't dare look up. Then a familiar voice said, 'Hey Josie, are you asleep? I'm sorry if I woke you.'

She took a deep breath and nerved herself to look up. Bright, friendly eyes and an engaging smile met her gaze.

'Koji,' she said. 'I didn't expect to see you here.'

'No, I didn't expect to be here, either,' said Koji easily. 'I was lucky to get this train – I must have been the last one on before the doors closed. The announcement was going *Don't jump onto the train, it's dangerous* just as I jumped onto the train.'

He laughed and Josie did her best to laugh with him, but it was difficult as her mind was racing. Was Koji there because of what she'd told him? Or did he have a genuine reason to be there? Was it an awful coincidence that he was on her train?

'Where have you been sitting?' she said.

'In the non-reserved seats, getting my breath back. But then I remembered you'd said you were planning to get this train so I thought I'd come and find you. Mind if I sit next to you? I don't suppose anyone's going to use that seat now.'

'Be my guest,' said Josie, twisting her knees to one side to make room for him to get by.

'But what are you doing here?' she said, as he settled himself in the seat next to her, leaving the window seat empty. 'Surely you should be on a train going the other way, down to Okayama.'

'If only,' said Koji. 'Mr Ozawa forgot to send some important papers over to the Nagoya office, so he asked me to rush them across. I don't mind. I can get a train from Nagoya back to Okayama after I drop the papers off. It'll only make me a bit late getting home and I didn't have any particular plans.'

'So you're only going as far as Nagoya?' said Josie.

'That's right,' said Koji. 'I wish I could come all the way to Tokyo with you, but I have to get back. It'll be gone ten o'clock before this train reaches Tokyo, too late to get a train back tonight.'

Josie mentally kicked herself. She should have checked that before she made her plan. She'd thought she'd been so clever but she'd failed to take the most basic precaution of checking the timetables for trains back. Now all her comforting assumptions about nothing happening for hours had gone out the window and she'd found herself on the back foot instead of being calm and on top of things.

All the same, she longed to believe Koji. After all, why shouldn't Mr Ozawa have forgotten about some urgent papers? In the rush of closing down the office it was only natural that something would get forgotten. Koji couldn't be the one she was waiting for. He was her friend.

She looked at her watch. It was only thirty minutes to Nagoya. Surely nothing could happen in that short time? She just had to keep her head. Take a deep breath and focus.

She looked at Koji smiling gently at her side, looking calm and pleased to see her. It could easily be a coincidence he'd got her train. She trusted him, why shouldn't she?

'I'm sorry I had to leave the party so early without saying a proper goodbye,' she said.

'No worries. It was winding down when you left anyway,' Koji said, setting his seat to recline and stretching out his legs. 'But Mack was sorry he missed you at the end. He left soon after you and I think he was hoping to run into you at the station.'

Mack, Josie thought. It could still be Mack. He could be on the train somewhere, biding his time.

'I'd have liked to stay longer,' said Josie. 'But you know how it is. I had to get back to Tokyo.'

'Of course. Everybody understood that,' said Koji. Was there an edge to his voice? An undercurrent of meaning?

A wave of fear swept over her. How could it be a coincidence that he was on her train? Hadn't she planned for just this to happen? For a moment she contemplated just getting up and going. Now, before anything could happen. Because, if it was him, then he'd got the upper hand in a way that she had never imagined. She was confused and her confidence that she knew what she was doing had deserted her. She wondered if he knew that.

Koji smiled at her, as relaxed as though they genuinely had met by chance and were going to spend a pleasant half hour together before the train reached Nagoya and they went their separate ways.

'Actually, I wasn't sorry to do this little errand for Mr Ozawa,' he said. 'I don't like long drawn out farewells. Better to move on. People forget you surprisingly quickly.'

I won't forget you, thought Josie. Not if this journey ends the way I think it might.

'Do you think people will forget about Saburo too?' she said, wondering how he'd react to the mention of Saburo's name.

'Of course,' said Koji calmly. 'They already have. Haven't you noticed that people don't mention him any more?'

'What about the police? They're still working on the case.'

'They don't have anything to go on. I could tell at that second interview they did. They're just casting around for something to latch onto, but there isn't anything. They'll keep pretending they're on the trail but in fact they're not going to do very much.'

He sounded confident, complacent, even. Was it the complacence of a killer who knows he's got away with it? Or just Koji's habitual self confidence? Josie didn't know any more.

'It's a tough case,' said Josie. 'And there's so much about it that seems strange.'

'Like what?' said Koji. He brought his seat back up to upright again so that he could turn and look straight at her. His eyes sparkled with interest and enthusiasm. 'Tell me, and I'll see if I can work it out for you.'

'Well, for instance, how could the murderer have persuaded Saburo not to get off the train at Shizuoka like he was supposed to?'

'Oh that,' said Koji. 'That's no big deal. There could be all sorts of ways to get him to stay. Maybe the murderer invited him to Tokyo for a night out. Or maybe the killer said he had something important to tell Saburo but there wasn't time before the train left Shizuoka.'

'I suppose that's possible,' said Josie. 'Especially if the murderer was someone he knew well. Someone from the office, maybe.'

Koji nodded. 'Someone from the office,' he echoed. 'That could be it.'

Josie took a deep breath, seeing a way to force him into the open.

'Oh, but there's a problem,' she said, shaping her face into an expression of naive innocence. 'You make it sound as though Saburo and the killer were friends, but actually Saburo wouldn't have wanted to have anything to do with that person.'

'Why not?' said Koji.

'Because they'd almost certainly had a bust up earlier in the day. Over the data theft. I think Saburo found out who did it and told the culprit he was going to report what he'd found out. That's why the killer followed him and it's also why Saburo wouldn't have been willing to talk to them. So I think you've got that one wrong.'

As Josie expected, Koji rose to the challenge.

'You're giving up too easily,' he said. 'Suppose the killer said they'd come to explain, that someone else was involved, someone Saburo wouldn't want to hurt. I think Saburo might be prepared to listen then, don't you?'

'Someone else? Who?' said Josie.

'Mimi,' said Koji.

'Mimi?' said Josie. 'How could she be involved?'

'Come on, Josie,' said Koji, sitting back in his seat with the complacent smile returning to his face. 'You know Mimi as well as I do. All she thinks about is money. She went out with me because I could get her a job at AZT, and once she was inside the door she changed to Saburo because she reckoned his prospects were better than mine. And now it's Mack, the one with the rich dad. See a pattern?'

Josie almost reeled back. That was what Taro had said too.

'Or maybe,' said Koji, with the air of someone who's just hit on the solution, 'maybe it was Mimi herself who persuaded him to stay on the train.'

Josie felt her head swim.

'Mimi?' she said. 'Mimi was on the train?'

'Think about it. Who had the most to lose? Who had spent all the money from the data theft? Mimi, that's who. She didn't want to be found out did she? It would shame her family.'

Shame her family, Josie thought. That was the reason Mimi had given for not telling the police about the false alibi she'd given Mack. But maybe his false alibi was her false alibi too. Maybe he'd played into her hands suggesting they said they were together.

Kōji was watching her closely.

'That would stop Saburo in his tracks, wouldn't it?' he said. 'His own girlfriend. What was he going to do? Maybe he needed to think again about the whole idea of turning in the person who'd stolen the data. If they'd only done it for Mimi then Saburo might do better to think again.'

'But then there would be no need to kill him.'

'Don't be stupid. So long as Saburo knew about the data he'd be a threat to Mimi's security.'

'So then what happened?' said Josie, forgetting in her confusion, to maintain the pretence they were talking hypothetically. Kōji didn't seem to notice the change.

'So then Mimi said that she'd had a change of heart. That she wanted to give the money back. That she'd brought the money with her to give to Saburo so he could put everything right again. But they needed to go somewhere private, somewhere she could hand over the money without anyone seeing.'

'The disabled toilet,' said Josie.

'The disabled toilet,' said Koji. 'Why else would Saburo have agreed to go there?'

'And when he got there…' Josie said, her imagination leaping ahead of her.

'And when he got there, Mimi killed him,' said Koji.

'No, she couldn't have,' said Josie, her whole being revolting against the suggestion. 'Mimi's not like that. And anyway, Mimi's tiny, Saburo would make two of her. There's no way she could have been strong enough.'

'You don't believe me?' said Koji. 'I can show you exactly how it was done. Come with me now. We've just got time before the train reaches Nagoya.'

Josie desperately tried to think. Koji knew too much for what he was saying to be mere speculation. But how much of it was true and how much was just a string of plausible lies? Had Mimi really been there that day? Or had Koji been the one who killed Saburo?

'You see, Josie,' said Koji softly. 'You don't really know Mimi at all. She's quite different to how you imagine her. She's cunning and determined and very subtle. So subtle that she's persuaded you into making this silly plan to trap the killer. But Mimi is the killer. And she's waiting for you too. Come with me and I'll show you.'

Koji was staring at her hypnotically, his eyes boring into hers. Josie couldn't think. Was Mimi really the killer? Or was it Koji? Was Mimi really waiting for them in the disabled toilet? Or was it Koji

277

she needed to fear, Koji with the crab knife hidden somewhere out of sight, confusing and disorienting her so she would make easy prey?

She thought briefly about just making a run for it then and there. But she knew it would get her nowhere. Where could she run to on a moving train? And no one would believe a hysterical foreigner who said someone was out to kill her but she didn't know who. No, her only course was to go along with Koji and hope to move fast enough when the moment came to avoid the attack, whoever it came from. Mimi or Koji… or both of them. Suddenly the odds were not looking so good, and her confidence in her plan ebbed way. She desperately wished that Dave was there to even things out, but there was nobody. Nobody on her side and a killer, or a pair of killers, ranged against her. She'd really blown it this time.

She sneaked a look at her watch. Fifteen minutes to Nagoya. She wondered if she could string it out and make a run for it when the train stopped, but she knew that was a forlorn hope. She had to see it through. And she'd need all her wits about her to do it.

'I don't believe you,' she said, as firmly as she could. 'Mimi's not on this train, and she won't be waiting in the disabled toilet. Just to show you, I'm going to go there now.'

'Alright,' said Koji. 'We'll both go. I'll show you how the door lock works. It's a bit complicated first time you use it.'

TWENTY ONE

Josie stood up, trying to stop her hands trembling. She didn't really believe what Koji had said about Mimi – or did she? She didn't know any more. Koji had muddled her thinking, thrown her off balance. Which, of course, was the point. Her advantage was supposed to come from being prepared, in control, knowing what was coming. But now her mind was seesawing madly between one idea and another. She had to get on top of it. Whatever happened when they got where they were going, she had to be ready.

She looked at Koji, waiting politely for her to lead the way down the aisle to compartment eleven. Whatever the truth was, Koji was not her friend. She knew that now. He was deliberately distracting her, driving her off course for his own advantage. Well, he wasn't going to get away with it.

She took a last look around the compartment. Nobody was taking any notice of them. The sleepers were still asleep, the readers didn't lift their eyes from their books and Kindles. There was nothing

special about Josie and Koji to make them look up –
they were just two people going to the space at the
end of the compartment to make a call on their
mobile phones, or to visit the smoking room for a
cigarette and a chat.

She took another quick look at her watch. Thirteen
minutes left until they arrived at Nagoya. It would
only take a couple of minutes to walk down to the
disabled toilet. Then, once they were inside, out
would come the knife, fast, before she had a chance
to react. How long did it take to kill someone? she
wondered. A few minutes? Leaving the murderer just
enough time to wash off any blood under the tap and
sidle out as the train drew in to Nagoya. She
wondered if Koji'd had it all planned, right from the
moment he left his seat and came to find her. Or if
Mimi had.

No, said the voice inside her head. Stop thinking
like that. That kind of thinking is what will get you
killed. Mimi isn't on the train. It's Koji you need to
be frightened of.

There wasn't much time left to think.
Mechanically, she started walking down the aisle. As
they reached the end of the compartment they passed
the coffee trolley; the girl behind it pulled into the
space behind the last row of seats and waited politely
for them to pass before continuing on her way. Josie
could have done with a cup of the fierce bullet train
coffee right then; it would have cleared her head
which was a swirl of confusion. But she knew Koji
would not let her stop.

Compartment eleven was as quiet as Koji had promised. The semicircular walls of the toilet took up most of the available space and nobody seemed much inclined to linger in the vicinity. Involuntarily, Josie glanced back the way they had come; nobody had taken any notice of them. The few people they'd passed on the way were too busy sending a final email or reaching their luggage down from the rack to pay any attention. As far as they were concerned it was just another Friday night on the bullet train.

The door of the toilet was shut, but Josie couldn't see whether it was locked or not as Koji stood between her and the lock button. He tapped on the door and called 'Mimi' softly. The door slid open.

In spite of herself, Josie hesitated, half expecting to see Mimi's face appear. The hesitation was enough to give Koji the advantage. He pushed her roughly and she stumbled over the threshold into the toilet. Koji followed her, pressing the lock button as he did so. She was trapped inside.

'Looks like Mimi couldn't make it after all,' said Koji. 'I'll have to look her up when all the fuss about this has died down. I bet she'll be sick of Mack by then.'

Josie moved quickly to get her back against the wall, as close as she could get to the door. She knew what was coming next.

'This isn't about Mimi,' she said. 'It's all about you. But it's over, Koji. You know that.'

'It's over for you,' Koji said, his eyes glinting in the harsh glare of the overhead lighting as his hand moved towards the pocket of his jacket.

Josie risked a glance towards the door. The light showing it was locked glowed red. Below it were the buttons that controlled the lock. She tried to memorise where they were, embed them in her muscle memory so she could reach them without looking.

Koji saw her looking at the door and his expression hardened. Swiftly he brought out the hand he'd tucked inside his jacket and Josie saw the knife in it.

'I'm sorry, Josie,' he said. 'I really liked you.'

The knife flashed in the light as he raised it to strike. It was the biggest of the knives from the block in Mimi's kitchen, with a thick blade and viciously sharp point. For a moment Josie was paralysed with fear. This can't be happening, said a panicky voice in her head. This isn't real. He's my friend. He wouldn't—

But even as the voice wittered mindlessly on, Josie's instinct for self-preservation kicked in. As Koji brought the knife down she dropped to the floor and grabbed him around the knees, throwing him off balance.

With a sharp cry he tumbled forward, hitting his head on the edge of the toilet bowl. Josie felt a thrill of satisfaction. One to me, she thought. You see, I'm not so easy to deal with as you thought.

But Koji moved faster than she expected. He was up on his feet again within seconds, the knife still firmly gripped in his hand. This time she wasn't going to catch him out so easily.

For a moment they stared at each other, the silence broken only by the sound of their breathing. Then Koji leapt forward, so fast that Josie barely had time to twist away. She felt the knife graze her hand as she moved, and drops of red blood fell on the pristine white floor. She wondered how bad the cut was, but she had no time to look as Koji pressed home his advantage, striking at her with such force that she knew she would have been a goner if she had not thrown herself to one side just in time.

I can't go on doing this, she thought. Next time I won't be so lucky. He's only got to be a bit faster and he'll get me. I've got to do something different.

She looked at Koji. He was vicious and desperate, but he was smaller than her. She was big, fit and had the advantage of being a foreigner, someone who wouldn't think like he did. She had to use that to her advantage.

She looked at her bloody hand and screamed, 'Oh my God! My hand – I'm bleeding. What have you done?'

Koji's gaze followed hers as she brought the hand up as though to cradle it in her good other hand. But as her hands met she locked them together and spun round so that her double fist struck Koji in the jaw with all her force. He was knocked off his feet with the force of the blow and Josie followed up her advantage by kicking him hard in the pit of his stomach. He groaned and the knife dropped from his hand, skittering across the polished floor.

Josie went to grab it, but Koji moved faster. He seized the knife and rolled over, staring up at her with a look of pure malevolence.

Josie took a deep breath and stamped on his hand. She gave it all the strength she had and he screamed in pain but somehow managed to keep a hold on the knife, though his hand was bloody and Josie doubted whether he'd be able to summon enough strength to stab her with it. She kicked him again, her foot connecting this time with his shoulder, and saw with satisfaction that his grip on the knife loosened. She stepped forward and wrenched it from his hand, feeling a thrill of satisfaction as he winced in pain.

For a moment they both stayed stock still, staring at one another. Then Josie hurled herself towards the door, feeling rather than seeing her fingers reach the button that released the lock. There was an agonising delay before anything happened, but then the semicircle of the door moved gently to one side, to reveal the shocked face of the ticket collector, and behind him a crowd of commuters, staring in with expressions of fascinated horror. Josie looked behind her. Koji lay whimpering in the floor. In the mirror was the reflection of a mad woman, with hair like a witch and a murderous look on her face. Blood dripped from one hand and in the other she held a bloody knife.

Ladies and gentlemen, said a voice over their heads. *We will shortly be arriving at Nagoya. Please remember to take all your belongings with you when leaving the train. Nagoya will be the next stop.*

TWENTY TWO

'Fortunately,' said Josie, 'The ticket collector was more interested in getting the pair of us off his train so he could stick to his schedule than in working out what had happened. The police were there in minutes and just took charge of everything.'

She scratched behind Rin's ears and the cat stretched luxuriously and yawned.

'I still shake when I think about it,' said Dave handing Josie a steaming cup of green tea. Shizuoka tea. The best. Josie took it with her good hand, trying not to look at the white bandage around her other one. It was still painful if she forgot and tried to move her fingers, but the doctor had said there was no lasting damage.

'Suppose Koji had moved just a second faster?' Dave went on. 'I could have been identifying your body right now.'

'Stop thinking like that,' said Josie. 'It didn't happen.' She picked up Rin and cuddled her, partly for comfort as the memory of that awful scene flooded back, and partly so Dave shouldn't see that her hands had started shaking again. She tried to blank out the image of the knife flashing as Koji brought it down, but she knew it would be with her for a long time to come.

'And then, when you got the door open, Koji could easily have spun them a line, saying you attacked him. After all, you were the one holding the knife.'

'Koji was in no state to spin anybody any lines,' said Josie. 'And anyway the police knew I couldn't have killed Saburo because I was still in the office when his train left. So that made it pretty obvious it was Koji the second time too. Plus Mimi corroborated my story.'

'I should have been there,' said Dave. 'You should have told me what you were planning to do. I should have been there right from the start.'

He sat down on the sofa next to Josie, put his arm around her and took a big consoling slurp from his mug of builder's tea. Josie snuggled close to him, much to Rin's disgust as she lost her place on Josie's lap.

'Don't think about it,' said Josie, deliberately failing to mention how hard she found it to keep her mind from replaying the scene. 'It doesn't do any good. Nothing awful happened and the police took Koji away. I expect they're questioning him now and I bet he'll be telling them everything. There's so much evidence against him, it's an open and shut case. And the bonus is, Mimi's in the clear. She won't have to admit to giving Mack a false alibi.'

'Suppose Mack had turned out to be the murderer?'

'Then she'd have had to come forward. But luckily it didn't come to that.'

'Or suppose it had been Mimi herself that was behind it all, like Koji said?'

'That's the one thing I can't ever forgive Koji for,' Josie said, the anger rising again as she thought of Koji's lies. 'It shows what a manipulative person he really was. I nearly believed him, you know, even though deep down I felt it couldn't be true. He used it to throw me off balance and it worked.'

'Well, Mimi owes you, big time,' said Dave, putting his arm around Josie and holding her close. 'Do you think the police would ever have caught Koji if you hadn't done what you did?'

'I'm not sure. He was clever, but he had a big problem with his alibi. Waiting until the train was near the end of its journey to Tokyo had its advantages, but it meant he wasted a lot of time getting to Tokyo and back to Okayama. The police were obviously probing people's alibis and I think they'd have broken his before too long. But then, Mack and Mimi lied about where they were and what they were doing that day, so I think Koji might have managed to deflect suspicion onto one of them quite successfully.'

'But Koji loved Mimi. That was why he stole the data and killed Saburo when he found out.'

'Koji used to love Mimi. But once she left him for

Saburo he just wanted revenge. He wanted to taunt her with all the money he'd got when she was stuck waiting for Saburo to start earning big.'

Dave drank the last of his tea and sat back. Rin seized the chance to reclaim her place on Josie's lap.

'So, no more early trains to Osaka,' he said.

'No, I won't miss those. But I might try and stay in touch with Mimi and Taro. I liked Taro. I think he'll go far. And I think maybe Mimi is starting to realise that too. He's got everything she wants – he's clever, he's bound to get the job in Tokyo that Saburo and Koji were after, and he worships the ground she walks on. A girl can't ask for more than that.'

'Just like you and me,' said Dave, putting his arm around her and pulling her towards him for a kiss.

'It's so nice being in our own flat, just the two of us and Rin,' Josie said, enjoying the warmth and comfort of being held close. 'I wish this could just go on forever.'

'I hate to break the mood,' said Dave. 'But you know it can't. I've got to go back to London next week, and you've got a decision to make.'

Josie opened her mouth to speak, but Dave stopped her.

'No, you can't put it off. You've put it off too long already. I'm a patient guy, but I need to know where I stand. We need to make decisions about where to live in London, what to do about this flat, whether to take Rin – all sorts of things.'

'And if I decide not to come?' said Josie.

Dave took a deep breath.

'If you decide not to come,' he said. 'That's it. It's over. I can't live in limbo any longer. It's time to make up your mind.'

Josie was silent. Dave disentangled himself, got up and took their empty cups to the kitchen.

'I'm going down to the café on the corner,' he called. 'I'll bring you back a croissant and a matcha latte. You can tell me what your answer is when I get back.'

She heard the door shut behind him and his footsteps going down the corridor to the lift. The flat seemed very quiet when he was gone. The only sound was Rin's tongue as she languorously washed her chest and then stretched, sighed and went back to sleep. Josie picked her up and buried her face in Rin's thick fur. Wherever I go, you're going with me, she whispered but Rin ungratefully struggled away and settled herself in a furry ball on the sofa.

Josie looked around. She loved this flat. It was a perfect size, in a pretty neighbourhood that was lively in the daytime and quiet at night, surprisingly close to the centre of Tokyo. She'd wanted a place like this ever since she'd come to Japan. Could she afford to keep it on without Dave to share the rent? It would be tight, but she reckoned she could manage it. And with no trips to Osaka, Tokyo would be at her feet. She and Keiko could go out every night, shopping and eating in the latest cafés, having a good time together like they always used to do before Dave had come to Japan. She'd missed being a single girl with no one to think about but herself.

And there was so much of Japan she still wanted to see. She knew Hokkaido in the far north well, having spent her first years in Japan there. And she'd been to Shikoku, the smallest of Japan's five islands. But she'd never crossed over to volcanic Kyushu, or looked out on the Sea of Japan with Korea on its far side, or followed Basho's trail to the deep north. She'd never seen the monkeys bathing in the snow-covered hot springs of Jigokudani, never sunbathed in the tropical paradise of Okinawa, never eaten fresh crab straight from the sea in Kanazawa, never climbed Mount Fuji.

Japan had been her dream. She'd worked so hard to get there, to learn the language, to make friends, find a job, become part of a new world. She thought of everything she'd miss if she went with Dave; the rich aroma of thinly sliced beef bubbling in a *shabu shabu* pot, the pulsing energy of the crowded streets, the cawing of crows disturbed by a temple bell. And cherry blossom. If they went back to London she wouldn't see the amazing sight of massed ranks of thousands of cherry trees in bloom ever again.

Then she thought of London. It would be just starting to get warm there. People would be sitting in the parks enjoying the lengthening evenings and standing outside pubs in great noisy happy groups on Friday nights. In Soho they would be crowding into bars and clubs and restaurants and theatres. There was so much to do in London, and so many friends to do it with. And family. She'd be able to see her Mum whenever she liked. Just like Cherie had said, your family had to come top of your list.

Plus, she'd be a tiny part of the incredible diverse mass of humanity that filled London, the most cosmopolitan city in the world. In London she wouldn't always be the foreigner, the one who stood out, who was taller than everyone else and who struggled to obey the complex rules of a hierarchical society. In London she'd fit in. She'd be at home. She'd be free. She had a sudden yearning to feel that freedom again.

She looked around her pretty flat and thought how empty it would feel when Dave was gone. Keiko had her own life to lead, she couldn't always be going out with Josie. She would be condemning herself to a life of lonely suppers in front of the television or in ramen houses where every other table was occupied by someone eating alone. Of having no one to share her triumphs and disasters with. No one to help her when she got herself into danger, and no one to share the relief when it was over. No one to share her bed with. No one to love and be loved by. Working later and later and coming home to watch the television with no one but Rin for company.

She got up and looked out of the window at the rooftops and balconies, each with a futon draped over it to air in the warm sunshine. Soon it would be June and the rains would sweep in, then the overpowering heat and humidity of summer. September brought typhoons, then a long warm peaceful autumn before the end of year parties and New Year celebrations.

And then the cherry blossom would bloom and the year would begin again.

Japan wasn't going to go away. If she went back to London with Dave it would still be here, the seasons still turning, the restaurants still bright with warmth and laughter. If she wanted to come back she could pick up the threads of her life again. Her friends would welcome her back as though she had never been away. It wasn't an either/or decision. She could have it all if she wanted.

She heard Dave's key in the door, his voice calling out to her and the warm scent of freshly baked croissant wafting through the air. She turned to see his big frame and ever-present grin and a wave of love washed over her. He was right for her and she for him. They were meant to be together, but she'd never been willing to admit it. Japan would wait for her. It was time to give London a chance. As Dave looked at her with hope in his eyes, she knew what her answer would be.

ACKNOWLEDGEMENTS

Grateful thanks to my beta reader, Yannick Pucci, and to my cover designer, Andrew Brown of Design for Writers.

AUTHOR'S NOTE

If you enjoyed this book, I hope you'll like the other stories in the Josie Clark in Japan mystery series:

The Tokyo Karaoke Murder – A night at the karaoke goes badly wrong for expat Londoner Josie Clark when she is accused of murder, leaving her just an hour to prove her innocence. Can she do it? (Prequel novella).

The Cherry Blossom Murder – Josie goes backstage at Japan's unique and spectacular Takarazuka Revue to expose a murderer and save a priceless treasure.

The Haiku Murder – Josie goes on a haiku-writing trip that turns to tragedy when a charismatic financier falls from the top of Matsuyama castle. But was he pushed?

To find out more about the Josie Clark in Japan mystery series, please visit my website, franpickering.com.

14196761R00176

Printed in Poland
by Amazon Fulfillment
Poland Sp. z o.o., Wrocław